WYNTER REIGN

STORM BLOODLINE SAGA: BOOK 3

EMMY R. BENNETT

DREAM SCRIPT MEDIA LLC

DEDICATION

To my grandma June: Thank you for believing in me.

WYNTER'S THOUGHTS

All those years of my childhood spent with Dad and Aunt Fran, grooming me for the future, were steering me to the gates of Ashengale, leading to this...

The biggest discovery of all, I know who I am...

"Time heals all wounds they say... And yet here I am, and they are still clearly open..."

Wynter Storm

1

IT HAPPENED IN THE LIBRARY

"*WHO IS HE?*" I ask my aunt. He glances at us as though he, too, can hear my thoughts.

"*Shh, not now. You will find out soon enough.*" She gives Garrick a gentle smile and he returns it equally.

Aunt Fran and I follow him through the enormous courtyard to the opposite side from where we entered the grounds. French doors made of decorative black iron open automatically and then abruptly close once we pass.

"It's good to see you home, Francesca. I've missed you." He speaks to my aunt as though they're longtime friends or lovers. I see it in both their eyes.

We cross over a cobblestone breezeway. On either side of the bridge walls, green ivy and white blossoms spiral up pillars that attach to the eaves of a mural roof. Small strange-looking birds with long beaks, colorful feathered wings, and razor-sharp talons suck the nectar from the flowers.

"Hummingbirds?"

More birds chirp, and the smell of jasmine distracts me.

Garrick turns around, noticing my surprise. "Similar, yes. These are dragon nectars. While they may look elegant and fragile, they are quite venomous. One sting will send you to the medical facility. They're not aggressive unless they feel threatened, and they love drinking the nectar from the many flowers that flourish around the castle. Their long beaks are used not only for nutrients but aid in defense when needed." Garrick motions his hand for us to keep moving.

"Yes, of course, sorry." Beyond the bridge walls the breezeway continues, crossing over a ravine. The views are spectacular, and I stop once more. A waterfall sprawls downward to an endless bottom, while birds of different shapes and size fly about in the vast space. "Long way down."

"Very," Garrick agrees. "It leads to another community underground. Shall we proceed? We don't want to keep the queen waiting."

"Queen? You mean my great-grandmother Sara is here?"

Garrick laughs. "Oh, My Princess, no." He scowls at Aunt Fran. "You really did a number on her head, didn't you."

"Oh, Rick, stop. I did not. Would you rather her find out everything prematurely?"

He grunts. "You do have a point there."

"You love me, and you know it." She smiles and kisses his cheek.

I squint. There is something more going on with those two. *"Aunt Fran, what are you not telling me?"*

"Shh, I'll tell you later."

"Right, you'll tell me later. Like I haven't heard that one before." She glares at me.

We come to a second set of iron doors on the other side of the bridge and pass through them to a grand foyer. The similarities to Storm River Manor are incredible. The difference here is the large entrance doesn't have a roof, and I can see the cave ceiling when I look above my head but the rest of the castle is a mirror image right down to the center foyer and staircase that stops midway to veer left or right. A wall supports the staircase, with open windows allowing the eye to trace the views of the deep valley below. A few dragons fly in the far distance. They circle the cave's ceiling, as though hunting or guarding.

"Spectacular view, isn't it?" Garrick says, coming near my ear and startling me.

"Yes. I'm still trying to grasp the reality that this morning we passed through the Hall of Secrets. I'm still in awe that it's a nexus that's been hidden away from all the realms, dimensions, and galaxies. All these magical places are a little overwhelming. And I still can't grasp the thought the circular room can jump us through space and time."

"Ah, yes, I imagine so. You will get used to it in time." He guides us to a spiral stairwell. "Come this way. The queen is beyond these steps," Garrick says. Aunt Fran walks next to him, and he puts his arm around her. She lays her head on his shoulder. They are talking, but I can't make out what they're saying.

I fall back, amazed at the colors, sights, smells, and wonder of it all.

Aunt Fran laughs, pauses, and turns around saying, "Wynter, keep up before you get lost."

"Who is he? Your boyfriend?"

She smiles. *"Much more than that."*

I follow them to another corridor, also like that of Storm River Manor, with many doors on one side and windows on the other. More marble pillars separate the space between the frames. Ivy vines circle around them, while more dragon nectars flitter to bloomed flowers, grabbing hold of the limbs and stabbing their beaks deep into the blossoms.

"At last we are here," Garrick says, and he raps on dark wooded french doors.

A servant opens the entrance, bows, and widens the door for us to pass through. "Your Majesty, she's here," the servant says.

A WOMAN WITH LIGHT brown hair, high cheekbones and thin rosy lips comes forward. "Come, child, let me have a look at you."

She wears a lovely A-frame pale pink sleeveless gown with lace decorating the front. A matching white scarf is tied around her shoulders. Setting aside the book she reads, she stands to hug me.

The awkwardness has me fumbling my hands into a closed fist, not knowing where to put them. How do I react to a stranger in my personal space? I give a slight sideways smile when she releases me.

"Oh, I'm sorry for being so forward. I'm a hugger. I should have asked. You haven't a clue who I am, do you?"

I smile. "No, not really. You look familiar, though. You look like my mother's mother."

She snorts. "And you would be right. I understand why you don't remember me that well. You were a small child when we were last together."

I think back to the vision Isalora showed me when the wraith came for Eleena at the cottage, when I still lived at the manor. She had similar features. "It isn't that. I remember seeing you in a dream. You're Eleena, aren't you?"

She nods. "A dream you say?" She gestures toward a chair. "Please, have a seat."

"Yes, I have visions when I sleep. Often times, they come true. Sometimes they are past events that I discover later." I sit. "Pardon me, but it was assumed you were dead. There are no books telling what happened to you after the escape from Ladorielle."

"That assumption is a good thing to hear, Wynter. And I'm glad we were able to pull that off." She stops. "Garrick, would you have Annah grab some refreshments please?" She looks at me. "I imagine you're starved."

"Not entirely. I had a huge meal not too long ago." *I'm still full from devouring that Trek at Geneviève's.*

"Certainly, My lady," Garrick says and bows, taking his leave through the doors.

I tilt my head. "You want people to think you're dead, don't you?"

"Hmm? Yes, it's for the best. At least until—" She's momentarily distracted and glances at my aunt. "My dear daughter. I do say, you have some explaining to do, young lady. What on Ladorielle happened to you?" She crosses her arms waiting for an answer.

I look at my aunt, and then down at my feet, avoiding eye contact. *"This ought to go over well."*

"Shh, let me handle this," Aunt Fran says.

My aunt hesitates to answer.

"Can she hear us?" I ask.

"No, she's not a Deagon, nor a ghost. Now, keep quiet. I'll explain later."

"Right..."

"Drelanda Francesca Deagon-Storm, answer me." Eleena sits in a red winged-back chair, staring across the sitting area at Fran.

"A giant got the best of me, Mama." My aunt struggles to meet Eleena's eyes. She doesn't appear fearful, only ashamed.

"I see." Eleena takes a deep breath and pauses a few minutes. I don't know whether Eleena is angry or sad.

"Mother, it was an accident. No one could have seen it coming."

"And what was that, exactly?" Eleena raises her voice. "That you couldn't see coming, that is..."

"A sword," I blurt. "It was Dad's—"

Eleena puts up her hand. "No need to explain, Wynter." Her stern stare at my aunt is terrifying. "It must have been some battle." Her face looks angry. She takes another deep breath, gets up, and walks to a bookshelf. There, she thumbs through book titles. "I presume you have already gone to see Nyta, else I wouldn't be seeing you right now. You know, Drelanda, we had plans for you. Who is to carry on the bloodline now?"

"Yes, I know, Mother. Nyta has my heart preserved in the healing coffer. Everything will be fine. Then we can start the ritual. Think of my body as being in a deep sleep. Besides, this might pose as an advantage against the—"

"We can discuss that later," Eleena says.

While my aunt appeared real to the natural eye, I see right through her, and the tension in her frame speaks volumes. *Is that what it is? A healing coffer?*

My aunt ignores me. "Mama, everything will be fine."

Eleena turns around. "Fine?" She looks my aunt up and down. "Does this situation look *fine* to you?"

"I know you're disappointed, Mother, but we can train Wynter, at least until we—"

"Is that what you think?" Her eyes glow a light green, unlike the glowing of my dad's blue eyes. "Wynter has other priorities." Eleena briefly glances at me then back to my aunt. Turning back to the bookshelf, she takes a book and skims the pages then puts it back in its place. "Where is your body now? You said it's with Nyta, but where?"

"What's going on? What are you not telling me, Aunt Fran?"

Still ignoring me, she says, "I don't know, but I assure you it's safe with Nyta."

"Your body should be in the crypt where it's supposed to be when something like this happens."

"Mama, no. I know what you're thinking."

"Do you?" She turns back again, squinting. "How do you expect to pull this off, Fran? This was not in the cards." Eleena purses her lips and scans more book spines. "Where is it!" The tension in the room escalates.

I ask again, hoping this time my aunt will answer me, *"What is she talking about?"*

"I said I'll tell you later." Fran sounds worried. "Wynter is fully capable of going through her trials without me, Mother—" My aunt paces toward Eleena and Aunt Fran's steps cease, like when the giants were fixated to the ground when Fran cast a spell on them.

"Mother, please let me explain."

Eleena ignores Aunt Fran as she continues thumbing through the shelf, looking for a certain book.

"What is she looking for, Aunt Fran? And how are you fixated in place? Did Eleena do that to you?"

"Yes. My mother is upset with me, and this is her way of coping. She's looking for the Spellbook of Immortality, I believe, so she can cast a spell to hold me here forever."

"I thought you already cast an immortality spell. That's why you're able to still be on the ghostly plane. You mean there is a spellbook? Plus, how is she able to keep you motionless? You're a ghost."

"Yes, it's presumed that I am, isn't it.

"What's that supposed to mean?"

"This isn't the same immortality spell you're thinking of. Remember when Isalora told you she cast a spell that allows her to look human, but it weakens her should she cross over to our world?"

"She mentioned she couldn't come with us, yes, I remember."

"Mother's looking for that spell. Except...well...the jewelry we wear is much more magical than you know."

"That's great, more surprises. So, what else are you hiding from me?"

"I'm not really dead. Just stuck on the Undead Plane until my spirit can reunite with my body. I'm a Deagon, immortal with only one way to die."

"I don't understand."

"Don't you get it, yet? No. Of course, you wouldn't. You still have that memory stamp in place."

"Francesca, dear, you're awfully quiet," Eleena says, still looking through the shelves. "What are you feeding my granddaughter? Do be careful, she mustn't find revelations too quickly. It will render her memory frozen."

"Yes, Mother, I know."

"I thought you said she can't hear us?"

"She can't."

"Are you saying my mother is like you? I mean that she can become whole again, too? That's what you're saying, right? That your body isn't really dead?" The memory of when Dad, Aunt Fran, and I turned to ash in our house in Washington comes to mind.

"Yes, with one exception."

"Which is?"

"She can pass through on the Plane of Undead to Ladorielle. If caught doing so, the undead of evil can steal your soul forever."

"So, you're saying that between the physical and spiritual worlds, a soul can die?"

"Yes, something like that. It's like the In-between. Some refer to it as Purgatory, but it's neither of those. We spirits call it the Plane of Undead, or Scarlet Hollow, where the immortal spirits go if they have had unfinished business while alive. If captured by an evil undead spirit, they will live a life in hell for eternity."

"Is this why my mother Isalora remains near the cottage most of the time? To avoid capture?"

"Yes, and no. She stays to protect you. To make sure you continue on the path to your destiny."

"Where's that book?" Eleena stops browsing through the bookshelf and turns to face us. "It appears it is missing. Someone has taken the *Spellbook of Immortality.*"

I think back to the book my mother gave me before I left the cottage to come to Ladorielle. I remember the front binding having the inscription S.O.I. I thought they were initials.

"Grandmother," I interject.

"Yes?"

I hesitate when she addresses me. "What exactly is this *Spellbook of Immortality*?" I stand next to Aunt Fran, who is still stuck in place.

Eleena sighs and comes to sit in the chair opposite of us. "It's a book that has spells of every imaginable recipe to keep beings in an immortal state as well as healing spells to cure curses."

"Hang on a minute," I say, trying to collect my thoughts. "You mean, there's more than one way to stay immortal? This is nuts."

She smiles and folds her hands. "Several ways, my dear. In this book, not only are there spells to live forever, but there are spells for the silver dire wolves that need the magic of the silver moon to stay alive. There are also spells on how to protect Light Witches and defeat the dark ones."

"So, what Great Grandmother Sara said was true? There is a cure for Redmae?"

"Who's Redmae?" Eleena asks.

"Geneviève's daughter, Mother," Fran reminds her.

"Ahh, right. I forget she's not called Mae, much anymore." Eleena laughs. "You kids and your nicknames. Anyway, this book was entrusted into the hands of Ashengale for safekeeping, but it appears we are not exactly keeping it safe when it's gone missing."

"Grandmother," I interrupt again, "what is in this book that is so important?"

"Besides casting a spell to give your aunt here," —she gives an annoying point to Aunt Fran— "life on Ladorielle, there is one spell in there that will protect those that would have normally died to acquire a regenerating state."

"What do you mean by that? I don't understand."

My grandmother smiles. "A true Light Witch can cast a resurrection spell. They can take many forms. We cannot raise the dead, like a necromancer, but what we can do is enchant an item such as a ring, necklace, or bracelet, and embed the piece with a healing stone. This magic will keep the person who otherwise would have been killed, from dying. The body will sleep until it's fully healed. It's a rather unique spell because the soul remains in the physical world." She points to my aunt as a reference. "As long as they wear this item in battle, they cannot die. It's called a preservation spell. Of course, these pieces are a rare find, and the recipe to create more would require the bloodline of a Light Witch."

"And you want to make this ring for Aunt Fran?"

"Oh, dear Ladorielle, no. This charmed jewelry would be for you to wear, dear."

"What, me?" I look at my aunt. "Hang on a second. That's what you meant by saying you're not really dead." I look at her necklace. "The ruby in that charm you wear around your neck is imbued with such magic you call a preservation spell, isn't it?"

My aunt nods.

I turn back to my grandmother Eleena. "And my mother?"

She gives a slight chuckle. "Sarmira will do anything to stand in our way and keep you from doing what you're meant to finish. And she thinks by taking the hearts of her foes, it will prevent her demise. Killing all the Light Witches was a tactic she almost fulfilled."

"I see. It still doesn't answer my question, though. Does my mother have the same preservation spell?"

Eleena's hesitation to answer, makes me feel nauseous. "She didn't succeed, I take it?"

"No. it came with a severe price. Your mother gave her necklace to you." She points.

I touch the chain, remembering back when Moyer was jolted, attempting to strike me down in the basement of the manor. "Are you saying the magic is already embedded in the locket?"

"Yes, and no. Your mother gave that necklace to your father the night you were born. She thought, by giving it to you to wear, it would protect you from Sarmira."

I cup the locket with my left hand.

"It would have protected Isalora from death because of the preservation spell embedded into the labradorite. While it protects you now from various wickedness, and it has done its job shielding you from evil thoughts, harm, and your location, it will not protect you from death. The reason why your mother can never come back to life is because each spell is unique to the individual. And for that reason, your necklace needs to be imbued again."

"Like DNA?" A tear trails down my cheek.

"Yes. A Light Witch long ago saved the future witches, but it came at a cost. There's only one *Spellbook of Immortality* left—if it, too, isn't lost." Eleena looks worried pointing to the shelf. "Secondly, a Light Witch must cast it."

"Are you saying that you're a—I mean—"

"A Light Witch, yes. One of the last on Ladorielle, trained to read the book. Sarmira has done a grand job of finding every Light Witch and killing us off one by one. She thinks I died in the battle when the commander of her unit offed the heads of Sara and Ailbert." She lowers her voice. "There are many untrained witches that have gone underground. Most don't know their potential."

"And yet, my great grandparents are still alive, as well as you. You must have enchanted something of your own."

Eleena lifts her right hand to show a ring with a red stone in the center. "The immortality spell that was cast on the land before you were carted off at five years old to safety is what saved the kingdom, yes. This ring is what kept me alive. I enchanted it with the preservation spell, as well as half the entire kingdom. I was able—with the help of Sara, of course—

to save everyone who wore a piece of jewelry. The ones who perished were people who did not have such items on their person. Mostly the poor, unfortunately. An incredible, terrible moment in time. A memory I wish I could erase."

"My mother and Aunt Fran had such items, which saved them, too."

"Indeed." She looks at Fran. "Once your aunt's heart regenerates, Nyta will be able to place it back in her preserved body." She scowls. "Which is why your body should be in the crypt, Fran."

I look at Aunt Fran. "The night we left the house in Washington, is that the spell she means? Is that what saved the Kingdom of Ladorielle, too?"

"Sort of, yes," Fran confesses. "They're similar, but the spell Mother is referring to is a regenerative spell that will embed in jewelry to protect you from death, while the other is more like an illusion, making others believe one doesn't exist."

"And just so I'm clear, the spell didn't get to the king and queen, Great-Grandfather Ailbert and Great-Grandmother Sara, in time, which is why they were beheaded?"

"Oh no, the spell worked on them," Eleena says.

I stop to think. The heart I carried in the coffer comes to mind. I turn to my aunt. "That's why the heart in those containers are so important, isn't it? Because those hearts have a preservation spell protecting them."

My aunt smiles.

"Now do you understand why keeping my secret of being alive was so important?"

I nod. "And why Great-Grandmother has asked Cory to try and locate Great-Grandfather Ailbert's heart as well. Wait a minute...do you think Cory could find my mother's, too?"

"Perhaps, but remember, I told you your mother will never regenerate back. She wasn't wearing the necklace when Sarmira killed her," Eleena reiterates.

I take in this new revelation and it dawns on me. "That means I, too, have the bloodline of a Light Witch?" I stare in shock at my grandmother. "Sarmira knows about this spellbook, doesn't she." I look at my aunt. *That's what you meant when you said to Eleena, 'you can train me,' isn't it?*

Fran firms her lips, not showing any emotion except for a slight nod. *"Which is also why you must remain on Ashengale Island. At least until Mother can conjure up another preservation spell for you. We cannot risk your death."*

I look at Eleena. "And so, you wish to imbue this necklace again rather than make a ring?"

She nods.

"I'm beginning to feel like we're in a losing battle, and Sarmira has the upper hand," I say.

"Not entirely. I'm still alive, and she believes all Light Witches are dead. New Light Witches need a mentor to hone their craft, to learn spells, and to be able to control their magic. Without the proper training, they are vulnerable to evil. I think Sarmira was counting on you not sharpening your skills—skills you hadn't known you had. I mean, after all, the bloodline of a Deagon and a Storm with matching traits of a Light Witch, what more could an evil sorceress ask for?"

"The mystery thickens even more," I whisper.

"Yes, and she knows we have the spellbook, or rather it exists. She knows there is a spell that could destroy her once and for all. Even though she believes all Light Witches are gone, she doesn't want to take any chances. She's been searching for the book for centuries."

"What about The Sword of Valor, I thought that is what will destroy her?" I ask.

Eleena smiles again and nods. "Indeed, you're correct. There is an enchanting spell in that book that has embossed powers into the sword, as well. It was created by the strongest of Light Witches long ago."

"I need to give the book to her, Aunt Fran."

"I know."

I pull out the spellbook from the inside pocket of my jacket. "Is this what you're looking for? My mother said I was to give it to Dragonscale."

Eleena comes forward, taking the book from my hands. "Isalora had this, you say?"

I nod. "Is it the *Spellbook of Immortality?*"

She flips open the pages and nods. "Yes." The delight and relief on my grandmother's face eases the tension. "This book has been carried down through the centuries, guiding the Light Witches through whatever evil stood in their path. It appears you had it all along."

She hands back the book. "If Isalora said for you to give it to Dragonscale, I'm guessing she hasn't let on to the others I'm still alive. I want you to keep it with you. It will help you along your journey and might get you out of sticky situations you will be up against going through your trials. It's the reason I was thumbing through my library a moment ago, looking for it. I wanted to give it to you."

She nods, pointing to the book. "The immortality spell is in there. We can cast the spell on your aunt and the kingdom while we wait for Dragonscale's return. It will keep people here safe from war. And your Aunt Fran will have the power to keep the wraiths from crossing realms from our world to others. I only ask one thing. That we make a copy of the Spellbook of Immortality for this library."

"But of course." I hand the book back to Eleena. "How do we do that?"

"Like this." She takes the book and places it on the shelf among the other books, taps the spine three times while saying an incantation and in seconds where there was only one Spellbook of Immortality, there are now three.

I gap in awe.

Eleena's eyes twinkle. "It's not as easy as it looks making duplicates. It weighs heavy on my mental state. I will need a nap soon to rest. First, I must help you through the next step in your trials."

"My trials? But I haven't started them."

"Oh, my dear child, but you most certainly have. It started the day Madame Moyer had you kidnapped to the manor."

"How do you know—"

"I know more than you think."

A knock at the library door sounds and a woman enters, carting with her a tray of teacups, biscuits, and a kettle of tea. "Refreshments, Your Majesty?"

"Yes indeed, Annah, thank you. Please set them there." She points to an end table next to her chair.

With the flick of my grandmother's wrist, Aunt Fran is finally released from her frozen state and comes to stand by my side. "Thank you, Mother," she says, sounding a little annoyed.

"You're not off the hook yet, Francesca. You and I will have some choice words later." My grandmother smiles at the servant. "That is all, Annah. Thank you."

Annah bows and exits the library.

Eleena grabs the kettle of hot water and pours a cup. "Tea, anyone?"

I try to be polite, despite the tension. "Yes, please." She hands me the cup and saucer with a biscuit balanced on the side.

Eleena finishes the last cup by filling it to the brim, and says, "You must have many questions about these trials Wynter, and I'm hoping I can help you with that. These trials you're about to embark on must finish before our Super Blue Blood Moon Eclipse. You have less than a month's time to complete your trials for ascension. Once that is accomplished, you will be ready for Sarmira." She pauses, as though deciding whether to say more. "Redmae must accompany you along the way, as well as a few others. You must all work as a team."

After a few minutes of clanking dishes and careful sips from the burning liquid of chamomile, my grandmother says, clasping her hands, "Now that we have settled our stomachs, I have something to show you."

2
HIDDEN GATEWAY

S ETTING MY TEACUP DOWN, I follow Eleena out of the library.

I ask my aunt, *"Are you coming?"*

"You go on. I have a few things I need to work on here."

I nod, and Eleena leads the way out to the grand hall and down a corridor to another set of french doors. She flicks her wrist and they open on their own, revealing a beautiful sight beyond.

"It's a large garden solarium." To the right is a stone wall, but to the left, marble circular pillars stand in a row, and beyond it a magnificent oasis with water falling into a pool below. I hear the singing of birds and the trickle of water along with more dragon nectars suckling the blossoms sprawled along rosebush vines that crawl up the sides of the interior walls with bright colors of yellow, fuchsia, and purple. "It's so peaceful in here."

"I do admit, it's the closest to Heaven anyone will get without dying," Eleena says. "I'd love to tell you a story that isn't written in any history book. Are you interested?"

"Absolutely. History is one of my favorite subjects."

Eleena smiles. "Walk with me." She guides me around the pool as she speaks. "Long ago, before these lands were corrupted by evil, this whole world of Ladorielle was a euphoric place of peace and tranquility. Vothule, the Ruler of the Underworld, lived on the other planet of Elleirodal. His planet and ours have a polarity that keeps the magic in both realms alive. However, Vothule was greedy and was bound and determined to overtake the twin planet Ladorielle. Eddar, a god of light, refused to allow such evil into his world."

"I have heard parts of this story, I think," I interrupt.

"Ah, yes, I'm sure you have, but there are a few details that have been kept from many who do not know. Eddar was a king and ruler of peace, and he was tricked. He had let his guard down, allowing the ruler of evil into his home. This evil ruler took the form of a woman and she seduced him. He thought she was the Goddess of Love, Tranquility, and Peace: his equal. When he found out the deception, he realized no living being should ever have such power as she. Evil would always seek to overthrow all that is good in the world, and good always needs to protect the innocent." Eleena stops and overlooks the beautiful solarium.

"What happened?"

"He cast a protection spell over all the land. The whole planet. In doing so, he gave free will, destiny, and fate to all living beings. Allowing the living to choose their fate."

"And where is this god now?"

"Everywhere." She smiles. "He can take shape in anything, as he wishes. He is a god, after all. But he did do one thing..." Eleena moves toward the stairs and descends to the garden below.

"What was that?" I ask, curious, following beside her.

"He gave a man of pure heart and soul of this land we call Ladorielle a glimpse of his power, to protect the people and their innocents, and condemn the evil that seeks to destroy it. That man would soon become the new king. You might know his name as Dragonscale."

My mind reels with this new information. I stop a moment and gaze on the beautiful fruit trees growing in the solarium as I step onto the soft plush grass beneath my feet. "What are you saying? That this Dragonscale is some sort of demigod?"

"Dear Ladorielle, no, my child." She moves to a bench under a willow tree in the center of the garden and sits. "That would be someone that is half god. No, he's more like an immortal king with divine powers. And anyone born into his bloodline shall be bestowed the same gift as he, passing down from generation to generation. The first-born child is to be the reigning king or queen, should the previous ruler expire."

"But I thought you said he's immortal?"

"Aye, that I did. Just because one is of immortal flesh, doesn't mean one can't be killed. The Elvin people will live forever, too, unless they die in time of war. They are, in most cases, immune to sickness. It is no different in this situation."

"How does this pertain to me, Grandmother? Please don't tell me I must marry now, too?"

She laughs. "I should hope not yet. Traditions of the past have many marrying young, but I would hope you would wait a while."

That's a relief.

"Come sit with me." She pats the empty spot on the stone bench. "I will say this, my sweet granddaughter, the ancient ones have seen your future and you will be the one to carry out the replacement of Dragonscale's duties someday. This is why it's so important to go through your trials. It must be done before your ascension."

"Are you saying I'm related somehow to this Dragonscale? I'm not ready to be someone's queen." I think my grandmother can see I'm not fond of the idea, too.

"We don't have to discuss it now. In time, you will understand. I did say *someday*." She grunts. "I do hope it won't be an immediate coronation just yet. Although we must be prepared in any event."

"I understand." *Definitely not something I'm interested in, however.* "Tell me more about this prophecy, Grandmother."

"Well, during the reign of your great-great-grandfather Greyson Deagon—who had taken on the title of reigning king from his father before him—knighted a man named Bryce Storm and gave him command of the royal guard.

"War again broke out throughout the land, with Sir Bryce in command, leading his soldiers to battle. Years passed, and the king agreed to a truce with the Lord of the Underworld, Vothule.

"The hopeful King Greyson invited The Council of Twelve for a meeting. He confided with the Priestess of the Royal Court, not knowing that she had been influenced by one of Vothule's assistants. She was the one who convinced King Greyson to go through with the feast of peace. But there would be bloodshed that day instead."

"Are you saying this priestess had a memory stamp placed?"

"I suppose you could say that, yes."

"Sarmira."

Eleena's mouth curves into a smile of disgust. "Yes."

"What happened next?"

"The king didn't know it at the time, of course, but his wife was poisoned. He later found out this priestess was the one who had given the queen the fatal dose. Vulnerable from heartbreak, he could not see past a life without her. He knew his beloved queen would die and leave his daughters without a mother. The king went mad.

"The priestess had tricked the king into having a feast, inviting the Houses of each coven to form a truce. A treaty of peace." She pauses to stand, taking my hand in hers, and pulls me over to a different bench placed near the waterfall. Goldfish swim in the pond, and an abundance of ferns that look much like the Waxlily surround the rocks, and green vines with yellow flowers cascade down throughout the cracks.

"It was a trap," she continues. "The dark side of the Underworld covens massacred most everyone in the realm. Word traveled fast claiming the king was accused of treason. Most of the leaders died, and it nearly destroyed the assembly of balance.

"When the king realized what had transpired, he locked himself in the throne room. I imagine he had thoughts of taking his own life."

"Is that what happened? Surely, he didn't take the coward's way out."

Eleena shakes her head. "No one knows. He disappeared. A body has never been found. When Sarmira realized she had won, she knew she had one last task to finish. Kill the one who betrayed her the most."

"Who was that?"

"Her daughter Petra."

"Wait, what?" I nearly choke hearing the words come from my grandmother's mouth. "Come again?"

She takes my hand and squeezes it. "Petra didn't want to live the life of evil like her mother and she escaped her world of Elleirodal, and with help from some, she fled through the gates between our worlds. Such a long story to tell but know that your great-great-grandmother Petra was pure of heart. She knew such evil would destroy all that is virtuous and elected not to be on that side and is living proof that even if a soul is born to evil, they have the free will to make a choice to do good. Because she chose the light and to do all things moral, the wrath of Sarmira's destruction began."

"So, she's angry with her daughter and takes it out on every single bloodline that follows?"

"More pieces of the puzzle, I imagine, you have been wondering about, huh?" Eleena asks.

I nod. "At least I now know why she's hellbent on destroying me."

"When Bryce discovered his beloved lying on the ground nearly lifeless, watching Sarmira about to take her fatal blow to Petra, he did the most spontaneous thing anyone would do in protecting the ones they love, and he stabbed Sarmira in the back. She didn't see him coming. She shattered into a million pieces of glass."

"The Sword of Valor," I whisper.

"Yes." My grandmother grabs my hand. "You may have heard this part of the story already, but it's worth repeating. In doing so, Bryce was stabbed by the fragments of jagged shards and nearly bled to death next to Petra. Petra had never used her magic in all the years she was with Bryce, but she couldn't bear the thought of her sons growing up without parents. She knew her time was coming to an end. She didn't have the energy to heal herself and save Bryce, so she did the only thing she could—saved her husband. The damage Sarmira had done to both of them was fatal."

"How do you know such details?"

"See this waterfall?" She glances up and watches water flow to the pool below. A mist forms, and it cools my skin. She takes my hand and guides me behind the cascade of water where a door hides.

"More surprises?"

She smiles as she opens the door. "You may find more answers beyond here."

As I pass through the enchanting entrance, I'm struck with immediate love and pure joy. I'm in awe of the existence of such a glorious place. The room reminds me of being in a cave, yet it feels like an extension of the solarium garden we came from. In the center of this serene area is a pool in the shape of a square, with pillars in each corner. From these pillars, there are faucet-like spouts attached to them. One pillar emits water while the opposite one looks to be pouring out endless amounts of sand. Neither element appears to overflow the pool.

"This place is magnificent," I say.

As we draw closer, Eleena says, "This is the Elemental Pool of Balance. As you can see, each pillar holds one of the four elements."

I turn to the left and see fire coming from the third pillar that was hidden from view when we first walked in.

"The pillar to your right is the element of air. If you stand near it, you will feel a breeze," Eleena adds.

"It's so euphoric," I say, as I look up and see a painted mural of clouds and stars above the pool.

Eleena appears pleased with my fascination. "And to your left is the Pillar of Fire."

Four benches set between each pillar. Eleena sits between air and fire, and again pats the bench next to her, gesturing for me to sit. Taking my hand in hers, she says, "Do you know why I've brought you here?"

I shake my head.

As though our sitting is a signal, four figures form in the pool, each unique in their own way. I can tell they represent the four elements. I gasp in awe.

One is dressed in blue and has white hair flowing down to her ankles. She carries a pitcher in one hand. Her ears are pointed, her nose thin, and her lips white. She comes forward and bows. "I am the Keeper of Water."

The second figures steps forward. "I'm the Keeper of Life," she says. "What many on the human planet refer to as Earth. But I have a different name here. I'm called Terra." Her hair is black, and her eyes a golden brown. Her skin matches the color of her eyes and she shimmers gold in the lighting. She carries an urn filled with fresh soil. "I plant the seeds, and the Keeper of Water gives them nourishment to grow."

The next elemental steps forward, saying, "I am the Keeper of Air."

A breeze passes through my hair and strands tickle my face.

She's translucent and doesn't have solid flesh as the others. Her gown is white, and she hasn't any hair on her head. "I bend the wind and give you air to breathe. I can move sailboats and glide birds as they fly. I also can call upon the storms when needed."

The final keeper steps forward. She wears a red gown, and her hair glows with shades of reds, oranges, and yellows. "I am the Keeper of Fire that gives one warmth from the sun and the lava that flows from mountains. I will burn those who dare to trespass where they do not belong. I will help those needing to build a fire for warmth, and with the help of the wind, ignite the wood from Terra."

"As you can see," Eleena begins, "this hidden oasis is to be protected at all cost. Should anyone know of its existence, it could jeopardize this magical place."

"I imagine Ashengale is part of this safe haven?"

"Yes," Eleena says. "And I hear you have two of these elemental gifts."

"I do?"

She nods. "Water and fire."

"You mean that's why I have the power to throw fire and water?"

"Correct. There hasn't been a Deagon that has carried two elements of power for a very long time. Part of your training in the trials will be to master these elemental powers."

"Has there been someone else with such power?"

"Yes. They have not discovered what they can do. They will in time."

"Who are they?"

"Ah, the curious question. This is not the time for that to be revealed."

I feel the blue gem in my pocket Aoes gave to me before I passed through to Dragonscale Island, heat up. I pull it out and it glows in my hands. "What's going on?"

"The stone knows it's time."

"Time for what, exactly?" As though the stone knows what to do, it lifts out of my hands and floats to the Elementals. They pass the glowing rock to one another. And each time the stone is taken into an Elemental's hands, the glow of the gem grows brighter.

"What's happening?"

Eleena smiles. "Watch closely."

"Your necklace, may we have it please?" Fire asks.

I hesitate. "But I'm not to—"

Eleena places her hand over mine. "It's all right. We're safe here. Protected. Sarmira cannot find you within these walls."

Trusting Eleena, I unclasp the chain and hand it to Fire. She takes the gem, and places it inside my locket and then releases the necklace. Instead of it dropping to the ground, it floats in the air to the center of the pool. There, each Elemental takes their right hand, and places a hand over hand, while the glowing locket hovers, chanting something in a language I don't understand. Their bodies match the glow of the locket. Then without warning, the glowing stops, the locket falls into the pool, and all the Elemental Keepers disappear.

"Where did they go?"

"Do not fear, they went back to their Elemental realms. Go on, dear, pick up the necklace."

I step forward and plunge my hand into the water to retrieve my locket. Immediately, I noticed something different. "What is this?"

Eleena comes forward. "You have received a very valuable gift from the Elementals. Look closer."

Where the locket once only showed a rose and sword on one side, and the dragon on the other, now shows additional characteristics. The gem Aoes gave me has been broken into tiny bits that are now strategically placed throughout the outer casing, set into the silver. It's as though a master jeweler cut each stone with exquisite precision. "It looks like I'm gazing into a galaxy of stars. Can you tell me what this means?"

She smiles. "Look inside. There you will find your answer."

I open the locket, relieved to still see the portraits of my great-grandfather and great-grandmother still intact, but something else has been added: a clock hand. "Is this what I think it is?"

"A compass, yes. It will help lead you to the Sword of Valor, but it is much more than that, you will soon discover." Eleena pats my shoulder, signaling that it's time to leave.

Aunt Fran waits in her translucent state, in the garden like a guard, when we return from behind the waterfall.

"I thought you had things to research in the library. Done so soon?" Fran laughs lightly. "You've been gone a few hours."

"Have I? It doesn't feel that long."

"The garden will do that to you."

"Let's take a break for a while, shall we?" Eleena says. "Fran, would you mind showing Wynter to her room? The day has grown to evening, and we need her to be at her full strength in preparation for tomorrow."

"What's going on tomorrow?"

"You will know soon enough. I've kept you entirely too long. You need your rest."

Aunt Fran nods. "Come with me, my dear niece. There is so much I have been dying to show you."

As I follow my aunt, I look back to observe Eleena engaging in conversation with Garrick. *Has he been there the whole time?*

Fran answers my thoughts. *"Not entirely, no."*

We walk together through some doors on the opposite end from which we entered the solarium and down a corridor. "You must be exhausted from your day."

"I am, yes, but what has been revealed to me thus far has me wanting to know much more."

"That necklace you wear is key to the answers you seek, but I have much more to show you," she says.

3

I'M HOME

WE WALK BACK THE way we had come through the corridor and past the library where I first met Eleena and descend a spiral staircase. In some ways, it reminds me of the stairs that led to the basement at Storm River Manor. But these steps are made of polished stone. Flecks of silver reflect from the lighted crystal chandeliers seated in the ceiling. We continue downward until we reach an opening to a grand foyer that's more like a gathering hall.

In the center of this large room is an oval table and several chairs. A large sectional is set to the side. If I wasn't aware of the fact I'm in another world, I'd swear I was in a random mansion back home.

There are several staircases in different directions, leading to different levels. Some go farther down the castle caves and tunnels, as other staircases scale upward around large cliffs. Some of the walls appear to be made of the same polished stone as the floors, while random spots of the castle interior remain rough and in raw boulder form. The unique style is not anything I've seen before.

"This area is the living quarters. Much of our day-to-day is spent either here or in our rooms. Unless we venture out into the city. This way, and I'll show you to your bedroom. I don't believe it's been touched since you left."

"Since I left? I don't remember any of this."

"In time you will."

We cross the open space to the opposite side and descend more stairs. "Tell me something. Is this the home we lived in before we fled? To Washington state, I mean."

"Sort of. You lived here in Ashengale City from the time you were about five years old. When you fell off that rock near Storm Castle, your screams were heard from across the lands."

"Yes, I vaguely remember something like that."

Aunt Fran sighs. "The whole world knew who you were in that brief moment. It opened a conduit to your whereabouts. We all were petrified that *she* would come for you. It was Queen Sara's idea to hide you away. She instructed Geneviève to gather all the druids and begin a mass exodus to the hidden veil of the underground. She could only take ten people at a time.

"This place is where she instructed Geneviève to bring you. Here you were safe. She also brought her daughters, Redmae and Rory, as well as Cory, Cole, Casey, Blair...and a few others."

"Is this when Sarmira captured Chad and Dad?"

"Your dad, no, but Chad, yes. Along with Derek and Daniel. As my mother mentioned earlier, Vothule and Sarmira slaughtered most of the kingdom. When they realized you were nowhere to be found, they left Storm Castle in ruins. It took years to rebuild the kingdom."

"I can't help but think it was my—"

"It's not your fault. Don't ever think that. Sarmira is evil and this was her doing, and hers alone, except maybe the help from her father."

We reach the end of the steps that lead to a hallway, and I follow Aunt Fran as she continues her story.

"Once the massacre was over, Nyta immediately went to work repairing the king and queen, removing their hearts and placing them in coffers. At one point, Sara's box was stolen. We've managed to recover hers, thanks to you, but as you know, Ailbert's coffer remains missing. And we still are unable to find Isalora's."

"Eleena said my mother will never be brought back, so why does it matter if we find her coffer?"

There's a twinkle of hope in Aunt Fran's eyes, "This is true. Many priestesses have confirmed your mother will never come back. I'm still looking for the one cleric that will tell me different." My aunt smiles, somberly. "She can still roam the lands of Dragonscale Island, having a form much like mine, though. That would be easier to accept than her being trapped on Earth."

"Moyer has it somewhere, I bet, keeping it as leverage."

"I have the same feeling, my dear niece. And I'm determined to find out where it is if it's the last thing I do."

"I'll gladly take on the task if you'll let me."

My aunt laughs. "You'll take on the task? My sweet girl, you have enough to worry about. I have no doubt if I gave you that responsibility, you'd be the first to seek out the assignment." She stops to give me a hug. "We already have people searching for your mother's heart, trust me. Your job—your main job—is to bring back your erased memories and focus on your ascension trials."

"And what about you, Aunt Fran?"

"What...you mean this?" she asks, gesturing to her own body. "You heard my mother. As soon as my body is regenerated, I'll be back. I, too, am able to stay solid-looking because I'm on Dragonscale Island, and anyone can see me. There is a tree that holds the source of all magic. The way to that source most do not know—not even me. That magic tree is protected by the Elementals." She pauses. "I'm going off on a tangent again. Like your mother, if I were to venture off the Island, I would turn into spirit form, and no one could see me."

"Except my mother used a spell at the cottage to look human as well. This sounds a bit like what you're explaining to me now."

"It is the same spell; the only difference is the cottage is her kingdom. If she were to leave, she'd turn to spirit form just like I would."

"So, what you're telling me is this spell anchors to a certain place."

"Yes. And going beyond the space, you lose the enchantment."

"Interesting."

"Of course, there are also those who have the innate ability to see ghosts." She turns to me. "Like you."

"How is all of this possible? Technically you're dead. I mean, once someone dies, they are presumed to move on. It's how life is supposed to work."

"I imagine you're right, Wynter. It's not exactly a conventional way of life, though, here I am." She huffs. "Now, if we were in the realm of Earth's atmosphere, none of this would be possible. They're in a different galaxy."

That thought sent an uneasy feeling to the pit of my stomach thinking at how far I am from Earth.

"The bigger test at hand is defeating Sarmira. I'm one of many guardians that will be shoulder-to-shoulder with other guardians once I'm called upon." She gives a side grin, stops, and points to a door. "Here you go."

"Wait, Aunt Fran. There is so much more I want to know." I hesitate to find the right words. "That day I saw you stabbed by the giant, I thought I lost you for good. If I knew then what I know now...I mean, I felt like my heart had been ripped out when you fell." Tears begin to form.

"Wynter, what are you saying?"

"I'm saying while Isalora is, indeed, my biological mother and holds a special place in my heart, you're my mom. I can't bear to lose you again. I need my mom."

Tears form in her eyes, too. She opens her arms and embraces me tightly. "Sweetheart. I get it. I will be okay." She runs her hands down the back of my hair and then pulls away saying, "I will be fine. Trust me." She looks into my eyes. "No harm will come to me. I promise."

"Promises again," I say.

"A promise I know I can keep. Now, enough of the water-works. Go into your room and tell me what you remember."

I veer in the direction of an oval wooden door. It has a loop handle rather than a knob to open it. A key sticks out from the keyhole.

"Go on, unlock it. What are you waiting for?" she asks.

I hesitate before turning the key. I hear it unlatch and the door squeaks open, revealing my room on the other side. Fran pulls the key from the latch and hands it to me. "Keep it safe. You will use it in the future. It is your portal passport to opening many doors to other realms. Might I suggest putting it on a chain? Perhaps the same one around your neck. Then it, too, will be invisible to the evil lurking."

"What do you mean by portal passport?"

"This key holds the combination to those doors you saw in the Hall of Secrets, much of them need a key such as this to open them." Her lips curve into a smile. "Except of course the portal doors that lay dormant."

"You're saying this key will help in my trials?"

She doesn't answer me, adding to the mystery, but her silence gives me my answer.

"Come, reacquaint yourself with your room." My aunt leads the way.

"This room is almost the exact replica as the one I had in Washington. Only bigger." Memories of the past flit across my mind.

"The nice thing about memory stamps, some things can be similarly duplicated," my aunt says. "I tried to make it as comfortable as possible. The furniture is different, of course, but as you can see, the window is also in the same place."

"But h-how did you—"

Fran puts her fingers to her lips and bites her nail. "Don't think, just enjoy the moment."

A vanity sits against a wall near the window with a gold-detailed framed mirror, which brings my eyes past it to enjoy the lands across the lava valley. A silhouette of Storm Castle resides across the water cliffs. Dragons soar in the sky, scouting Dragonscale Island territory.

I pause from the view and look around the room. A four-poster bed sits off to one corner, decorated in my favorite shades of purple, lavender, plum, and deep mauve with two nightstands on either side. A trunk rests at the foot of the bed, with a purple and white crochet blanket with crochet lavender rose accents applique stitched on top.

"This was my room after I fell. I remember." My mind swells with memories of how it use to be.

"Yes."

"I recall Namari sleeping in this room with me, too." At that time, he wasn't as large as a full-grown Dragongryph. I walk to the other side of the bed to see his sleeping nest still intact.

"Occasionally, he will come in through the large window, there." She points. "I'm told he still sleeps in here. He missed you. Don't be surprised if you see him tonight."

"I missed him, too. I mean now that I remember him." I turn to face my aunt.

She folds her hands. "Dinner is in about thirty minutes. I'll let you settle and wash up. We have more work to do before your third trial begins tomorrow evening."

"Third trial? When was my first and second?"

Aunt Fran grins. "When you learned the truth about where you came from."

"You mean my self-discovery when I was still locked away in that evil place at Storm River Manor? I never want to go back there."

"I understand that you have scars. It will take time to heal. You overcame a lot. You pushed through the dream stamp Sarmira invoked upon you. And you discovered who you are."

"Okay what was the second?"

"Trusting yourself and the power you're capable of."

"I'm still not sure who I am."

"Don't worry, your journey is just beginning."

"I'd hate to know what my past trials were, if this is my beginning."

"Wynter, it will be okay. You're almost through your first set of trials."

First set? "Sure, okay."

Fran shuts the door, and I turn to take in the lost memories. *I'm home.*

I scan my room again. A similar bookshelf rests against the wall housing all my paperbacks, and the desk I did homework on, is next to it. I glance out the window to see the moons have joined.

The moonlight reflects on the ocean waters below. Hanging there on the window frame is the labradorite, or at least a replica of the one I had in my faux home. I laugh under my breath. "It's the little things, isn't it?" I whisper.

Even the door to the bathroom is the same. The dresser and closet is filled with clothes, and I glance to the abundance of fluffy pillows on my bed—Charlie. He sits hiding among the soft luxuries of accessories lying on the bedspread. I pick him up. "How did you get here?"

Still clutching the key Fran gave me in my hand, I place it on the chain around my neck. It feels good to be back. Back to a place where I belong. I didn't realize how much I missed it until then. I grab Charlie off the bed, hug him tight, recline against the pillows, and close my eyes as I reflect on my life thus far. Ironically, for the first time in a long time, I feel peace, and I want to enjoy the moment.

A KNOCK AT THE door startles me from my meditation followed by a loud grumble from the side of my bed. That too, distracts me. Namari opens one eye.

I must have fallen asleep. The sunlight shows through the window, and what I see flying outside isn't birds, but dragons.

Another knock raps at my door.

Namari stands and yawns. *"Well, aren't you going to answer it?"* Thankfully, my room is big enough for Namari to outstretch his wings.

A little sidetracked by seeing Namari, I say, *"Yes, of course."*

A knock sounds once more as I reach for the knob and open it. "Aunt Fran."

"There you are," she says, stepping into my old room. "I waited for you in the hall last night, but after an hour passed, I decided to check on you."

"I'm sorry, I must've fallen asleep."

"Indeed. I don't blame you. It was a long day yesterday. Today might be even longer though."

"Oh? Does Grandmother have me starting so early already?"

"More like Dragonscale this time." Her words I'm sure were meant to tease, but the thought of more training has me a little anxious.

"Can you give me about thirty minutes to get ready?"

"Sure." She smiles. "I'll see you in a few minutes." She shuts the door behind her, leaving Namari and I alone.

I look at my dragon hybrid who has since laid his head down on the floor, saying, *"Well, Namari, it appears I'm late for a date with Dragonscale."*

"He's probably planning to take you on a tour of the city."

I squint at Namari. *"Hang on a second. You're talking inside my head. It didn't register until now that you were telling me to answer the door."*

His nostrils blow out steam.

"Was that supposed to be a chuckle?"

His grumble gets louder, and I feel like he's not at all pleased.

"Oh, come now, why are you giving me the silent treatment? Namari, what is it?"

He grunts, again. *"You best get a move on, Princess, and not keep Her Ladyship waiting."*

"No, Namari, it can wait. What's wrong? Why do you look so sad? And how are you able to communicate without me being on your back?"

"I'm sad because you will no longer need me once you learn to fly, and you don't need to ride me to communicate while under the umbrella of Dragonscale Island."

"Hold up...fly?"

"I've said too much. You will see."

"Namari, I will always need you. You're my friend. My dragon brother. I will never leave you. I don't know what to expect after the trials, but I will always call upon you. No matter what happens, we will always be friends. Why do you worry so much?" I wrap my small arms around his giant neck.

"You will understand, once you have completed your last trial," he reiterates.

"Don't be sad, Namari." I swear his eyes glisten, but I see no tears. I know in my heart, though, he is worried I will forget him. *"Remember, I love you, always."*

"I love you, too, my Princess. Go on, get ready. We haven't much time. I urge you to find something comfortable to wear."

I nod. Gathering my things, I head to the bathroom. *"I'll see you later today, then?"*

"I'm close by, always. You know how to call me."

A KNOCK ON MY door startles me as I come out of the bathroom. "Wynter, we haven't all day."

It's my aunt. I look back at Namari resting on his bed. *"Here goes nothing, I suppose. Wish me luck."*

He gives a loud huff, and steam emits through his nostrils. *"You will do great."* He stretches his wings and lowers his head, as if he's bowing, then takes off through the large window of my room, fit for a dragon, letting out a loud roar.

A second knock sounds, prompting me to answer.

"Are you ready?" my aunt asks.

"Yes." I turn around taking a quick look around my room.

"Wynter, is everything all right?"

"Yes, fine." I look at her and smile. "I'm happy to be home."

4

THE THIRD TRIAL

T HE WALK DOWN THE dark corridor with Aunt Fran by my side feels like we're moving in slow motion.

My thoughts reflect to when I arrived at the castle yesterday. There was so much I wanted to know, so many unanswered questions. Now I wonder if I am ready for those answers.

I'm beginning to understand why my dad taught me how to wield a sword, or the projections Cory helped me through in maneuvering my directional intentions—that was hard. The focus to light my fingers on fire by just thinking about it took a lot of mental strength. And Aunt Fran tried to guide me around to understanding the truth about our family. Looking back at that now, I realize she'd been throwing hints at me all through high school. It all led to this moment. I have a heavy feeling I am about to know the entire truth.

"How are you feeling?" Aunt Fran asks.

"I don't know yet." My heart races. The anticipation sends a chill up my spine. Time will tell if I'm worthy enough to possess so much power.

"Don't be nervous. He's waited a long time to see you. This will be your last lesson, but it will be liberating, Wynter. You will soon understand who you are."

Lesson. Like a schoolgirl on her first day. Aoes said this was needed to grow my abilities. I don't need to stand in front of a mirror to know I have physically and emotionally changed. I still have long white hair, and my eyes are no longer green but blue from coming into my power, however it's my heart—my soul—which knows the truth, and it stares back at me as though I should have known all these years.

My thoughts are interrupted by the hard knocks on an iron door that stands in the pathway of meeting the famous Dragonscale. I was so consumed with my recent past I didn't realize how quickly we'd arrived at the training hall.

"Remember Wynter, you're a warrior, and one day will be queen. You will overcome this. Keep a clear mind, and focus," my aunt says.

The doors open. Together, we walk shoulder-to-shoulder to the center of the circular room.

"Father." Aunt Fran bows. She nudges me to follow suit.

"Father? I'm confused. Where is he? I see no one. I thought we were to meet Dragonscale?"

A grumble intrudes my thoughts. *"I'm here I assure you."*

"Hold your head high and keep your posture straight. Own it. Stay confident." She kisses my forehead and slips out between the doors, leaving me in the large arena, alone.

A breeze passes over my skin giving me goosebumps.

The room isn't dark except around the perimeter where the colossal pillars hold the second floor above. Seats line the balcony. It feels like I'm in a fighting arena from ancient roman times. To my left and right are iron gates leading down dark hallways. Above us is a painted mural of dragons fighting dragons, giants fighting elves and fire colliding with ice. Is it an ancient war? The background places planets and stars in the distance.

Hot breath behind my neck brings me back from my deep thoughts and I turn around to see nothing there.

A deep laugh follows.

"Aunt Fran?"

"Focus. It's a test. Your thoughts are distracted. I am with you but not beside you."

I look up into the seating area to see she's watching from above.

A blurry figure passes by me and it's like looking through liquid glass. It has a shape I can't quite grasp but whatever it is, it's massive. My eyes follow it as the outline moves.

"Good. You catch on quick," the unfamiliar voice says.

The entity thrusts forward and I leap out of the way. Something else comes at me, forcing me to jump. *A tail?* It whips forward and I instinctively spring upward a second time. It all seems to happen in slow motion and before I realize it, I tuck and roll, and land on my feet. My body instinctively knew what to do before my brain did. *"What was that?"*

"Your instincts kicked in," Aunt Fran answers.

"She has great reflexes, Fran. You've taught her well." The voice speaking has a deep rasp.

"Sadly, I can't take credit. It wasn't me who taught her that move."

The voice grunts. "I should have expected that answer."

His vibrations sends energy through my body. A feeling of peace and love. Much like how Cory does when he tries to calm my emotions, only this feels different.

"If she's anything like her father—"

"In some ways she's better. She has come a long way, Father."

"Time will tell if she is ready," the voice without a face speaks.

"Hey, I'm right here. Third person is child's play. Why are you invisible? I may feel calm on the inside, and I imagine it's to keep me from a fight or flight situation, but hiding from me feels cowardly."

The voice laughs, and slowly reveals himself. A massive dragon appears. "Cowardly, you say?"

I gasp and take a step backward. *Eleena is my grandmother and queen. It doesn't click until this moment. Is Dragonscale... my grandfather?*

His black coat glistens gold, along with talons and winged, matching tips. His eyes blink a fiery orange. And as quickly as he appears, he disappears in the same instant, changing into his human form right before my eyes. "It's a test. You passed—barely." He looks up at Aunt Fran. "She needs much more training."

Aunt Fran bows her head. "Yes, Father."

I've never physically seen my grandfather. In the visions he was much younger and called himself Ian. The man who stands before me has deep blue eyes, white hair and a beard. Tall and lean and wearing chainmail, he still comes across as strong. His breastplate matches the banner flags displayed in the front courtyard entrance. I'm assuming it's the Deagon's Coat of Arms.

"Are you ready for the truth?" He takes a key from his pocket.

It's a key that looks much like the one used to release the cuffs around the others that wore valiancium steel in the past. I nod, standing confident. "I was born ready, sir."

He grunts. "Yes, I suppose you were. You've had one hand tied behind your back since birth, it's time to spread your wings." The doors to the training room swing closed. He unlocks the valiancium cuffs and then transforms back to a dragon.

A surge of power ignites within my body. I didn't understand freedom until now. My magic comes at me in full force. The flow of energy burns as it slowly travels through my veins from the tips of my fingers down to my toes, like a river of fire. A numbing sensation sparks my nerves, and everything tingles. My entire body feels warm, like I'm sitting next to searing flames. My skin burns, my eyes see things I didn't see before, and my mind knows things that were not lucid a moment ago.

The temperature rises and the energy almost feels overwhelming, but something is preventing the power from consuming me.

"This is only level one, child. Are you ready to continue?"

"Yes."

"Deep breaths, my niece. Focus and remember what we've taught you."

The power that held me anchored releases, and this time my bones ache, my head feels like it's on fire, my heart races, and my eyes blur. "My veins burn! What is going on with me? I can't control it!" I scream.

"Yes, you can. Concentrate," he says.

"You say that, but it's easier said than done. It's too overpowering." My skin feels like it's about to rip from my body and peel away from my bones. It's pure agony. I feel my bones breaking and the throbbing twinges are almost unbearable. "Make it stop!"

"The change is inevitable. Trust me, the first time is always the hardest." He pauses to bend down to my level, looking me in the eyes. "It was excruciating for me, too, but I know you can do this."

I drop to the floor, my knees weak from so much pain. The pressure inside my shoes intensify forcing me to pull off my boots. Pointed nails push through my toes. My spine breaks, forcing me downward and I double over in pain.

"Why do you think that the poison given to me all those years ago as a child didn't kill me?" Aunt Fran questions as she stands against the wall, witnessing my suffering. "Or Sara, for that matter? Have you ever thought why Sarmira stole your mother's heart from her chest in the first place? Wynter, think! Use your intuition." I sense the frustration from my aunt.

I can't speak. The pain is so intolerable. My thoughts barely carry. *"Why?"*

My trainer comes forward, laughing as though I'm ignorant. "Don't you get it, Wynter? You're a Deagon."

"You all keep telling me that." I breathe a heavy and exhausting breath. "But I still don't see what it has to do with this." More stabbing discomfort erupts through my skin as it breaks open, revealing white scales with a shimmer of silver and I scream in a panic. "What is happening?"

He grunts and touches my forehead with his thumb. "Remember who you are."

My body lifts as my whole frame changes and some of the pain melts away. The heat builds and the winds kick up, like a tornado.

Flashes of the past come racing back, a power of strength coming with it. Rage, happiness, sadness, it all consumes me like a vacuum. It all lines up with each piece falling together like a puzzle — lost pieces of my life suddenly found. I gasp in confusion.

Flames shoot out my mouth and wings grow from my back. My legs turned to talons.

It's at this moment my memories come full circle.

Aunt Fran smiles and Garrick smirks.

"See, I told you she could do it," Garrick boasts. "I knew you had it in you, Wynter, the first day I saw you enter the palace, I knew."

"Where did he come from?" I ask.

"He snuck in while you were—occupied," she answers.

Dragonscale, my trainer, sits back watching me, as I explore the *new me*. He joins my thoughts, saying, *"You've awakened."*

My mind becomes clear. It's at this moment my memories come full circle. "I remember—everything."

"Now, you're ready," Dragonscale says.

WHEN I ENTERED THE arena before my transition, it looked like nothing out of the ordinary, but now I can see every detail all the way down to the speck of dirt hiding in the cracks of stone, or the fine line brush strokes of the painted mural above. Even the grainy bumps that are left behind after iron is crafted and cooled, I see present on the entrance doors. Colors appear brighter, my sense of smell peaks and aromas that were not present before, fill my nostrils. My mind feels like it will explode at any moment, with all the whispers I hear from afar. "I'm sorry, Grandfather. There is so much to take in."

"In time you will grow comfortable. It's going to be a while before you will be used to your true identity."

Now that I've released the beast that has craved freedom within my soul for so long, I stand here in a different form than my human body. I glance down to my feet. "Seeing me in this shifted form is going to take some getting used to."

I have the scales of a lizard, but my feet are talons. I stretch my wings, and they spread so far that if not for the large area we're in, I would have possibly injured one. My head feels heavy, and I have the urge to open my mouth and blow flames. It's as though I have a cold, and all I want to do is blow my nose to relieve the pressure. "How long am I to stay like this? I feel like my skull will explode at any moment."

Dragonscale's eyes are bright gold this time instead of fiery orange and his scales have a red tinge near the skin that I didn't notice before and while he is mostly black in color, I'm silverly white with blue edging, having a silver shimmer. He chuckles.

"I didn't realize I was so amusing to you, Grandfather." My nerves flare, I want to flame something out of anger.

"It's all right, Wynter. I'm not laughing at you, I'm laughing with you, because I'm joyful you finally found your true form." He transforms back to human once again and paces away from me to one of the dark tunnels.

"Where are we going?"

"To an area where target boards line the wall. And you can practice your new dragon abilities. Come, let me show you." Aunt Fran and Garrick follow behind me.

The tunnel leads a short distance away to another room. It reminds me of a gym except it set up like an obstacle course.

"See the dummy over there?" He points. "Turn it to charcoal. You may feel better."

I do as he instructs and release a path of destruction along with it. Not only did I destroy the doll, but I made a hole in the floor. Charred rocks crumble through the opening to the level below. "Whoops."

"Well, I see your strength is improving. We will have that fixed. Not to worry, my student."

My mind is clearer now. I sense his strength and can feel he's truly not worried, but proud of what I did. Our minds are connected, as well as body and soul. His power consumes me. It's everything I ever imagined. Love, honor, respect for the living, peace of mind, the strength of power, and the madness that comes with it. I see inside his mind, as he shows me the wars of the past, the births of children, and the deaths of loved ones.

Not only can I remember my own past, but I'm also flooded with the memories of all those who call Ladorielle their home. Even the Trek and goblins are in my mind. I can see King Zeelx the goblin leader sorting out a map trying to locate me, and Sarmira's devious plans about whom to destroy first, my very existence or the kingdom Dragonscale rules. I can also see how Sarmira has taken possession of Maura Moyer. How my grandmother Moyer's soul is helpless to stop Sarmira from her ploy to destroy everyone around her. I'm torn between sympathy for Moyer and anger. Her human form has caused great chaos to my family line and of others, but I also see it was her own choice to save— I gasp. Me.

"What is all of this you're showing me in my head?" I ask. "And my grandmother Moyer—she sacrificed—"

"It's who you are. What you were born to do. All that ever was, is, and will be, is now in you for you to see. You're to take the crown as Queen of Ladorielle," he says. "Do not allow the past to define you, Wynter. Take this knowledge and use it wisely."

"But why now? There is so much more I want to explore, to do."

"And you should do them. I'm not going to hold you back from your dreams."

"But I don't know if I want this." I pause, taking in what he's telling me. Every question I ever had is answered. "How is it that I'm able to know so much?"

"You have but a glimpse of what I see because I've invited you into my mind. Most of what you see you will forget. You must make your own decisions. The memories that remain will be because I choose for you to remember to carry out the mission at hand."

I dig closer into the channels of his thoughts. All of what he has witnessed would make any ordinary person go insane.

One of the iron gates opens. "Come with me."

I look behind me, and both Aunt Fran and Garrick nod, urging me to go with my grandfather.

The long tunnel leads to a ledge overlooking the entire valley. He comes to sit next to me. "It's like looking into a hidden world within a mountain." It is massive, with dragons flying about. Ashengale's village is set along a river that flows to the mouth of the cave where the cliff edge greets the ocean below.

"As you can see," Dragonscale begins, "the realm you will rule will be a big responsibility, which is why your training is so important. Rest assured, I will not leave your side until you're fully ready to take on the duty."

"I have much to learn. I want to explore this *new* me. To see this whole world through my new eyes. Defeat Sarmira and free Maura Moyer from the grasp of evil."

"And what's stopping you?" he asks. "Let me show you something else."

To the left of us a large castle window overlooks the volcanic terrain below on Dragonscale island.

"The views are spectacular. A window carved into a mountainside. How extraordinary." Through the glass, fissures erupt spontaneously with lava rivers flowing throughout the sulfuric land mass. More dragons circle about scouting for foolish intruders attempting to trespass.

"The glass is made of the same valiancium steel as the cuffs you wore, except through the magical touch of Elvin magic it has been turn to glass. Master craftsmen are trained specifically to make such work."

"Are you implying the glass is as strong as steel?"

"Stronger."

"The dragons outside fly as though they expect a war to break out at any moment," I say.

"You're not wrong in making that observation. We're nine days away from the Super Blue Blood Moon Eclipse here on Ladorielle," he says. "In Earth's galaxy, it's a little over four weeks. We must be ready for anything."

"I keep forgetting about the time difference. Can we pull it off? Winning the war, that is?"

"Only time will tell."

He shows me every possible outcome flowing through my head, but free will is the ultimate decision-maker. I understand that now. It is the only thing that changes. The images flipping through my brain almost becomes overwhelming.

"I could tell you the outcome of a million more possibilities, each having a different ending, but that would overload you right now. We need to allow your body time to adjust. Can you imagine if I gave you all of them now? You're not ready yet to see everything I see."

"I understand. I see there is a possible outcome for every act made, there are a million more possibilities that can result in one acting decision. I feel overstimulated as it is."

"Yes indeed. That is where free will comes in...and why whatever decision a person makes is so important. Can you imagine if others had the gift I do? They would go mad. I show only a glimpse of it to you, to help you understand the vast energy potential you have inside you."

Knowing the power Dragonscale has, frightens me, but it also gives me comfort at the same time.

"Do all the dragons carry the Deagon name?"

"No. Deagon is the name from the royal court. You will find many with different surnames. Once you have finished your trials, you will be crowned Wyndreana, Queen of the Dragons and Ruler of Ladorielle."

"I really don't like that name. Is there a way to eliminate it entirely and just call me Wynter?"

"We might be able to compromise on something, but remember, your name has meaning."

I nod, looking out at the horizon line where a faint silhouette of Storm Castle resides. "And the Storms?"

"They will still have their land. Your father, Lord Jeoffrey Storm, will take the helm when the realm is ready."

"Why not give my father the title of king here on Dragonscale Island? Surely, he's more fit to rule than me."

"He's a direct descendant to the Storms. Your great grandmother, Queen Sara, is a direct descendent of dragons. Sara is your great-grandmother and my mother. She is a Deagon who married a Storm. Our two daughters, your aunt Fran and your mother Isalora, belong in this line. You are first in line to Deagon, and second in line to Storm. Queen Sara is your father's great aunt, which has you ruling both kingdoms when the time comes."

"I see." So much to absorb, so much more to learn.

5

A HAUNTED PAST

H E SHOWS ME HOW Sarmira had taken possession of Maura Moyer. How her soul is helpless from stopping Sarmira at her ploy to destroy everyone around her.

"The one thing nobody else can see," he says, "is Maura's heart, and how she feels responsible for all that has transpired. She begs for forgiveness but cannot seem to find a way to ask for it."

"How can one think they can have forgiveness for the atrocities they have bestowed on others? She may ask, but how do I come to forgive her?"

"Because not forgiving her will harden your heart, child. It's how hate is invited in, in the first place. You must find a way to forgive, only then will you reach the peace you need to move on and become stronger."

"I see her face. Her features are very similar to mine," I say.

"Yes. Moyer was Sarmira's intended target for years."

Rage clouds my mind. "She allowed Sarmira in, and as a result, the tyrant took her soul. Why do I not feel sorry for her? I'm angry."

"Do not allow the anger to fog your thoughts with false information. Look closer, what else do you see?"

"She looks like a woman in her late twenties as though she never aged. She has emerald eyes—not the black coal irises I'm familiar with. The Moyer I see now, is inside a cell block of her own mind, has the face of a woman with stress lines and eyes sunk into her sockets. I see the veins through her near-translucent skin, but no heart beats within her chest. She sits on a bench in a room. The walls around her are made of stone. It's a cell block that looks similar to the ones located in the basement of Storm River Manor." The phenomenal thing about my new powers is I can see exactly what she sees, as though I'm inside her body, and I can feel what she feels. The helplessness is spine-chilling and it leaves me grief-stricken.

"You're seeing the imprisoned mind of Maura Moyer's soul," Dragonscale says. "All she can do now is sit back and watch with torment the pain she has inflicted upon our family and those of others. Even though her soul hasn't done these awful things, her body has. And when people see Maura, they don't see that Sarmira is the one possessing her."

"She looks so broken," I say. "But how can I forgive such a wicked monster that has inflicted so much pain?"

"Give it time. Remember, Wynter, Maura isn't the monster. Sarmira is. Evil possession has penetrated her soul, and you must also set her free by forgiving her."

He shows me flashes of the past.

"What are you revealing to me now?"

"You will see," Dragonscale says.

He shows me lush green grasses and land as far as the eye can see. A stone castle sets on a hillside, overlooking a valley with two magnificent towers and a center courtyard. I'm guided inside to one of the halls, where two boys are laughing and a woman is covering her eyes, counting. The children scatter, seeking a hiding spot. One hides under a dining room table while the other boy goes up some tower steps. Giggling can still be heard after she's stopped counting. "Here I come," she says. "I'm going to find you. You cannot hide from me for long." I'm astounded when I see her face and realize it's Maura Moyer.

She goes up the tower steps after hearing a noise that sounded like something falling to the ground and opens the attic door. The room is filled with trunks and old possessions. A wooden chair is on its side, appearing to have fallen to the floor. As she picks it up, a breeze whisks by. She grabs her arms, to warm herself from the cold chill. "Jeoffrey, are you in here?" she asks. Her face looks worried while searching for the hidden boy. I can see her thoughts and hear what she hears. She knows he's hiding. She's heard his footsteps from below. Her other child doesn't have the same stride. Every time they play this silly game, she finds him somewhere in this room. "Jeoffrey, you know the rules, son, this room is off limits.

The game is over. Please come out. I give you a free pass to go hide again someplace else." I can feel what Moyer feels, and it's a sense of dread, and danger.

I see the boy hiding behind a large old chest. Still thinking it's a game, he covers his mouth, trying with all his might to be quiet.

The wind from outside passes through an open window of the attic, and a white sheet drops to the floor, revealing a large mirror. I can see the image standing on the other side of the frame. "Is that who I think it is?" I ask.

Dragonscale nods. "Keep watching."

I hear the temptations of evil call my grandmother Maura. Its whispers are loud, as she moves toward the object in a trance.

"Can she see what we see? I mean, that 'thing' in the reflection?"

"You are seeing through her eyes, much the way Cory sees through yours. But to answer your question, no. This is a moment in Maura's past."

"So, can Cory see what I'm seeing now?"

"No. When under Ashengale's protection everyone's thoughts are shielded and blocked. Even yours, Wynter. Although you will need to learn how to block out the obtrusive thoughts of others. Now, watch, my child. Learn. You must see the history of what has transpired before forgoing your future trials."

"Maura..." the mirror calls again, drawing my grandmother's attention away from finding the boy. "It is time..."

Beautiful black hair flows down her back in long locks, waving in the breeze from the open window. She appears transfixed, staring at her reflection as though admiring herself. The vision I receive through Moyer's mind is a wraith on the other side of the glass with a black gown that flows down its ghostly body, stopping a couple inches from the floor. It holds a scythe in one hand while in the other a crystal globe. There isn't a face visible in the darkness behind the cowl. It seeks her soul as it admires her, pulling her inward for possession. Maura Moyer stares back at the same wraith I saw in my dream the day it came to attack the Storm family.

"So, this is how Sarmira possessed Maura?"

"Yes," Dragonscale confesses. "The mirror was supposed to be destroyed years ago when it attempted to take her as a child. Her mother came in her room in time to see the evil about to be bestowed upon Maura and protected her daughter from fate that day."

"Maura...come to me," the wicked voice murmurs. "You must fulfill your fate as promised. Shall I remind you of what will happen if you do not?"

The eerie sound sends chills up my spine as I watch what unfolds. "I'm not ready. It's too soon," Maura protests. She backs away.

My father watches as he peeks around the trunk, not knowing the danger his mother is in. He stays quiet, hiding, thinking they are still playing this silly game.

"No wonder my father never told anyone this secret. He blames himself for this curse, doesn't he?" I ask.

"Your father holds more guilt than you will ever know, even though he isn't responsible for what happened that day. Focus on the now, my child, not that past. Now, you know why Jeoffrey is the way he is with you. He knows if Sarmira had the chance—"

"This is what Sarmira was planning, wasn't it? Using Moyer to take my soul once she had the opportunity—not just my power?"

"Yes. The necklace protected you from that. It still protects you."

"And so, she knows I'm a Deagon therefore, she knows what my power truly holds?"

"Yes. Can you imagine what would happen to Ashengale if she took possession of your soul? We must finish your trials. Only then will you be strong enough to resist her dark magic."

Flashes of the past come to the forefront again, like in the vision I had at Storm River Manor, when Isalora came to me in a dream showing me the past. The images focus, and I see the land of Ladorielle with lush hills and deep valleys, again. "What is this you're showing me now?"

Down in a meadow near a different castle than before, where animals graze and people are tending a field, I see a quaint chalet nestling near a river.

"This is a countryside that is in desperate need of a strong ruler," he says. He shows me the war, and the life that has been taken. The souls that have been possessed, and the souls that have made it to the light.

Stunned from the visions, I say, "She would have destroyed this kingdom. But you can see the past, present, and future. You know how this ends. Why do you not show me that?"

"As I've explained before, I know every possible outcome, but making the right choices will change your destiny. Making the wrong ones will set your fate. This is how I know. In time, perhaps, you will, too, but for now, we must focus on what lies ahead—defeating Sarmira and freeing Moyer from possession. Besides, free will can change, remember?"

"How can we help her?" This newfound information gives me mixed feelings.

"You mean Maura?" he asks.

I nod.

"By following through with what destiny has bestowed upon you."

"She will die, won't she?" I ask. "If it's like the history books have claimed it to be, it means one strike at Moyer and Sarmira will be released, but at the sacrifice of Maura Moyer."

"I'm afraid so. I see no other option. Do you?"

"No. But her spirit will be released, will it not? Will her soul be saved? I see my grandmother locked away within her own mind. I can hear her and feel her."

"Yes, Moyer's soul will release, along with Sarmira's, unfortunately. We cannot perform an immortality spell on Maura, or it will also transfer to Sarmira."

I don't know why, but I feel sorry for Maura Moyer now, knowing what I know. It's like Sarmira had chosen her long before, she had a chance to make a choice.

"It must have frustrated Sarmira when she failed to capture Maura as a child." There must be a way to defeat this evil witch once and for all.

I can forgive Maura, now knowing she made a fatal choice to save our bloodline. I'm furious knowing that Sarmira has ruined my family. I will get revenge if it's the last thing I do.

6

A REVEALED TRUTH

I'M MESMERIZED BY THE beauty of the walls and upper caverns made of precious gems and rock. The ceiling appears to consist of raw, unpolished gold. When light reflects on it, it produces a prism on the interior.

"What can you tell me about the Sword of Valor? Aoes and my Grandmother Sara said you would be able to guide Cory and me to its whereabouts. I noticed you did not show me the location with your mind. Why?"

"The sword will reveal itself when the time is right. Trust your instincts. You have about ten percent of your power. As you remain in your shifted dragon state, you will soon begin to gain more energy than you ever thought imaginable. You can also change back to your humanoid form at any time." He pauses. "However, in your human form you're more vulnerable outside of the protection of this island. The enemy—a tracker to be more specific—will know your location. It's because you have not yet learned how to control your mind from the influence of others, the dark dragons will know how to find you. That is a skill you must acquire. It's part of this final phase in your trial."

My necklace comes to mind. "When will I start learning that segment of the trial?"

"You must complete your transition first. You've already passed the first two."

"I have?" I look at him, perplexed.

He laughs. "Of course. Your first was learning the truth of your family and finding out who you are."

"I discovered that while staying at Storm River Manor."

"Yes. Unbeknownst to you, your trials began the day your father came into your room to tell you about the family line. He should have told you sooner, so you'd be properly prepared, but that's the past now."

"Somehow, I'm not surprised you know about that. What was the second? When I discovered my powers?"

"Part of it, yes. Trust was your second trial. Learning to trust yourself and yielding magic is the key to being a strong dragon."

"So, this is the third and final phase?"

"Shifted transformation, yes. And choosing to fight the evil that has plagued these lands will be the first test. You were raised to be a paladin warrior."

"A paladin warrior?"

My grandfather who is still in his human form, smiles. "Not many great paladins exist anymore. Many of those warrior class fighters came from the Storm kingdom long ago." He points across the water. "Long before that Storm Castle ever existed. Storm paladins were fierce. A force to be reckoned with. Alas, that is a story of another time. I will say, your title comes with great responsibility and talents that with time will grow and become skilled." He pauses and turns to look at me. "I hear you often complain about seeing ghosts."

I nod. "It's such a boring talent."

"Seeing ghosts—or what we here on Ladorielle refer to as the undead—is a great gift given to a paladin warrior. And because the paladin are so scarce in numbers, we've had to rely on the witches to create spells so we can see them during this time of war."

"It seems no matter how much I learn, more of my life's mysteries surface. Will it ever end? My life feels like a never-ending loop. As soon as I feel I've accomplished one goal, another appears in its place. Am I ever going to be done with searching?"

He smiles. "You never stop learning, Wynter, and you will always have tribulations. You will always have a path you're destined to follow as long as you breathe life into your lungs. Keep in mind, you may be immortal, but you can be killed. However, you can make choices of your own free will."

Immortal? His words make my heart beat fast. "I never thought of being immortal. Great-Grandmother Sara, Aunt Fran, my mother, they're all eternal in a sense, aren't they?"

Dragonscale nods. "Spirits live on forever, in most cases, whether good or evil. They can also be vanquished. Evil spirits go back to the hell where they belong, and the good will be sent to the light. In your aunt, great-grandmother, and mother's case, what they have done is a little different. They have cast a spell of immortality, where they walk the Planes of the Undead. The caveat to this is the evil side can do the same. They stay there until the superiors of these two worlds, good and evil, have decided they have done the work they need to complete before they are called home. Driving an object through the heart of a dragon is the only true way to kill an immortal shifter."

"And yet Aunt Fran will soon breathe life through her lungs again."

"Yes, I see why you may be confused. Nyta preserved your aunt's heart before it grew cold. If a heart is damaged and not repaired before this happens, then it's death to the dragon shifter, but your aunt was lucky."

"And my mother is dead forever."

"Unfortunately, yes. Unless by some miraculous event that took place I don't know about before she died, she will remain a ghost forever."

"You mean like the necklace she gave me that was charmed with a spell that would keep her alive?"

"Is your head beginning to hurt?"

I let out a deep sigh.

"Your mother called upon the souls of the undead, so that she may be granted temporary life to keep on task. She bound her life with the Spirits of Immortality to keep her 'alive' so she could help complete your destiny."

"And who are these Spirits of Immortality?"

He doesn't answer, instead saying, "Come with me." He shifts back to a dragon. "I want to show you something."

I walk beside him but he's much larger than me which makes it difficult to keep up. "Do all the dragons have different colors?"

"The color on a dragon is its fingerprint. No two have the same shade combination. Certainly, one may have similarities, but we are all unique in our own way."

He spreads his wings and takes off flying. I follow, trying to keep up, but he's much faster.

"Speaking to you telepathically might be easier while we soar through the air, but to answer your question, flying will become second nature. Your true form has been revealed, Wynter. Enjoy the journey." He shoots through the caverns as I try and keep up. *"No longer can anyone impose on your mind, not even Sarmira, when you're in dragon form."* He grunts flippantly. *"Unless you're another dragon shifter among our clan, I will teach you how to keep your thoughts private. You are safe from the dark dragons. Communication is cut off between us and them as long as you remain here on Dragonscale Island. Though we can sense when they are near. It's like keeping a door shut, and if you decide to open it, you can."*

I think about the necklace that still dangles from my neck. In my dragon form it nestles in a pocket under one of my scales. *"Does the locket I wear still serve a purpose?"*

"It will continue to shield your location and protect your thoughts."

I soar behind Dragonscale as we fly. He leads me to an open cave entrance set on the other side of the mountain. The sounds of ocean waves crashing and smell of sultry air clings to my senses.

This side of the island isn't as brazen with ash and heat as it is from the other end. We fly toward the shoreline where I see two figures. As we come closer, the silhouette of who it is becomes clear. It's a woman, looking much like Geneviève—the real Geneviève—and she's beside another dragon.

We land on the shore near them. Before I can get a word in, I hear the unfamiliar dragon say, *"You finally made it."* His silver scales with light blue edging and golden shine remind me of my colors. His talons are black with gold tips.

"Have you waited long?" Dragonscale questions.

"No, I thought I would bring Geneviève to this side of the shore away from the burning ash so she may breathe easier. She wanted to get a bit of fresh air."

Geneviève smiles. "Good day, Wynter. I'm so happy to see you finally made it home."

"So, this is the famous Geneviève, the druid we have been trying so hard to find. She's been on Ashengale all along, hasn't she?"

Dragonscale doesn't answer me.

I transform back to myself. And quite surprised to see I'm clothed. I look at my grandfather.

He answers my thoughts without me having to ask. *"Magic, my dear. Our bodies have memory and remembers what we were wearing before we shifted."*

"I see." I look at Geneviève. "Rory is worried about you."

"Yes, I imagine she is, but she should know Jeff and I got out safely from the Grengore mines." She pauses to introduce the colorful dragon before me. "Wynter, I would like for you to meet my dragon brother, Gottfried."

"Gottfried. I remember hearing that name once before." I look at Dragonscale. *"Like Namari?"*

"Similar, yes. Namari is a dragongryph, but Gottfried is not."

Gottfried says, *"It's good to see you, Wynter. I see you have successfully passed your third and final trial of your first phase of many."*

Ignoring how he knows that, I ask, *"Who are you? And how can you read my mind? I admit you seem familiar, yet I haven't a clue who you are."*

I cannot yet see into another dragon's mind. Dragonscale has not taught me that. I only see into his because he's invited me into it. I remember Namari once told me when a human bonded to a dragon they could read each other's thoughts when riding together. Is this what Geneviève is implying? I will need to learn to protect my thoughts more closely. Can he hear them now, this Gottfried?

"You have come a long way, Wynter. We've been patiently waiting for you. Dragonscale assured us you were safe and on the right path. That we would be meeting up again soon," Gottfried says.

"Forgive me, again, but who are you?"

In the blink of an eye, he shifts into his humanoid form.

"No, it can't be. All this time, you were a dragon, and you never let on that you were a shifter?" I think back to the accident and when the car was consumed in flames. When Chad told me my family died from the explosion, he said, *'Even a supernatural can't survive after that.'* Now here, standing before me, the one man who has always had my unconditional love: my father. He's not the supernatural I thought he was, but a dragon.

I give him a hug. "Dad, is it really you? I have so many questions. I don't know where to begin." I stop and look to the woman standing next to him. "I get it now why you and my dad were so close. Well, I mean, why the Trek pretending to be you back at the ranch laid it on so thick, as though you two were having an affair—Dad is sort of like your familiar."

"More like my protector. Some call them warders, others refer to your dad as a guardian," she says.

I stop, pondering the past, and look over at Dad. "You suspected from the very beginning, that it was a Trek impersonating Geneviève, didn't you?"

He nods. "That's my job. I was trying to protect you, too. My cover was blown the night you lost your control with Nyta. I filled her in on what I knew."

"You're not a vampire, Nytemire, or a Shadow Walker, are you?" I ask.

"No. But I had to make you believe it. It was the only way to get you here safely. If anyone found out the truth, the memory stamps that have been placed on the rest of our family would have prematurely triggered their true identity, which would have paralyzed them from learning about their past. You must have many questions. Shall we all go back inside?" Dad shifts back to his dragon form, and Geneviève climbs on his back. I do the same, and we all fly back to the cave's opening to the castle of Ashengale.

7

A SHIFTED MOMENT

WE APPROACH THE LANDING and Dragonscale steps first with grace and strength, followed by Dad and me. Geneviève slides down Dad's wing, landing feet first, as though she's done this thousands of times. At the entrance to the castle Aunt Fran stands next to another dragon, which has me wondering if that is Garrick. My mind reflects back to the large lizard-like eye, which peeped through the hole in the entrance to the gate of Ashengale when my aunt and I first arrived. This dragon is green in color with reddish-brown edging, and his coat shines gold. His talons and winged tips are black. I never got a good glimpse at what Garrick looked like as a dragon.

"Good to see you again, Jeff," the dragon says.

Dad bows. *"And you, too. I see you have found Fran."*

"Yes, not the way I expected her to be, of course."

"Boys, now is not the time to discuss this," my aunt says, looking over my way. *"She's still in her dragon form and can hear all of you."* My aunt nods toward me, saying, "Go on, Wynter, you can change back to your original form."

I do as she instructs, and notice that once I'm back to myself again, I no longer have the magical ability to see past, present, and future. I hadn't noticed that on the beach, but I was too caught up with seeing Dad and Geneviève. It's like waking from a dream and slowly forgetting everything, except for one difference—I do remember *my* past. All of it. The truth of who I really am, and the truth of what has happened in the last eighteen years. The memory stamp that prevented me from remembering is gone.

The dragon shifts to his human form, confirming he indeed is Garrick, and laces his hand with Aunt Fran's. He kisses her forehead.

"Shall we continue your tour of the castle, Wynter?" my grandfather asks. He shifts back to his human form.

I follow beside him. He gestures toward the french doors, leading into the grand foyer. "I have an important meeting to handle. I know you have many inquiries, Wynter. We'll meet this evening and go over the groundwork for your next task. You have successfully completed your third trial. You are officially a dragon shifter. Your next phase in your journey to complete your ascension will come tonight during dinner." He turns to Dad and the others. "I trust you will prepare her for tonight?"

"Certainly, Father," Aunt Fran answers.

Garrick bows. "She's in good hands, sir."

Dad and Geneviève nod in agreement.

Dragonscale—the man—walks away wearing black leather boots that clap the marble floors, and his dark cloak waving behind him. A few soldiers follow close behind and in front of him, as they disappear through a side corridor.

"Well, you heard the man," Dad says. "Let's start by showing you around, Wynter. Now might be a good time to reacquaint yourself with the city. Perhaps it will jog some of the memories."

"Dad, I have my memories back."

"Wait, all your memories?" He looks over at Fran, Garrick, and Geneviève.

I smile. "Yes, Dad. Can we go to Scale Café & Grill for lunch?"

"Well, this does call for celebration. I think that restaurant is the perfect place to start our day."

"I'm sorry, love, I wish I could join you, but I have guard duty." Garrick kisses Fran. "It must be a wonderful feeling to finally remember who you are, Wynter. We'll meet up again soon." He transitions and flies off.

"I can't go, either," Geneviève says. "I've been called to Queen Sara's court for a matter that needs resolution. Hopefully, I can finish before this evening's meal.

Fran stops walking and turns around. "Oh Gen, surely you're not going to leave me alone with these two, are you?"

My heart sinks at Aunt Fran's words.

Dad nudges my shoulder. "She's referring to me."

Fran glares at Dad.

"I'm sorry, Fran. I promise, I'll be back soon." She pulls a rock from her palm, and it glows, forming a bubble around her, and she disappears.

Dad wraps an arm across my back and grabs one shoulder, saying with great enthusiasm, "It's just the three of us again...like old times."

I grunt, slightly cowering from his bear hug. The family outings would sometimes get rather embarrassing. Dad would think it was funny. Especially if he knew any of my friends were around. He never missed a moment to take his cue. "Do we walk or fly?"

They both laugh. "Let's walk, shall we?" he says.

Dad hooks his arm around mine. "I look forward to showing you around, reintroducing you to the places you have seen before."

A walk down memory lane. Yay!

8

MEMORY LANE

WE WALK THROUGH THE courtyard to the outer gates of the castle where ahead of us is a landing station, but it isn't just for dragons. It's also for other flying creatures. "Dragongryphs are flying transportation?" I ask. "That's something I don't remember."

"Druids are still the preferable way to travel but yes, Dragongryphs, are resourceful beasts," Dad says.

They line in the air like planes waiting to land on the docking pad.

Dad adds, "We recruited them for travel because of their exceptional cloaking abilities. They help provide safety for people who seek refuge."

We hike up the ramp to the landing dock and off to the side is a walkway. Dad guides us around the waiting line. People of all shapes and sizes remain behind a chain for their turn to travel. The walkway follows along a wall, which turns into a dark tunnel.

"Where are we going?" I ask.

"To the stables," Dad answers.

I squint, confused by what he means. "And why not fly?"

He chuckles. "You'll understand once we get there."

Aunt Fran grunts, thwarting Dad's suspenseful ploy by answering, "Until we win the war, shifters are not safe to transform. Only here, on the island, can we spread our wings. A shifter can walk the planet undetected by anyone and surprise foes with their strength, but they can also be surprised by one particular talent—a tracker. They can see us, but we can't see them. It didn't used to be that way. Something or someone has disrupted the magic that keeps us protected."

"I'm assuming that's why the giant pursued us?"

"Yes," Fran confesses. "We've been—rather Nyta has been—working tirelessly on developing a potion that will help us detect when a tracker is near."

"That explains why hiding me as a shifter before I even knew I was one, was the best possible solution. I'm guessing the necklace hid that, too?"

"It did, yes," she answers.

"Does Cory know?"

"He should, but then again he may not remember."

"Hang on...not remember? Are you telling me he, too, has a memory stamp placed?"

"He does. Whether he's recovered those memories, or not, is unknown to us."

"It's hard to wrap my head around this. You're a dragon, Aunt Fran. This whole time, you were a dragon!"

She raises a brow. "Yes, we all are. What are you getting at?"

"If we're protected under this mountain volcano, and we're more difficult to kill in our dragon form, then tell me again why we're not flying to Scale Café & Grill since we're still protected under Dragonscale's kingdom?"

Dad chuckles. "For nostalgic purposes."

"Jeff, wait, seriously she needs to fully understand. This isn't supposed to be about the long-lost void you've had about spending time with your daughter. She needs to know the truth!"

Dad's joyful demeaner changes. "You're right, Fran."

"Dad?"

He grunts. I can tell he doesn't want to share his thoughts. "What your aunt is trying to say is the dark dragons scout the lands like we do here on Dragonscale Island, and once out from the protection of this land, dragons can sense other dragons, differentiating ally from foe. I assure you, my dear, you will eventually learn how to do that. Right now, you're too vulnerable to let us out of your sight. Once Sarmira is destroyed, we can then again perhaps plan for peace. Sarmira's magic empowers her commanders, making them stronger, stronger than some of us."

I dig deep into what Dad's telling me. "Okay, that doesn't surprise me that dark dragons scout the lands. I would think we do the same."

Dad veers a concerned glare at Fran before adding, "We think there are spies among us—here on the Island, already."

I mull over Dad's theory. "You're saying we can't detect them, is that it?"

"It's the giants we worry about, more... off the island." Dads says. "They have cloaking abilities and they're getting cleverer every year. As for the Iknes Shaw, they too, have tracking abilities, but we can sense them from several feet away because they leave an unpleasant odor. But—"

"But we don't want to worry you, not yet anyway. We don't have proof of any dark dragons getting past the perimeter," Aunt Fran adds.

"I get it now. That's the real reason you don't want us to fly into town."

"Aww, come on," Dad says, trying to make light of things. "It's a perfect time for us to bond as a family."

I smirk. "Okay...sure."

"Look at it this way, Wynter," Dad goes on, "it gives you a chance to discern between your abilities in both shifted states."

Fran glances at Dad and says, "And you have an innate ability to see ghosts, Wynter."

"How creative of me." My sarcastic tone doesn't sit well with them. "I am intrigued by what Grandfather said to me today, though, that I'm a paladin warrior."

"Wynter, I've told you before, you have amazing gifts," Aunt Fran says. "You can form fireballs, and generate icicles from your fingers, run at the speed of light like a vampire, and the ability to create spells from a long line of witches. Wynter, you will do great things. Your father has seen it."

Dad smiles. "Your Deagon side of the bloodline, as you're fully aware, is a dragon shifter, and you can read minds. Your ascension will complete your training. Don't underestimate your abilities, Wynter. You're stronger than you think."

Coming around the corner of the dark tunnel we arrive at a stable. "I arranged this ahead of time." His smile is filled with excitement.

"A horse and buggy? Really, Dad?"

Dad winks.

Rolling my eyes I humor him.

He approaches a man with a young girl who is tending to horses and clears his throat.

The man looks up. "Lord Gottfried, my apologies I didn't see you walk up, sire." The man bows.

Dad nods. "Jeff seems to fit me better, don't you think, Cyrus?"

"Yes, sir." The man bows, again. "Quinn, are the horses ready for Sir Jeff and his family?"

The young woman looks up. She wears a brown apron and hat with golden curls tied in the back. She takes her mitts off and bows. "Yes, Father. These horses are shoed, fed, and ready for a city stroll." She pats the croup of one horse.

A glint of silver hides a secret behind her eyes. Golden tones around her iris' show her true nature. *Is she a vampire?*

Dad grabs my hand and helps pull me up, then does the same for Fran. "I thought we could enjoy the moment. We haven't done something like this in years," Dad says, as he sits opposite from my aunt and me.

"Memory lane, is that it, Dad?" I think back to his warning us of his nostalgic intention for the afternoon. "A sports car would have been nice."

He chuckles. "I'm sure you would like that, too, huh? Those vehicles are not allowed in this world. Too much pollution. Besides, why have cars when you have magic?" He snaps his fingers, and appearing in his hand is a single rose. He hands it to me.

Ignoring his comment, I say, "They do have electric cars. Why not do something like that here?"

"And spoil the fun riding in something like this?"

"Fine, I'll give you your moment." I smell the rose. "Since we're going down memory lane, Dad, tell me are Cory, Cole, and Blair dragons or vampires?"

"They were born as vampires as you are already aware. If they were dragon shifters they would have transitioned when they turned eighteen.

"My brother Chad, on the other hand, was bitten. I watched it happen and I couldn't save him. To this day, I don't know how I escaped. Something more powerful than myself released from within me. The valiancium cuffs Moyer had chained to my ankles busted, and I shifted right before the both of them, at Storm River Manor." He laughs and shakes his head. "The look on Moyer's face was priceless. I knew then she, too, had no clue what had transpired. Anyway, I didn't care how it happened or why... all I knew was by burning a vampire it would execute any poisonous venom my brother endured. The look in Chad's eyes begging me to end his life, haunts me to this day. She'd turned him."

"What happened next? Obviously, Uncle Chad is walking around—not dead."

"I burned my brother to ashes. Moyer was furious, but before I could get to her, she fled the basement and up the spiral stairs. After I shifted back to my human form and saw Chad's ashes on the ground, it changed me." Dad gets lost in his thoughts.

"I don't understand. How is Chad still alive?"

It takes a second before Dad answers, but first he asks again, as though he wasn't convinced the first time, "How much do you remember?"

"All of it. I remember everything."

"Everything?" He gives me a stern look.

"Yes, I remember when Rory and I were playing along the river a few days before falling from the rock, and I was almost swept away downstream, but Namari came just in time to swoop me up, right before the waterfall. I'm not sure Rory remembers, though. Dad, what are you getting at?" I look over at Fran and she shakes her head, staying silent.

"Dad, you're avoiding my question. How is it that Chad is still alive?"

He turns his head away and looks out among the trees that line the road.

"You're not going to answer me, are you?"

Fran places her hand on mine. I know it's her way to not press the issue. "Fine." I fold my arms and look out as well. My thoughts wonder off on a tangent. Is Moyer a vampire, too? I thought she was a powerful Necromancer witch.

Aunt Fran answers my private thoughts, *"Oh, she is. Don't underestimate that. You didn't think she would pass up having added powers, did you? Keen sense of hearing, speed, the mind control—my dear, she's their queen—the Shadow Walker's creator."*

"I asked Cory once, and he said she was just a greedy witch with a purpose."

"A very powerful purpose, yes, and then some."

"Do you know the answer of why Uncle Chad is still alive?"

"No. And your Dad has never told me."

Dad sits back in his seat and stares off into space.

"I don't understand any of this and I am tired of the secrets!"

"You're not supposed to understand, yet." Dad glares. You're supposed to follow directions." He changes his posture, drawing my attention. "There is something else Fran and I haven't told you yet." He glances her way.

She nods as though she knows what he's about to say.

Dad hesitates a moment before saying, "There is a school that all shifters must attend before—"

"Wait, a school for dragons?"

"Something like that yes," he answers.

I laugh. "Whoever heard of such a thing."

"This isn't just any school. This is a prerequisite to get into Dragon University."

"You're joking. There's really a college for dragon shifters?"

"Yes, more like an academy for dragons—" He pinches his nose.

He wants to say more. "Dad, what is it?"

"It's a supernatural academy for magic. Where one goes after their ascension."

"Meaning?"

"Meaning, Light Witches–if we can manage to find the bloodlines that are in hiding, wolf shifters—not to confuse you with the werewolves, there is a difference—"

"Hang on, next you're going to say vampires—"

Dad nods. "Vampires, wizards, druids—pick your poison, Wynter."

"Well, I admit I didn't see this coming. And when am I supposed to begin going to this—college?"

"In September."

"Don't ask, just do. Is that it? What if I don't want to go?"

"You don't have a choice. If you want to wield magic this is the only way."

"But of course it is."

"Have I ever steered you astray?"

"No. But you did keep a big secret from me. Am I supposed to forget that even though you thought what you were doing was right? And now you spring this on me?"

"I can understand your concern. But knowing what you know now, can you blame me?"

"No. But can you blame me for questioning you, Dad?"

He stays silent. Dad leans back in his seat again. "This isn't how I thought our ride to your favorite restaurant would go at all."

The carriage drops us off in front of an old wooden building that looks like it belongs in a Western movie.

"Here we are," the driver says. "This place makes the best Trek steak."

"Indeed, they do," Dad says smiling. "Thank you for the ride, Davis."

"Always a pleasure, sir." He tilts his head.

The thought of devouring the Trek imposter at Rory's home comes to mind and my nostrils flare. "Do they have to cook the meat? I like them rare."

"Well," Dad says, "it appears the flavor of blood hasn't left your taste buds."

"We may pull this off after all, dear brother-in-law." Fran gives a devilish grin.

"Again, with the third person...hello, I'm right here!"

"No shifting," Dad reminds me, ignoring my outburst.

9

SCALE CAFÉ & GRILL

D AD OPENS THE DOOR and a hostess greets us. People of all ages are drinking, laughing, and eating. I feel like I've walked into a rowdy sports bar and grill. There are televisions on the walls showing football playoffs while others watch basketball.

"They're American games," I say.

"Our kingdom has the ability to tap into Earth's network, as well as some other planets. Many of our people enjoy human sports. We used to come here a lot when you were a small child," Dad says.

"I remember. There was a train set and tracks in the kids' section."

Dad grins. "Would you like to sit in there, for old times' sake?"

"Why not?" I grin.

The hostess smiles. "How many?"

"A table for three in the kids' area, please," Dad answers.

She gives a surprised grin. "Sure, let me see what's available." She leaves to check on the section.

Dad pulls my arm, and we sit down on a bench near the door and wait.

The hostess comes back. "It will be about ten minutes. Can I get your name please?"

"Jeff." I observe her jot down his name, but not before I see a hint of red in her eyes. Her hair is long and black, and she wears an all-black uniform. She notices me staring and smiles. Fangs peek out on either side of her mouth, but they're not extended. I don't need any more hints to know what she is.

I nudge my dad. "Are vampires a thing, now?"

"Hmm?" He looks up to see what I'm referring to. "Oh. All are welcome to live under the protection of the kingdom, as long as there isn't any trouble. If she lives here, then it means she's an immigrant in hiding."

I observe families with children eating in booths while in the bar area brutish-looking men sit on stools. Some folks are mesmerized by football playing on the big screen. Shouts roar out, as one team makes a touchdown. In the back of the restaurant, people play pool in another room while others throw a game of darts. "Talk about your catch-all diner," I mumble.

"This is a popular hangout for the townspeople," Fran says. "It's changed ownership since you were here last."

Another group of people come through the entrance doors, seek the hostess, and take a seat opposite from us—a man, his wife, a teen girl, and a child. I can tell they, too, are vampires, including the child. The kid appears shy and pops up on the mother's lap while the teen stands against a wall engrossed with her phone.

Two more people enter the restaurant before the hostess comes up to us, saying, "Excuse me, folks, your table is ready."

We make our way to a corner booth. As we sit down, the hostess hands us our menus. "Your server will be with you shortly."

I pick up my menu. "Do they still have the cricket burgers?"

"A niece after my own heart." Fran laughs. "Yes, they do."

I squint, trying to read the menu, and I think Dad notices. "Don't tell me you forgot how to read Elvin."

"Is it that obvious? It's fine, I'm sure it will come back to me. I just need practice."

"Here, allow me," he says, taking the menu from my hands. "I'll order for the both of us. Any clue what you want, Fran? Oh wait, that's right, you're dead."

"Ha, ha, I almost forgot to laugh. Whatever, Jeff, I'm immune to your teasing. Besides, it does pose as good practice to try and fool others that I'm still human. Order me a calamari."

"Hmm, that was always your favorite."

"Would you two stop badgering each other and play nice for once?"

The server approaches. She has a pen and pad in her hand, chewing gum. "Hi there, my name is-s Halle, may I take your order?" Her dark hair and scaly, yellow-brown skin remind me of Nora's features when she pushed me against the wall that day she caught me in the hall at the manor. Her eyes have a snake-like look, too, and I immediately recognize her as being an Iknes Shaw.

"Why's she in this town? I thought they were our enemy."

Dad gives me a glare, saying to the server, "We aren't quite ready yet, Halle. Give us a few more minutes, please."

"Some Iknes Shaw have sought sanctuary from the brutal poisonous clan in the mountains," Fran says.

The girl stares at me, as though she can see my thoughts. "What about drinks-s?"

"I might remind you, Wynter, some Iknes Shaw have the ability to read thoughts."

Distracted by the glare of the server, I stutter, "I-It's been a long time since I've been here. Do you still serve Moggle Pops?"

"Who is she? She shouldn't be making me so nervous."

Halle grins. "Sure do, darlin'. What's-s your flavor?"

"Pardon us," Dad says. "It's been a long time since my daughter has visited this restaurant."

"For sure..." She smacks her gum, making popping sounds. "We have Pink Lily, Gooey Green, Tropical Tangerine, and Black Widow Berry."

"You mean there is more than root beer now?" I ask, amazed.

"Mmm, Black Widow Berry sounds great," Dad says.

I stare at him, thinking he's nuts. Even the sound of spiders gives me chills.

"Try the Pink Lily Moggle Pop," Aunt Fran says.

"Oh yeah, that's my favorite," Halle interrupts. "It tastes like a Shirley Temple but with a kick."

"I'll take a Pink Lily, then," I say.

"Make that two," my aunt says and puts the menu down, smiling.

"Is there s-something els-se I can get you? Appetizers-s, perhaps-s," Halle says, looking up from her notepad, still smacking her gum.

"How about an order of Spike Dip, too," Dad replies.

"Coming right up." She twirls around and darts off to order our food.

"Spike Dip? Do you know what the urchin did to Rory, and you're ordering it to eat? And furthermore, she's a—"

"Yes, she is," Dad interrupts. "Her family, among a few others, fled when the war came to the Storm Castle—"

"The day I fell from the rock," I say.

"Yes."

"I'm beginning to understand how much of an impact my screaming rendered that day."

"You have no idea," Dad says.

"Nyta found Halle on the beach one day, near the rocks by the cave in Pine Willow Valley, abandoned as a baby. Well, not really abandoned, but she was near death. Her mother, father, and brother were gutted. All that remained were their skins. I don't think the enemy knew of the child's existence. The mother must have had an egg stashed somewhere and was able to hide it under a rock, keeping it safe."

"Hang on a minute. Iknes Shaw are born from eggs?"

"Of course, they're snakes. They are born looking like a human, but they have the scaled skin of a reptile. Her name, Halle, means rock. Nyta named her. Said her name brings meaning, that she's strong, and she felt it fitting."

"So Nyta raised her?"

"Like one of her own, yes."

Halle comes back with our drinks. "Three Moggle pops-s," she says and sets them down on the table. "Your appetizer will be on the way. Are you ready to order?"

"I think so," Dad states. "Wynter?"

"Cricket burger."

"And kale cobbler fries-s?" Halle asks. "They're a blend of kale, potatoes from Earth, and Ladorielle sea plankton fried in bat oil."

"Oh yes, please. I forgot about those. They are the best in town."

"Very well." She jots down my order, glancing at Aunt Fran. "Oh, I'm not hungry," Fran says.

Dad and I hide a smile. "I'll have what she's having, a cricket burger," Dad says, "and calamari."

Fran glares at Dad.

"Great," Halle says and leaves to put in our order.

I look down at this strange drink in front of me. "So, this is a Pink Lily Moggle Pop?"

Fran smiles. "Tastes like bubbling lemonade," she says, taking her first sip.

I take a swig of mine. "Tastes like lemonade, but with a tart, sweet kick."

Fran gives a gentle laugh. "Remember coming here as a kid? You would hang out here after school under Nyta's care."

I look at Dad. "Yeah, I remember. You were always gone, Dad, leaving Aunt Fran and I alone many times."

"You weren't alone. You had family everywhere. There was always someone to play with. You and Rory would go scout tadpoles in the Rock Water Pond. Remember?"

Fran smiles, grabbing my hand. "Give it time, Wynter." She takes another sip of her drink. "I mean, come on, you just came into your power a few days ago. What's it been, like a week? You discovered you're a shifter, and you have so much on your plate...give yourself a break. You're worrying. It will be fine. I will be right by your side every step of the way."

I huff. "Has it only been a week? Feels like it's been months already."

Halle comes back and sets our appetizer on the table. "Can I get you anything else?"

"No," Dad answers, "this will be good. Thank you."

Halle turns away.

"So this is Spike Dip? I don't think I have ever had it. How do I know it won't blind me like it tried to do Rory?"

"Once it's been cooked, the poison dissipates. Besides, it's the outer shell that's harmful, not the flesh underneath," Fran answers.

I take a spoonful of dip and dap it on my plate and grab a small handful of chips. "So, Dad, tell me more about what happened to Uncle Chad." Taking my first bite, I savor it as it has a party in my mouth. "Wow, this is amazing."

Dad laughs. "Yes, it's one of Scale Café & Grill's most popular dishes."

Dad appears to avoid my initial question, and I shoot him an irritated look.

"Right, Chad. Well, as you may have guessed dragons cannot die by fire. They can't die by fire in human form, either."

"Go on..."

"We can be killed by a strike to the heart. If it grows cold, without getting the proper attention, we die—as you know." He looks at Fran. "In your aunt's case, her body has perished, but her spirit lives on. The magic of Dragonscale Island allows her to keep her physical form while her body regenerates. If she ventures off the Island, she will revert back to a spirit." He takes a sip of his drink.

Aunt Fran gives a grim smile. "Not exactly the perfect way to live an immortal life, but it's something, I guess. Nyta, has my body safe somewhere." She lays her hand on top of mine. "Rest assured."

I take another bite of spike dip.

"Besides, there is a silver lining, my dear niece." She gives a wicked smile. *"If I was solid looking and not of spirit form, I wouldn't be able to help with the eclipse happening at the end of the month."*

I provide a slight chuckle, nearly choking on my mouth full of food. *"I'd love to see Sarmira be beaten at her own game. Instead of possessing a body, you're using this regenerating spell against her. She isn't going to suspect that you're really alive, is she?"*

My aunt and Dad both beam.

"Our thoughts are not as protected in public," she says. *"I mean we can only hold up our shield for so long. It will drain our energy. Let's change the subject and just eat."*

"Okay, so what about Uncle Chad?" I press for the third time.

Dad grunts. "You're not going to let this go, are you?"

I shake my head, sipping on my Moggle Pop. "Nope."

"Well, of course, I didn't know I was of Deagon blood until that day I changed into a fiery ball of rage. Magic isn't as strong on Earth as here."

"Are you saying magic on Earth could be stronger than it is?"

"Precisely. During a Super Blue Blood Moon is when magic is at its strongest."

I reach back to my memories of reading when the last time the Storm family was strong enough to flee. When the Storm family tried to escape the first time, or when Sara was poisoned. "I'm going to take a guess that all those different times the family tried to escape Sarmira's grasp, it was during a Super Blue Blood Moon eclipse, am I right?"

"Yes, Super Blue Blood Moons are one of the strongest, but any full moon will give us an added edge on magic. Blair's younger sons, Cory and Cole, were really young on Ladorielle during the time of the last Super Blue Blood Moon eclipse. Sara and Isobel were at their strongest in defeating Moyer during one of these moon phases.

"But I wasn't born during any eclipse, was I?"

"No."

"Then how did you have the strength to save us?"

"Isalora called upon the Spirits of Immortality." Fran leans in, whispering, "Remember the book?"

"Yes."

"She bound her spirit with the Spirits of Immortality. By doing that, she gave us enough power to escape. Namari, your little dragon, hatched the same night you were born, and his magic showed us the way to Geneviève, and we all left."

"Sounds like my mother beat Moyer at her own game, too, didn't she?"

"Perhaps, but the last Super Blue Blood Moon gave Sara enough power to use magic to keep the cottage protected for another hundred and fifty years. It's that power that has protected it since, and the magic in the cottage grows stronger, allowing Isalora to do her work away from Ladorielle's universe. Remember, Wynter, during that small amount of time when you fell from the rock all those years ago, it has given Sarmira ample time for her to raise a supernatural army."

"It goes both ways, though, right?"

"I'm afraid so. Sarmira has more power to direct Moyer's body into doing unfathomable things."

Halle comes back, bringing our main course. "Here you are. I have two cricket burgers and kale cobbler fries. Is there anything else I can get you?"

I shake my head and she walks off.

"So back to Chad," I say, "What happened?"

Dad sighs, knowing I'm not letting this go. "His ashes rose up."

"You're saying like a phoenix?"

"Similar, maybe. I should remind you, I thought Chad was dead, that I killed him. This dragon shifter secret was kept from me all my life. I didn't stick around to find out what happened to my brother. Instead, I ran after Moyer but she disappeared. I fled to the cottage to warn Sara, told her of what happened, and she informed me that it was the magic of the Super Blue Blood Moon that reengaged my shifting form."

"And that's how Sarmira found out I was a Deagon. Am I right?" I ask.

"Yes. And she knew Chad would be reborn, as he is my brother."

"But Moyer had to already know this. You're her sons, and she's my grandmother."

"But Sarmira didn't. Somehow, Maura Moyer, imprisoned within her own mind and body, kept that secret from Sarmira, until the day I shifted."

A familiar face walks into the restaurant. It's Garrick standing at the door, waving his hand, and trying to grab our attention. I nudge Aunt Fran.

She looks in my direction. "What does he want?"

"I don't know, but it seems important."

"He's not at his post," Dad says. "That can't be good."

I frown and nearly choke on the food in my mouth as I swallow it down. "What do you mean, not good?"

"Hang on, you two. Wait here, and I'll find out what's up." Aunt Fran gets up and walks to Garrick, and he whispers in her ear.

"Dad, can you make out what they're saying?"

"No, it's too loud."

Two soldiers squeeze by Garrick and approach our table, wearing silver chainmail. "Dad?" They wear the same filigree emblem on their chest as I have on my necklace. It's our crest symbol.

One of them bends down by Dad's ear. My keen hearing hears him say, *"They are here. We must leave now."* I look at Aunt Fran and Garrick still by the door. She gives a nod, indicating our meal is over.

"Let's scoot, kid. Time to vacate." Dad throws down a wad of cash, grabs my hand, and pulls me to the door with two soldiers following close behind us.

Startled by the abrupt departure, I ask, "What's going on?"

Dad wears a look of concern on his face. "Something's come up. We can't talk here."

As we leave the restaurant, Garrick says, "Dragonscale requests you return to the castle grounds immediately."

Fran says, *"We've been followed."*

Fran and I tail behind Dad and Garrick while the two soldiers follow behind us. A third and fourth soldier come in on my left and right. I'm boxed in on all sides.

I'm led down a path to an unfamiliar home. More guards stand at the entrance while Dad opens the door.

"Whose home does this belong to? We can't barge into someone's house." The soldiers thrust me inside. "Hey!"

"It's not a home," Garrick says, "it's a station made to look like one. Blending in is what we shifters do."

"Soldiers go, where you go, Wynter, they always have," my aunt says.

"I don't remember them from earlier. Where have they been hiding?"

"The soldiers stay back a little, mixing in to allow space so that you can have a little bit of privacy. But we have word that there is a mole in Ashengale."

"A mole? So, your suspicions earlier were spot on. Someone has breached the perimeter."

"It appears that way. We can't risk having you out in the open anymore. This is the safest path back to the castle."

We come to a stairwell and descend quickly. Memories of the basement at Storm River Manor again bear its ugly head. A rush of unpleasant emotions surface. "What's down there?"

"The way out," Garrick says. There's a sudden movement, and the walls begin to shake.

I scream.

"Everything is fine. Keep moving," Garrick calls out.

Pictures fall, and I hear glass smash to the floor.

"What is that? Are we having an earthquake?" *"Earth" quake. The irony.*

"No," Garrick answers. "Ashengale is under attack." He pressures me to run faster. "Move, move, move!"

10

DOWNWARD SPIRAL

GARRICK RUSHES IN FRONT while Dad stays behind me and the soldiers stand behind him. "The Trek know you're here," Garrick says. We reach the basement and a loud crash from above blasts like fireworks, shaking the whole building.

Garrick gives a stern look at Fran.

Behind me, the soldiers who escorted us out of the restaurant follow us, keeping a close distance.

"Dad, you said we were safe." Anger, rather than fear, consumes me. The blood in my veins boils with fury. I'm enraged that my family has been put me in harm's way.

Garrick opens another door to another set of spiral stairs, and we press further downward for what feels like the gateway to the depths of hell. The hallway is dim, and the stone walls are cold.

"Where are we going?"

"The back way to Ashengale castle," Garrick answers. "Dark shifters have made it past the island's valley of fissures. The Trek are here, fighting, riding in on dark dragons." We reach the bottom step. "C'mon, this way."

This corridor Garrick has led us to is pitch black. Dad's eyes glow to give us light. We follow him as he leads the way and Garrick tails behind me. "We're at the bottom tier of the basement," Dad says.

Panic sets in, but rage outweighs the fear soaring inside me. Knowing I must control my emotions, I work on focusing my anger, channeling the thoughts, and letting them fizzle. I want to shift badly, to leave this place, but the walls surrounding us prevent that. It's hard, but I have to trust these soldiers will get us to safety.

"Wynter, breathe," I hear my aunt whisper in my head. *"Fight this urge you're having. Think of this as another test. This is no different than all the other times you fought hard to not become the beast. Now, you must fight not to change, no matter how difficult it might be."*

"I imagine it's because I don't know how to control my emotions yet, is that it? I thought that was why Dragonscale was training me earlier this afternoon."

"You must remember, you're at the most vulnerable time right now. This is but one of the many trials you'll face ahead."

"I don't want to talk about it!" My brain, my skin, my whole body feels like it is crying for me to shift. Murmurs sound in my mind—different voices other than Aunt Fran. I feel their hate, their pain, their sadness. The tugging on my hand startles me.

"Move, let's go while we can," Dad says.

"There are so many voices." Realizing the voices are trying to pull me in, I fight through the noise, saying, "Dad, what is happening to me? I feel this burning. It didn't happen earlier when Dragonscale helped me change the first time. It's a different feeling."

"Fight it, Wynter. Now is not the time to break down," Dad calls. "Your fear of what is currently happening, this need to escape and be safe, is wanting to free itself."

"I do believe you have discovered what you can do with that mind of yours. You're hearing the sounds of both good and evil," Aunt Fran answers.

"Do you hear them? The muttering of different people. Can you hear them, too?"

"No, because I've shut the door in my mind. You try doing the same."

"How do I do that?"

"Imagine a door. Do you see one?"

"Yes. It's wide open."

"Visualize shutting it."

"I know how you feel. When I went through my trials long ago, the voices came to me, too," Dad says.

"Wait, you went through trials?"

"Every Storm does. It's how we gain our power to control the magic, remember?"

More vibrations from aboveground sound off and shake the floor beneath our feet. "We need to get to the lower caves." Garrick takes a key and unlocks a steel door. "This way."

He shuts the passageway once the last soldier passes through.

The voices in my head slowly dissipate the deeper we descend.

"I closed the door in my mind but some of the voices are persistent."

"Try to focus on other things. This island is supposed to protect you, but it appears even this place has its weaknesses."

"How is that possible? I still wear the necklace."

"The magic has been blocked out somehow. We're going to find out why. Don't you worry."

We come to an underground clearing much like the cave where Ashengale resides, but this place is much different. There are more flying creatures, however, they're not the same type of dragons. "Dragongryphs?"

Aunt Fran smiles.

There are other species flying as well. One that stands out is a bird-like creature having the head and wings of an eagle and the body of a lion. They each have their own unique color, just like the dragons.

Dad notices me staring. "Those are lyongryphs," he says. "They're quite rare to see, but here in the underground city caves, they flourish."

"This is their home, and where they are raised," Aunt Fran says. "Most of the dragongryphs come here to live if their humanoid brother or sister are killed. You will soon discover there are many other species that live deep down in these caves to avoid discovery. The ancient wars of the past have pushed many to live under the protection of Ashengale Mountain. This is a small community within the Ashengale Kingdom."

"Quickly, this way," Garrick says, drawing our attention. He opens another door, and we dart into a building. The entrance is a grand sight. It's like walking into a skyscraper of a large city. From the outside, it looked like a cave enclosure, but the smell of sulfur suffocates me.

I plug my nose.

"Don't worry, you will get used to the odor soon enough," Dad says.

Two guards stand on either side of the front desk. When they see us, they salute, questioning, "Sir?"

A petite woman wearing a white suit stands in between them, looking much like a human, and pulls off her glasses. "Can I help you?"

"We need to have access to Doctor Brekker's office," Garrick demands.

"Is everything all right?" she asks.

"No! Now open the door."

An entrance to the doctor's office opens to the side of them and I'm pulled across the threshold without warning.

"That was a little rude, don't you think?" I ask.

"There's no time to be amiable," Garrick says.

A jerk in an elevator sends my stomach reeling in knots. I feel us going upward. My stomach continues to sway from the motion, making me feel nauseous. "I hate elevators."

Dad huffs. "We'll be out of this contraption soon." The elevator stops abruptly and opens.

More sulfur smells linger through my nostrils as we pass down the corridor and come to another door. Garrick opens it, and we enter a new space.

"It looks like a doctor's office."

"That's because it is."

"Dad, I'm not sick."

"No, but that necklace is."

"Huh?"

"I'll explain later."

Of course, you will.

A lady behind a counter sees us enter, and Garrick goes to her.

"Good day to you, sir. Is everything all right? We can feel the quakes below the surface."

"Is Doctor Brekker here? It's an emergency."

"Let me buzz him. Have a seat, please."

Garrick grumbles as he paces with impatience.

I walk over to glass cases embedded in the walls. Each compartment has a split geode revealing a different sparkling crystal. The largest one is made of amethyst. The smallest made of clear quarts. "They're protection stones."

My aunt comes by my side. "Yes. You will find many of these scattered throughout the underground city of Crystal Cove."

At the opposite end of the office, windows expand the entire side. I peek outside at the community below. "Is that what this place is called?"

She nods. "This is our family physician's office for the community under the caves."

"I'm sure we'll be fine down here," Garrick says, standing next to Fran. "I don't understand how the dark dragons managed to penetrate our island barriers."

"Not to worry, Garrick, our soldiers have it handled," Dad says.

Garrick glares at Dad, then turns his attention to the lady behind the counter. "This waiting feels like an eternity."

I look for a chair and observe fish swimming in a tank opposite of me. Children's laughter comes from one section over in the play area. Books are stacked on a table and beside it is a box of toys. They play quietly while their mother reads a magazine.

The receptionist calls Garrick and we rise. "The doctor will see you now."

We follow her to a back room where she gestures to a patient area. Like any other doctor's office, it contains all the gadgets: an examination table set in the center of the room with paper lining the pad and beside it a countertop and sink. The adjacent wall has a cupboard with an attached shelf, housing a jar of cotton swabs and gauze.

Feeling a little confused, I say, "So why are we here?"

"The necklace you wear appears to be...broken," Dad says.

"And how do you know that?"

"The dark dragons found us and you're the only possible link. Doctor Brekker needs to find out why your location spell isn't working anymore."

The door swings open, and a man wearing a long white lab coat, goggles on his disheveled grey head, and a stethoscope around his neck, comes to greet us.

I feel like I've stepped into some bizarre place where a mad scientist popped through those doors.

11

MAGIC IN A JAR

"**G**ARRICK, GOTTFRIED, WHAT BRINGS both of you to see me at the same time? Is something wrong?"

"Call me Jeff, please," Dad says. "And yes." He points to me.

The doctor glances my way and nods. "I see. It's indeed been a long time, hasn't it." He comes closer. "You may not remember, but I know you very well, Wynter. Good to see you again. You've grown since I last saw you. How's the arm?"

I reach deep into my memory and realize that this is the doctor who put a cast on my arm. "Fine?" Confusion washes over me. "Was this the doctor's office I was brought to?"

Dr. Brekker nods. "In a manner of speaking, yes. We've since moved locations."

"I remember now, but Nyta was with you."

"Yes, she was here." He points. "I see it's healed quite nicely. You haven't had any problems with it, have you?"

I shake my head. "No."

Dad nods. "Potentially, yes. I mean, not her arm, but there's another issue." Dad directs attention to my necklace.

"Say nothing more until we're in my office." He steps back. "Please, right this way," he says gesturing through the office doors. "There's a room available down the hall. Last door on your right. I'll be right there."

Dad, Garrick, Fran and I walk the hall to an empty room while two guards stand watch outside, and the other two stay near the front desk. It's only a few seconds before Dr. Brekker enters. "Now, tell me, what exactly is happening with the necklace?" He directs his attention to my chain. "Does it have anything to do with the random tremors we're having?"

"I fear it does," Dad says. "We have reason to believe it's been compromised. I didn't put two and two together until the attack to Ashengale City above. That's why you're feeling the small quakes below."

"We're under attack? But that's impossible," the doctor says.

I sense the doctor's temperature rise.

"Yes, I agree, but apparently it isn't impossible after all," Dad says.

"We were trying to get Wynter safely to Ashengale Castle but no matter where we turned, we were followed."

"And so you lead them right to us, Garrick?" The doctor gives a concerned glare. He comes closer, peering down at my locket. "Who has come in contact with this necklace, Wynter?"

"Well," I begin. "I haven't taken it off for weeks. Except for yesterday when I was visited by the Elementals."

"No, that wouldn't cause such a disruption of magic," Dr. Brekker remarks. He looks up at Dad. "When did it start happening? I mean when did you start to think the necklace was weakened?"

"We were eating at Scale Café & Grill when it clicked. I realized once Garrick came to warn us that we were followed, something was wrong," Dad says. "No one can get past our perimeter."

"Which means prior to today, something else occurred to compromise the necklace and leads me to believe the necklace is tainted with evil." Dr. Brekker reaches out his hand. "May I?"

Dad nods. "Go on. There is no need to worry. We're already compromised, anyway. They already know you're here."

I unclasp the chain and hand it to the doctor. He puts on a jeweler's loupe and inspects the locket. "I would say my suspicions are confirmed." He points to a small crack on the stone. "See this?"

I nod. "How is that possible. I've not dropped it before."

Dr. Brekker grunts. "This fracture isn't from dropping the stone." He breathes deeply. A sigh that triggers fear that whatever has happened might not be fixable. He inspects it further, taking it over to a microscope. "This necklace has a homing device attached to it." He looks at Dad. "How long was she with Moyer?"

"Only a couple weeks," I say. "She placed a memory stamp on me, too. I've since had the spell broken, thanks to Dragonscale."

"No, that couldn't be it. Moyer can't touch the locket. She'd be electrocuted."

A feeling of satisfaction flints through my body remembering the jolt Moyer experienced when she attacked me in the basement of Storm River Manor. "Yeah, I know."

"Any recollections before that? What about the day you were kidnapped?"

"How is it you know all this?" I ask, perplexed.

He smiles, glancing at my dad. "Let's say I've been briefed on the matter." He lays the necklace down on the counter and brings out a full jar of clear liquid and places my locket inside.

"This should help cloud our exact location until we can determine the cause."

"What is that?" I ask.

"Fusing gel. It's basically the glue that keeps the magic intact."

"Is it supposed to look like that with blue crystals forming around the locket?"

I snag the doctor's attention. "Hmm?" He has an anxious moment, saying, "Has this locket gotten wet at any point?" He pulls the locket out of the jar quickly and washes off the goo, and then dips it in another solution.

"It fell into the Elemental healing water yesterday."

"No, that would not affect this chemical reaction."

"Well, how about the day before I was kidnapped, I forgot to take my necklace off in swim class, and the chain fell off landing at the bottom of the pool."

"Mmm, I see." The doctor seems to calm down knowing the possible cause. "Chlorine weakens the magic, yes, but it would not weaken it to the point that it would break the glue." He pauses and faces me. "What else can you tell me about that day?"

"I remember doing one more lap around the pool before getting out when another classmate by the name of Sadie tried to drown me. Well, I mean, I imagine she didn't want to kill me, but she definitely wanted to scare me. Bully me a bit, I guess. I fought back. The coach caught us, and Sadie seemed thrilled, knowing she got under my skin. The coach yelled at her to get back to the locker room and then asked if I was all right. I said I was fine. Coach told me he was going to file a report, and Sadie would be suspended."

"This Sadie...what did she look like?"

"Medium build, dark hair, brown eyes. I remember she had a scar above her left eyebrow."

"Pointed ears?"

"No. What kind of question is that?"

"Right, the human world. Elf ears would not be well received. Hmm." The doc rubs his chin while examining the locket through the glass jar.

"What are you getting at?" Dad asks.

Dr. Brekker furrows his brows. "That someone must have sent a dark witch to weave their way into Wynter's life to get that necklace disenchanted. It appears to have almost worked, too. The fusing gel has almost completely dissolved."

"Are you saying Sadie was a dark witch?" I ask.

"Possibly, yes. I mean dark witches know how to disenchant items such as jewelry."

I point to the jar. "And in that container, you're trying to re-infuse the magic back to the way it was?"

"Yes."

The ground shakes again, nearly knocking me down, but Dad catches me.

"The tremors are getting stronger," Aunt Fran says.

"I think we need to prepare to evacuate, sir," Garrick says, glancing at my dad.

"Agreed. Sound the alarm." Dad looks at me, concerned, and then at the doctor. "They know we're here."

Garrick leaves the doctor's office, and seconds later a siren wails.

"We better get out now," Dr. Brekker says. He grabs the jar. "Follow me."

Debris falls from the ceiling and the lights flicker.

"Do not shift, no matter how much you want to," my aunt says inside my head. *"You would lead the dark dragons directly to us."*

"Trust me I won't."

A fireball crashes through the office. The receptionist screams as she catches on fire. People in the office run down the hallway screaming. The mother that was in the waiting room with us lifts her two children and flees.

Dr. Brekker hands me the container. "Take this with you. In about five minutes you may remove it once it stops glowing blue. Do not let it out of your sight."

"Got it. What are you going to do?"

One of the soldiers in our group puts out the flames on the woman's back. She collapses.

"Help the injured, of course. Now go!"

As we turn for the door to flee, we're stopped by a hovering dark dragon with a Trek on its back. He takes aim with his arrow. "Duck!" I scream. The arrow nails a nurse in the shoulder.

"Okay, you said I'm not to shift, but you never said I couldn't do this." Before my aunt has time to react, I throw a ball of ice towards the intruder, freezing them both instantaneously like the wolf a few days ago in the mountains. Gravity forces the ice cube downward to the rocky valley below.

Dr. Brekker's eyes grow large. "It appears, Lord Jeoffrey, that you have some explaining to do once this is over. Never in the history of dragons has anyone had the power of water since—"

"Yes, I know, I know." Dad looks over the edge of the balcony. "Is there another way out of here?"

"Wait, let me heal her first," I say. "It looks like the same kind of arrow Rory was hit with."

"Rory?" the doc asks, sounding confused.

"Yes, my friend. I have a hunch it's tainted with Sea Spike poison. Don't touch the arrow, whatever you do." I glide my hand over the wound, sealing the shaft into the nurse's flesh. "Get her to Nyta, she will know what to do."

Doc nods.

"We should go, My Lord," Garrick says.

Dr. Brekker points. "Through those doors at the end of the hall is a stairwell leading to the lower caverns. But be careful, I'm sure it will be heavily guarded. If they can find their way to this office, they'll be waiting for you."

"Sounds like we're trapped," I say.

"Not yet." Dad pulls at my hand.

"Wait, what about Doctor Brekker and his staff?"

Dad looks to the two soldiers tagging along. "Can you men take these three to Geneviève's Ranch? This nurse needs immediate care."

"Sir?" one soldier protests.

"Wynter will be safe, trust me. Besides something tells me she can take care of herself. The folks injured need medical attention."

The woman that was scorched moans.

"Let me help her first, Dad." My hands glow once more. It takes a few seconds for me to gain control, but soon a cooling sensation washes over the woman's back and I feel her pain ease. I don't have the strength to completely heal her but at least I can give her some sort of relief.

"Okay, let's move..." Dad pulls at my hand again.

The two soldiers shift into dragons and lower to the ground, allowing Dr. Brekker to help the two injured women onto the dragon's backs.

"Can we please leave now?" Garrick presses. "Before it's too late."

I pick up the jar of liquid holding my necklace, and we flee through the back way out of the office. By this time, the blue glow begins to fade.

"Don't take it out too early, or it won't work," Dad says.

I nod and tuck the jar under my arm as Dad leads us out of danger.

12

SECRET TUNNEL

WE REACH THE SURFACE of Ashengale City. The area is devastating to witness. "How are we to get back to the castle? The city is in ruins." Many dead bodies are strewn about. A protective dome shields the entire area, while our dragons encircle the perimeter inside its boundaries. The enemy hurls fireballs from outside the armored sphere.

"They're trying to weaken our defenses," Fran says.

A commander calls from above. Standing on the stone wall that overlooks the valley, archers with bows and arrows prepare to shoot. "Get ready for round two, men!"

"Hurry," Garrick cries, "we need to get to the other end of the cave." He points in its direction.

I hear something similar to glass breaking.

"Shields are cracking!" the commander cries. "On my call..."

"Move," Garrick orders.

We run along the boundaries of the fencing.

Garrick shifts and so does my dad as the Trek soldiers invade. Now, it's a battle on the ground as well as in the air.

It's not just dragons fighting, but allies of many other different species, too, coming to defend our home. Soldiers combat with swords drawn against the intruders, wolves pounce on their enemy, elves ready their arrows in the trees and atop roofs, and even giants appear where I hadn't noticed them before. Wizards armed with balls of magic throw their weight into the battle and sorcerers call upon the natural elements to aid in the fight. All kinds of magical beings are coming out of the woodwork. It makes me realize this isn't just a sanctuary for misfits, this is their home, and everyone is defending it to the death.

The jar I hold still glows blue. *"When will this necklace be ready?"*

Fran frowns. *"We work with what we have for now. Isn't that what I always tell you?"* Her tone cuts like a knife, and I know this is a battle of survival now.

"I can't see Dad."

"He will be fine. He's stronger in his shifted state, unlike the dark dragons. Their weakness is their scales. They no longer hold the magic of good. Their only strength is the fire they breathe. Burning as much as they can."

A Trek charges toward us. My quick reflexes freezes him. *"Um okay, so that just happened."*

"Perhaps you may be more useful than we first hoped," Fran teases.

One of our allies doesn't hesitate, taking advantage of my frozen masterpiece and smashes it.

"Oh no."

"What?" I turn around and see nothing. *"What is it?"*

"You don't see that coming toward us?"

"See what?"

"Never mind," she says and swooshes past me in her ghost form. She fights with the airspace in front of her. There's nothing there. This doesn't make any sense. If it were another ghost, I would see them.

"What's going on?" I fight through the chaos, with each attacker that comes my way while still trying to keep tabs on my aunt.

"Run to the fence. I'll catch up," she says, *"as soon as I take care of this Trek on our tail."*

Whatever it is I can't see, it's giving Aunt Fran a tough fight. My hands cool and I think of a javelin. Ice forms from my fingers and soon a spear is in my hands. I hold an image in my mind of what I think this Trek might look like fighting Aunt Fran. I don't hesitate and send the weapon hurling forward, saying, *"Duck!"*

"Nice work. Direct hit to the heart. How did you—"

"I didn't see anything there I just trusted what you were fighting hoping my ice dagger would work. But it does concern me that I didn't see, what you saw considering I'm supposed to 'see ghosts.'"

"Don't worry, we will figure it out. Right now, let's focus on reaching the interior wall I pointed to earlier."

We reach the barrier as Fran suggested just in time for another round of attacks. *"Run to that tower ahead. I'll be right behind you,"* Fran urges.

Her words go in vain as another Trek runs forward, and successfully slams me against a rock. Dazed for a moment he raises a hand to deliver a deadly blow, but flames consume him before he has a chance. Garrick roars, then darts away to his next victim. The Trek crackles like coal before his body falls to the ground in a pile of ash.

Fran grabs my hand before I have time to absorb what just happened. "Quick, this way."

"Wait, the jar of liquid. I dropped it."

"We have to find it." Fran dashes away scouting the area.

I run back to the boulder where we first encountered trouble. *"I found it. It's wedged between the rock and the fencepost. Liquid is slowly seeping out of the container. Thankfully, the blue glow has disappeared."*

"Smash the glass, take the necklace, and put it on," my aunt says.

It oozes with goop, but I don't care. At least I can once again hide my location. *"What do we do now?"*

"Keep moving. The war isn't over just because you wear that necklace. We still need to get you safely out of here." Aunt Fran catches up to me. *"This way."*

Marksmen trail the upper edges of the fencing catwalk, shooting like madmen. Some fall to their deaths as we keep running.

We take cover by a willow tree, and it's immediately torched by a blasting fireball.

Fran points. *"Keep moving. We need to get to that tower."*

Many trees around us burn. Squawks from above ring out with horrid fighting. Two dark dragons spew fire, torching the homes and buildings around us. People are fleeing everywhere. Fiery bodies are burned alive as we sprint past them. My heart aches, knowing I can't help everybody. This is all my fault. The Underworld is looking for me, and all these people are perishing because of it. Animals bolt across the paths, trying to avoid the firestorm from above while the strong ones fight back the evil intruders. *"This is utter chaos."*

"The mountain beyond the tower, is our freedom to safety. That's why we must head that way."

"But the mountain looks like a dead end," I protest.

"Trust me, it's not."

A fireball hits another tree, urging us to move faster. All around me soldiers prepare cannons and marksmen ready more arrows from unscathed treetops. In the distance, knights fight alongside the elves, and more dragon shifters take to the air. Women and children continue screaming, searching for cover. Balls of flames catapult through the town and damage everything in their path. I can't tell who's winning and who's losing. There's so much death.

We leap over dead bodies, trying to avoid the fires moving across the ground. A shrieking scream catches my attention. A Trek chases a small child. The same child I remember seeing in the doctor's office. I freeze the Trek where he stands, allowing the child to run away to his frantic mother and sibling.

I stay close to Fran hurdling over more bodies as we round the corner of another large boulder. We tuck and roll as a fireball nearly misses us.

"We're going to have to make a run for that tower. But wait on my signal. I have an idea." She pops up onto a boulder. *"I can see the dragons are regrouping. Go now! There is a hidden trap door in the floorboards. It's made of steel. Open it and get out of here."*

"Let me guess, made of Valiancium steel?"

"Yes. Now go," Fran presses.

Arrows fly by my head as I make a break for the tower doors. A few straggling elves make a break for it, too.

My aunt stays behind distracting the enemy. "What can they do? Kill her?" I laugh. *Brilliant, Aunt Fran.*

I make it inside the tower walls. Soldiers protect the window opening, firing out ammo, as people pile down through the trap door that's already laying wide open. *Apparently, the trap door isn't a secret.*

Many people are huddled together waiting their turn to pass through. Some people are impatient and jump down instead.

By the time it's my turn, Fran is by my side in ghost form. *"Wynter, get ready, on three."*

It takes me a couple of seconds to realize she's warning me. Her ability to see what's coming before it comes.

She looks over my shoulder and from the expression on her face, it isn't good. I hear her scream aloud, "Three!" Before I have a chance to react, she yanks my hand, and I freefall down the stairwell, landing onto something soft, not realizing at first it's dead bodies that have fallen from impatiently waiting in line.

"Ewww!" I scream.

"No time for theatrics, let's go!"

We hurry deeper inside the tunnel along with many other elves and shifters trying to flee the battle. A fireball shoots through the hole, and I realize that's what prompted Fran to tell me to jump so quickly.

Again, my reflexes react before my brain, and the damage to the tunnel is reduced by my ice blast, cooling down the area.

"Nice!" Aunt Fran pats my shoulder. *"Follow the crowd. It leads out to a ravine."*

I look at the frightened faces around me. *"Their lives have been invaded and their homes destroyed. And it's all because of me. This was supposed to be a safe haven away from such brutal attacks. This is insane, Aunt Fran. Dragonscale said we were safe."*

"Yes, that's true, but something has clearly happened to break Ashengale's protection barrier. The first full moon has begun. This tragedy does not lie on your shoulders."

13
ASHENGALE MOUNTAIN

"*WHAT DO YOU MEAN the first full moon has begun?*" I ask. "*Are you saying Sarmira has gained greater power?*" Anxiety grows within me. "*Does this mean we failed?*"

"*No, we haven't failed,*" she answers. "*It means we need to hide you somewhere no one will find you. I'm sure my father will know what to do. I must prepare to go to the gates and hold off the invasion from the other worlds. Sarmira will try to enter this world now that the first full moon has started on Earth.*"

"*You're leaving me, aren't you.*"

"*I'm not leaving you alone just yet. We will wait for your dad or someone in his company to aid you to safety.*"

"*What about Namari?*"

"He can't travel these confined cavern walls. When we reach the valley at the end of this passageway, you can call to him then."

I cross my arms. "I feel so claustrophobic right now."

"I know the feeling," a woman says behind me. I turn around making eye contact. Her hair is disheveled and dirt powders across her cheeks. "We will be safe in the valley of Aegis."

I'm not sure what she means, but I'm assuming that's where this tunnel leads to.

"The woman's right. We'll be safe there." Aunt Fran looks at my necklace. *"We won't know if the fusing gel worked until darkness comes for you. No news is good news, as the saying goes. For now, we stick together."*

Sounds thud with movement from above our surroundings. The walls of the cave crumble with dirt and rock falling on our heads. People shriek in fear. Faint screams are heard above, along with the clanging sounds of swords. People cry in agony, and men shout as they fight. After a few more minutes of walking, the noises fade away. I don't know if it's because we've distanced ourselves from the hellacious sounds of death and destruction, or if it's because the battle is over. The line of people in front of us becomes stagnant and slow.

My head is consumed with visions of souls passing as death takes them. *"Aunt Fran, are you seeing what I'm seeing?"*

"Yes."

"So much death."

"Try not to think about it. The sadness will only lower your defenses. If you allow your emotions to take over, then evil has won."

She's right. I need to keep the horrid thoughts at bay and push the vision out of my mind. *"The good news is I haven't seen the passing of Dad."*

"Which is great news."

WE WALK FOR WHAT seems like hours before a light in the distance reveals itself. I half expect it to be my imagination. Ocean waves echo off the tunnel walls, giving me a sense of hope.

"We're coming to the end of the cave," Aunt Fran says.

The excitement of people and shouts of joy echo with relief. Reaching the end seems to take an eternity from so many people waiting.

More minutes roll by, when it's finally our turn to pass through to the fresh ocean air. What I didn't expect was that reaching the sea would mean a fifty-foot drop or more.

It isn't until I come out onto the edge of the underpass that I realize it juts out of the side of a cliff. A rolled-out bamboo ladder drapes over the edge with people descending to a ravine below. A waterfall cascades down, splashing onto large rocks to a raging pool of water that flows out to the ocean in the distance. Large trees line either side of the river. From my vantage point, I can't see a single person in the foliage because it's so thick, which under the circumstances is probably a good thing if someone was searching the sky.

There are trees everywhere, and the sun shines brightly in the afternoon air. *"How is it possible? We haven't left the island, have we?"*

"No," my aunt says aloud. "This is the back side of Ashengale Mountain. The ocean is beyond those trees." She points. "It's the only side that remains green with life. The dragons have protected it for centuries."

"What do we do when we get to the bottom?" People climb down the bamboo ladder, two at a time. "Why can't they shift and just fly down?"

"Not all these people are shifters. Many of them come from different factions. Like I said when you first arrived yesterday, many are refugees cast out from past wars, their homes were destroyed, and they have nowhere else to go."

A loud rumble rolls through the hollow dark tunnel. I turn around to confirm if we're the last of the people out of the cave. In the far, dark distance, a pair of eyes emerge. I nudge Aunt Fran. "Look." The glowing eyes come closer and closer slowly coming toward us.

Fran's face lights up. "Garrick!" She runs and hugs him tight.

He carries with him an injured soldier. They both seem to be in pain.

Garrick yowls. "Easy on the shoulder."

"Let me help you," she says. She props to the other side to aid the injured soldier.

"They're all gone," the wounded stranger mumbles. His breath is heavy.

Fran looks worried. "Garrick?"

"The invaders have been defeated, rest assured of that, my dear love, but we lost a lot of men, women, and children today. He takes his eyes off my aunt and looks up at me. "She didn't shift, did she?"

"No," My aunt smiles at me. "She was really brave today, though."

They set the soldier against the mouth of the cave. Garrick takes a canteen from his waist and gives the man some water. "Drink."

"Your shoulder is injured. Are you able to fly him down to the ravine below?" Aunt Fran asks.

"Yes." Garrick rotates his shoulder a bit. "I think so, anyway. Can you heal him first, Wynter?"

"Definitely. Perhaps you could use a light healing, too?" I hover my hand over the man's burned chest, and it clears up, leaving only a scar. Then I do the same to Garrick's shoulder.

"Thanks," he says.

It only takes a few minutes before the man comes to. He has blond hair, and his physique is nearly the same as Garrick. A tattoo is inked on his left bicep with an emblem I don't recognize, but somehow, I feel like I've seen it before.

"What is your name, soldier?" Garrick asks.

"Thane."

"Well, Thane, thank you for all you do in helping to defend our kingdom and homes. Can you walk?"

"I think so," he replies. "The pain has subsided quite a bit." He squints at me. "Are you a healer?"

Shyly, I say, "Not in the way I should be, I suppose. I just turned eighteen last week."

"I see. Well, I'm indebted to you, My Lady. Thank you."

"Are you well enough to climb?" Garrick asks. "I can fly you down if you prefer."

Thane shakes his head, nodding toward me. "No. I'm feeling much better now that she's healed me."

Garrick helps the man up. "You should still get looked at by a physician."

Fran notices the tattoo, too. "You're a druid?"

The man glances to his bicep. "Aye, that I am."

"We could use your help with these folks getting down to the valley below," my aunt says. "Do you think you're up to helping?"

"I think I might be able to help with that, yes."

"You're not a dragon shifter, then?" I ask.

"No. I'm a Dryad Druid."

It's then I take notice of his pointed ears and the texture of his arms. His skin looks rough like tree bark, but when I healed him, he felt smooth to the touch. "A Dryad? Huh."

Garrick gives a wink, and Aunt Fran smiles.

"I didn't realize Dryads came this far west." I stand back as he prepares for portal jumps. It's the same routine Rory does right before she jumps, too.

"Everyone hold hands and we can safely get down the mountain." His hand glows as he prepares for takeoff.

In seconds, we're on the ground near the river. The breeze wakens my body followed by a sudden chill. "Garrick, where's my father?"

14
VALLEY OF ÆGIS

"**I** HAVEN'T SEEN HIM."

Inside my mind, the world crumbles, hearing what Garrick said.

Aunt Fran interrupts my thoughts. *"Wynter, breathe. He must be fine, otherwise we both would have seen him by now."* She grabs my shoulders and forces me to look into her eyes. "Wynter, breathe. Your father is fine."

"It doesn't make it any easier. What if the Underworld captured him?" My mind thinks the worst possible things besides death. "If Dad isn't dead, then he must have been caught. Why aren't you two together? And Dragonscale, why isn't he here?"

"Dragonscale is still at the castle tending to the wounded," Garrick answers. "As for Jeff, we lost sight of each other in battle. Your dad is a brilliant man. He wouldn't be easy to kill, trust me."

Garrick attempts to touch my shoulder, and I shrug him away. "I've already gone through the loss of losing him once, now those feelings are rearing up again. The third time actually. How many times can one lose their father and then somehow miraculously hope they appear alive?"

"Fran's right. If he died, he would have come to say goodbye to you first."

Garrick shifts to a dragon. *"Climb on and we'll search for him together."*

His persistence forces me to smile. *"Am I ever going to understand how to control the thoughts of others getting in my mind?"*

He laughs. *"Get on and let's go find him? Shall we?"*

I concede, and climb onto Garrick's back, holding tight to the back of his scales. Garrick takes off, and we glide through the valley. This ride is much different than being on the back of Namari. Utter silence covers me, and I don't have the invitation into Garrick's thoughts like I did with my dragongryph.

Nearly an hour passes, and I hear a screech above in the sky. Several dragons come flying toward us, and my necklace begins to glow. *"Garrick, are those friends or foe?"* I ask, pointing.

"That would be Lord Gottfried and some surviving soldiers, My Princess." Garrick whirls around and heads back. *"See, nothing to worry about. Your father is alive and well."*

Someone is riding on his back, and I can only assume it's Geneviève. Relief settles in my bones knowing Dad is safe.

Garrick lands softly and quickly changes back to a human-looking form.

Aunt Fran sees us and waves, standing by a large tree near the river. "Back so soon?"

"Jeff is close behind us," Garrick says.

"Such good news." Aunt Fran's lighthearted face eases.

Dad lands with Geneviève sliding from his back and he swiftly changes to looking like his old self, followed by the men with him.

"Glad to hear you made it through the battle," Aunt Fran says. She kisses Dad's cheek. "Is it clear to come back yet?"

Dad dips his head. "We lost many refugees, more than our own. Many innocents died today. Not many dragons though since the Island makes us stronger. I think we might have lost one shifter. The rest were Pine Willow Elves, and those humanoids who migrated to our island for protection."

"Such a sad day. I'm glad you're safe. Wynter has been worried. I must go, though," Aunt Fran says.

"Leaving so soon?" Dad asks.

"So sorry, dear brother-in-law. I've been called upon to guard the gates of Scarlet Hollow."

Aunt Fran hugs me and kisses Garrick like she won't ever see him again.

"Where are you off to?" Geneviève asks.

"To keep the evil from entering our world—and Sarmira." She grins devilishly like she's looking forward to the battle and disappears.

"I wish she didn't have to go," I say.

"You're not alone in thinking that way," Garrick says. "As a sworn member of the Kingdom of Ashengale, it's our duty to protect you at all costs."

"And yet by protecting me, this is what the kingdom has suffered." I gesture to the wounded residents of Ashengale. Some moan in pain while others tend to the wounded. Some bathe in the river a few yards away, washing off the sweat, blood, and dirt. "Does my protection warrant such pain from our people? Look around, Garrick..."

I step away and begin to aid with some of the injured. At least I can alleviate some of their pain by attempting to heal them.

Geneviève follows me. "Fran will be okay."

"I know."

"The battle with the Underworld can only mean one thing—"

"Yes, it's already started," I say. "Apparently early. Something about the full moon on Earth. Geneviève, if you're trying to sooth me, don't. It's not helping." I step to an injured child and smile. "Are you in pain?"

The child nods and lifts her arm. Burns cover the back of her hand, up to the elbow. "Let me see if I can help." I hold out my hand and hover it over the girl's arm.

Geneviève smiles, resting a hand on my shoulder. "I'll get to work gathering the people ten at a time and take them to the castle. Will you help me with organizing? We need to get these people safely back inside the mountain."

"Sure." I look back to see Dad in a deep conversation with Garrick.

I overhear Garrick say, "We just came from there. Are you sure it's safe to go back?"

"They're all gone," Dad answers. "It's safe to go home." He sees me staring.

ABOUT AN HOUR PASSES when I hear Garrick ask Dad, "How many were there?"

"I don't know," Dad answers. "We need to get Wynter to the Underground Valley, where it's much safer than out here in the open."

"Underground Valley?" I ask, turning. I don't think they realize I can still hear them. My question goes unanswered, but not without Dad giving me a concerned look.

"How will she be able to complete her trials if we take her there?" Geneviève asks.

"Do you see any other choice?" Dad argues.

"Geneviève, are you almost finished with gathering folks to port out?" Garrick interrupts.

"Yes, I've entrusted a few druids who have taken the injured. This is the last of us."

"Very well," he says. "Wynter, call your dragon, please. We need to get you to the valley before round two occurs."

"Round two? Are you telling me to expect more attacks?" I look at my dad, concerned.

"Your trials are far from over, my dear. Call him now, please." Dad's tone is firm and urgent.

"But what about the people we just sent back to the mountain?"

"They are safe. Ashenville Rock was virtually untouched The only dark dragon that breached the city was the one who was killed at Doctor Brekker's office," Dad says.

Dubiously, I blow into my whistle and call my Dragongryph. I don't like my dad's answer. Within seconds, Namari soars through the sky, gliding down in my direction. The sight of him fills me with security. He's such a beautiful creature, bellowing as he lands to show his strength to protect. I don't hesitate to climb on his back.

"He will be able to shield your whereabouts," Dad says. "It might be best to stay on his back, at least until we can secure your location."

I look at my necklace, wondering if the fusing gel took hold.

"Take care of my daughter. Bring her to the Underground Valley. We'll be right behind you, and make sure you're not followed."

"You still think I'm being followed, Dad?"

"I'm not taking any chances, besides, it's not a secret that you're my daughter. They could still follow me. Now, get going!"

Namari takes off, flying over the ocean.

"What is the Underground Valley, Namari?"

"Somewhere safe. It's a small island off Ashengale. Only way to the Underground Valley is by ship. An invisible ship, that is. It's the headquarters of Dragonscale's lair."

"But I thought that was Ashengale."

"Sort of. It's where his people reside and are protected, and where most of the family functions occur, but where we're going, it's more of a military guard post. It isn't far from the large island. See there, that rock sticking out of the water?"

I peer above his head to see a small island in the middle of the ocean, and as we draw closer, I see it has many fir trees. There is a cave opening to one side, and Namari takes us there, landing flawlessly on the sand.

"Now what?"

"Now, we wait for the others. Stay on my back, though, so I can cloak you. If we were followed, they'll see only me and not you. Hang on tight. We're about to glide through the caverns."

15
THE GROTTO

T HE 'SMALL' ISLAND IS much bigger than it appears. Namari flies down the deep, dark, massive cave and veers left, then right, continuing to wind along until the sounds of the ocean are faint.

"This cavern is huge."

"Well, Princess, we are, after all, dragons."

Soon we come to a clearing much like the grounds outside of Ashengale City except there's no city beyond the perimeter, instead there are crystals of all sorts peeking through the cavern walls and sand that sparkles. *"An underground grotto."*

"Yes, but it's much more than that."

To the right is a waterfall, and to the left are heavy boulders. *"So many waterfalls in Ashengale."*

"That waterfall comes from the ocean. Believe it or not, we're underwater. This is a dormant volcano."

"It's amazing, Namari."

"There is magic in all things, My Princess. Waterfalls help to conceal our charming abilities, as well as give us healing and health. "That way" –he points with his head to the falling water– *"is the way to the Underground Valley."*

He lands on the ground walking toward the waterfall. *"Cover your head. You may get a bit wet. This is the way to the ship."* We pass through to the sight of a ship bobbing up and down, tied to a dock along a cavern river. Every few seconds rushing water waves in, confirming what Namari said about us being surrounded by the ocean.

"It looks like a small port, except there is only one boat."

"A grand vessel, to be exact," Namari says.

A couple guards keep watch at either end of the dock, with one other guard standing at the top of the ship in the crow's nest.

A black dragon with green wing tips and talons guards the mouth of the cave as we enter the small cove. He appears to be sleeping until a horn announces our arrival and wakes him. It doesn't take the dragon long to stand at attention, observing our presence.

"What is the problem, sir?" he asks Namari. This dragon is much larger than my dragongryph, yet Namari seems to hold higher rank.

Namari approaches and two more guards I didn't see before, gather near, not in dragon form, but as elves, having a dubious look to them.

"Ashengale has suffered an attack. I was instructed to guide Princess Wyndreana to the Underground Valley," Namari states.

"I see you have guided the princess safely, Namari," one unfamiliar voice says.

"Who is this in my head?" I ask.

It appears as though one of the elves is speaking telepathically. But I can't tell which one. How is that possible? I thought those of dragon descent and a handful of wizards could only have such talents. Rory comes to mind and she's an elf. However, she only 'sees' after being poisoned by Sea Spike.

"Wait a minute, you can read my dragon's thoughts?" I ask aloud.

"Of course, My Lady. Have you forgotten already?" The guard appears perplexed but hearing him talk confirms he was the one speaking within my mind.

"Forgive her, sir, she's still new at this. She's forgotten much of her past and needs gentle reminding once in a while. Besides, she hasn't completed her trials yet," my dragongryph reminds him.

The guard stands at attention. He's dressed in the same white and gold attire I have seen on the streets of Ashengale city. On his left breast are three red chevron patterns with a gold dragon symbol underneath. I recognized this symbol immediately, knowing he's a much higher rank than anyone else here. Why does he pose as a common guard, I wonder?

"How quickly one forgets, indeed," the guard says. *"This is Duncan."* He points to the dragon. *"The one you caught sleeping on post,*

and I am Sedrick, the commander of this grotto sworn to protect the entrance to the Underground Valley."

The large dragon bows his head as he's introduced. *"At your service, My Lady,"* he says.

I nod. *"Are you a shifter, too?"*

"Most certainly, Princess."

I look at Commander Sedrick, stunned. "But you're Elvin? I'm so confused."

"Ah...yes, looks can be deceiving, can't they?" He shifts right before my eyes into a golden dragon with black talons and wings. He gleams silver when the light hits his scales just right. *"Follow me,"* he says, turning around.

I gasp. *"A dragon shifter that's Elvin?"* Now it makes sense.

Sedrick chuckles but he ignores my curiosity. We follow him to the dock. *"The ship will add more protection until the others get here,"* he says.

Duncan follows behind us with the other soldier remaining in his Elvin form.

"Commander, I'm not feeling very confident. We may have been followed. Please keep a watchful eye for enemies that may approach," Namari presses. *"I feel we should move forward quickly."* He turns his neck to the side, looking behind him at the entrance where we came from.

"Duly noted, sir," Sedrick says.

The horn sounds, startling me. "We have intruders!" a scouting soldier shouts.

"Get her aboard the ship, now," Duncan says. *"Namari, it seems you may have been right."*

SEDRICK TAKES TO THE air, along with the rest of his crew. Even the soldier who paced behind us a moment ago shifts to his dragon form.

Within minutes, I hear a battle between beasts around the corner of the canal we passed through a moment ago. Namari rushes aboard along with a few soldiers who didn't shift.

Duncan has shifted back to his human form and climbs the deck to the porting bow. "Release the ropes!"

I lay low on Namari's back as we find a corner to hide. The ship is unbelievably huge, but so is the cave we're in.

Dad and Garrick fly in from the canal that led us here and join in the fighting. Dark dragons with Trek riders follow them in. It's an all-out battle in the grotto. They all circle, shooting fire at each other. Dad's talons grab one of the intruders, and they plummet to the water below.

"Dad!"

My screams grab the attention of another Trek rider, and he comes near the ship. *"I'm sorry, they know I'm here for sure, now."*

"The shield is invisible, they can't see it, but yes, they know you're here," Namari says.

Sedrick comes from behind and blows fire at the Trek intruder. Both dragons fight, good versus evil, neither getting the upper hand.

"I have to do something."

"Keep quiet. We can't risk it. Let them battle it out."

"I can't stand back and watch this." Anger builds within me once more. *"I will not shift for the sake of my people, but I also will not stand by and be a spectator."* Before Namari has a chance to catch me, I slide off his back and run to the edge of the ship, dousing the dark dragon and his rider with water.

The rage within me escalates, but I keep it in check. "You will not hurt my family!" I go much further than drenching this intruder with water. The anger in me is so strong. I feel it building, as though my veins will burst. I thrust my magic upon him so forcefully he's encased in ice, along with the beast he rides. They drop into the water below with a huge splash, bobbing up and down like an ice cube.

My rage burns more, and I have this sudden rush of energy. So much energy that somehow it fuels my strength even more, and I strike at another dark dragon heading right for me. He, too, meets his frozen fate. A third beast attacks, blasting toward me with his blue fire, and I douse his flame before it reaches the ship.

He flaps in the air, roaring with fury, as though he's lost his most valuable prize. One of our allies blasts the enemy with fire, and the force knocks the dark dragon backward toward the edge of the grotto's shore. The strength is so strong the dark dragon shifts to his human form, allowing our allies to capture him.

Namari scoops me up and tightens his grip, holding me on his back with his mane. *"You will not get away so easily next time, my dragon sister. What were you thinking? Do you know I could get in trouble for what you did?"*

"Please, Namari." I roll my eyes in anger. *"Something had to be done."*

"Not at the expense of you getting hurt."

"I'm not some fragile egg that needs to be handled with a pair of velvet gloves."

"Perhaps not, but you are a princess that needs protecting at all costs."

More dark dragons fly in the grotto, attacking.

"Get that ship out of here," Sedrick commands.

I feel the liner move as we head for another waterfall, and not the one we came through. *"What about my dad? Someone needs to see if he's okay."*

"Have you seen him pass?" Namari asks.

"You mean, is he a ghost? No." My mind is flooded with all kinds of emotion. I need to get myself in check. I must remember the gift I have. Knowing that is half the battle. He's okay as long as I don't see him pass, which leads to my next question…Where is he, if not dead? I haven't seen Garrick either, for that matter.

"Where does that lead to?" I point to the waterfall we're about to pass through.

"That's the way to the Underground Valley, and the enemy knows it."

Some of the fighting dissipates once we cross through the falling water. I feel the pain of fellow dragons with each slice and each stab inflicted on them.

"Can you feel this agony, too?" I ask Namari.

"Yes, and so can each and every dragon of the Kingdom of Ashengale."

"But I thought it was impossible to kill a dragon unless in human form?"

"We are not immune to death if the one we're fighting is another dragon."

"Of course. Dad and Fran failed to tell me that part."

"Probably because they didn't want to worry you. You have too much on your plate, and it's important to complete your trials."

Aunt Fran pops in, startling me, but not Namari. Somehow, he knew she was on the way to visit us. I hear a teasing tone in his voice. *"How's the new gatekeeper holding up?"*

"Not bad, considering," she remarks. *"How's my niece holding up?"* She smiles and adds, *"Isalora has her end secured, in turn, helping my end, too. Apparently, I'm not the only gatekeeper to this side of the universe. My mother has secured more than one gatekeeper to guard it. My guess is she anticipated I would need to be in two places at once. I've come to distract the dark dragons, so you may get to the Underground Valley safely."*

Without warning, it becomes quiet, prompting those hidden on the boat to become very still. A purr-like sound comes from behind the waterfall we passed through. I see some slight movement and then it appears. Only one, though. He's a massive beast and looks very much like the same dragon I froze a moment ago, but I know that's impossible. *"They just keep coming, don't they? Where's Dad and Garrick?"*

"I don't know. Do not make a sound," Fran says.

Another dark dragon comes through the waterfall. They both hop onto the walkway on either side of the canal. Their breathing is heavy. They clack and purr to each other, as though it's some sort of language only they know.

"Because they are no longer dragons of the light, they have lost the privilege to communicate with the minds of other light dragons. Likewise, we also cannot understand them," Namari says.

"Except for me," Aunt Fran smirks. *"I'm a ghost, remember. I can hear any living creature...and dead."*

The ship begins to ease slowly along the waterway toward a dead-end rock wall. The water currents grab the dark dragon's attention. Fran must have noticed because I hear her say, "Hello, boys," as she appears at the other end of the canal.

They run to her, roaring. She laughs. "Catch me if you can." She disappears and pops to the other side of the canal, right as one dragon runs into the wall of boulders. Rocks crumble on his head, and the dragon is dazed a moment. The other dragon is furious and goes to flame my aunt.

"Can't kill something that's already dead." She laughs. *"Almost dead anyway."* She winks at me.

I laugh. Her distraction is working. We head straight for the rock wall, and I begin to panic because we're going to crash.

"Relax, the wall is an illusion," Namari says, and we slip through the barrier, undetected.

I look over the side of the boat as we pass through to see both Garrick and Dad lying along the ledge, hurt. "Stop! We must get them aboard."

"We can't, My Lady, we must continue onward," Duncan says.

I'm powerless, held by Namari's mane. *"Please, dragon brother, please."*

The ship slows. "Hurry then," Duncan says. "I can't halt the ship from moving, though, so make it quick."

Dad and Garrick are in their human forms, both bleeding profusely.

One of the soldiers shifts into a dragon and flies to shore grabbing both men, taking them in each talon. *"They're still alive,"* he says, coming back to the ship. He lays them down on the deck, and other comrades come to aide in stopping the bleeding.

Namari releases me, and I go to them both, taking one hand to each of them, placing a healing glow to their hearts.

"You're a healer to others?" Duncan asks, sounding surprised.

"Yes," I whisper. My eyes well, and I can barely see, but I keep my focus on healing them. "Now, we wait. I hope it's enough to get them well," I say as the oozing of blood fades. They both appear to be sleeping. Their chests rise and fall with an even rhythm.

I stand and look around, taking notice of the hollow tunnel we're in. In the distance, a bright oval circle appears. *"Hang on, My Princess,"* Namari says, as he grabs me again with his mane, setting me onto his back. *"It's the way to the Underground Valley."*

"How do you do that?"

"Do what?"

"Hold me so tight with a horse's mane?"

He chuckles. *"Magic. Our mane can be as soft as hair or as strong as the bones of any man. Magic is what keeps it healthy."*

16
THE WAR ROOM

I LOOK OUT AT the endless water waiting to see where this ship will lead. It isn't long before we reach the walls of my new destination, and as though we pass an invisible line, what wasn't there a moment ago, is another small island like the one we left, in the distance.

"This doesn't look very underground to me," I say.

"The word is used metaphorically to throw those off who try to discover Dragonscale's headquarters. Only a select few know of its existence, and when we bring strangers such as you, normally you're blindfolded or put to sleep," Namari says.

"And so, why haven't I been shielded to its presence?"

"You're the heir."

"Right."

I look down to see both Garrick and Dad resting. Their injuries now healed. It prompts the memory of the first night that Aunt

Fran, Dad, and I huddled around the dining room table back at our little house in Washington. Finding out about Aunt Fran's healing abilities was a shock to say the least. I understand now that dragons have an innate ability to heal themselves, yet neither Garrick and Dad healed. I needed to do it. This has me puzzled.

The ship slows its pace, and we come to an abrupt halt. A foghorn sounds, announcing our arrival.

"Glad you made it back safely," one mariner says as he ties one end of the boat. Is he another Elvin shifter, I wonder?

Hearing others' thoughts flowing through my mind is going to take some getting used to.

"Did anyone see you?" He runs to the other end and anchors down the back end of the vessel.

"Yes, quite a few actually," Duncan says.

"To here? Are you mad, sir?"

"No, no. I mean they followed to the port before leaving through the waterfall. We were not followed; I assure you that we're safe. Lady Francesca took care of the trackers, allowing us to flee."

"Is the ship secure?" Dad asks. He attempts to get up.

I wasn't aware he'd woken. Garrick is alive as well, both of them looking as though they'd never been in battle. He turns his head to me and smiles. "My Lady, you may now get down off Namari's back. You're safe."

I slide down onto the deck floor and follow the rest of the ship's crew to the dock. The island looks like I've come to an Alaskan port except there isn't any snow. Housing sheds are scattered strategically about, each holding a boat of some sort, and at the end of the pier is a building I imagine is the tackle and fishing center.

"Did any of them appear to be imposters?" I overhear one shifter ask as he hurries in front.

"Imposters?" I ask. I receive a stern glance from Dad, as though I'm interrupting.

"No. I was able to see into each of their souls. We are good. But there is one," Duncan says.

"Tell me, please?" the man asks.

"This person had something protecting them. I couldn't break through his mind."

"That means only one thing."

"What do you mean? What's going on?" I interrupt. Again, I'm feeling out of the loop.

The man, Garrick, Duncan, and Dad turn to me with stern looks. "It means we have a mole in Ashengale," Dad answers.

G ENEVIÈVE APPEARS ON THE dock. Over her shoulder is a bag.

"You made it." Dad gives her a hug.

"I got what you asked. It wasn't easy though."

Dad pulls from the sack several jewelry enchantments.

"Are these what I think they are?" I ask.

Dad nods, handing me a ring. It is subtle, not at all looking fancy. It's a simple silver design that circles around a blue stone. "Lapis Lazuli." He hands out rings to his men, and Geneviève. "Wear them as though your life depended on it."

"Quite literally," Namari says.

Dad gives me an earring. "This is for Namari. The piercing will hurt but make him understand."

"Sure, Dad." I climb my beast and without hesitation he allows me to stick the jewelry in a conspicuous place behind his mane.

"We need to move," Garrick says.

Namari waits along the pier as I follow them down a corridor to solid steel doors. It feels like I'm in a completely new world. Florescent lighting above, walls made of concrete, and the floors have white tile. "Where are we going now, a hospital asylum?"

Duncan snorts. "A what? No, it's the headquarters where Dragonscale conducts his daily business," Garrick answers.

Dad remains silent.

The doors swiftly open. Greeting us is my grandfather in his human-looking form. "Were you seen or followed?"

"No, sire," Garrick answers.

Odd. Why would he ask a silly question like that? He showed me earlier that he knows all and can see the future. Shouldn't he know that answer already?

My grandfather gives me a glance as though he reads my thoughts. "Are you sure?" he asks.

He knows something but isn't leading on as to what it is. Is this a test?

Grandfather winks at me. "My dear, it is good to see you again. I imagine we're all hungry. We'll meet in the dining room."

"Dining room?" I ask. I squint, not sure if I fully trust what's going on.

"Yes, you do eat, do you not?"

"We're at war and Grandfather takes the time to feast?" No one answers me. "Yes, of course."

"Well, many might refer to it as a mess hall, perhaps, but I've spruced it up to my liking." He gestures with his hand. "This way."

We follow his lead, but I don't hesitate to ask more questions along the way. "How is it possible that Ashengale has come under attack? You said nobody could penetrate through to the island." I can tell my grandfather is uncomfortable in answering.

"That's true. Remember when I spoke earlier that all dragons are born here? Well, their roots are planted, yes, but they still have free will to make choices. Those choices will determine a path of good or evil. Because they are born here, they will always have the chance to change and come home, but if their true meaning of integrity is revealed, they will not be able to penetrate these walls."

I'm not convinced this is really him. "I don't understand. This doesn't make any sense. You're either evil or not. Good or not."

"Ah, but see, now there is where you're slightly misguided. You can be reckless having good intentions, but still doing something wrong. Like stealing, for example. Someone might steal because it's an act of survival. Doesn't mean they, themselves, are a bad person, it means they have made a bad choice." His eyes glint green.

"So, you're saying it's okay to steal?"

"Of course not. I'm saying people make poor choices. In this case, our people—dragon shifters—have made decisions that have impacted them and their lives, and they feel that they have nowhere to go."

"What are you saying, Grandfather? What does that have to do with us coming under attack?"

He stops before we pass through the last set of doors, smiles, and reaches his arm around my shoulders, giving me a huge hug. An uncomfortable hug. A gross hug. "Let's go inside and make our way to the dining room, shall we? I'll explain it all to you then."

Something is off about him.

We cross the threshold to a large, open room. Paintings hang on the wood-paneled walls. The craftsmanship is amazing with each outlined in detail. The ceilings are carved in the same way as the crystal chandeliers hanging every few feet apart. One minute I'm in a military setting with concrete walls and fluorescent lighting, and the next I'm surrounded by an extravagant dining hall. I can't keep up. There is even a grand fireplace from an old-world time period putting out flames to warm the room. The mantle has to be at least eight feet high.

In the center of this grand space is a dining table so large that it could easily fit fifty people. A much bigger table than the Hall of Secrets. Smaller tables are set off to the side and strategically placed throughout the rest of the area. The tabletop is already decked out with fruits, vegetables, and deli meats. Servants finish up placing dinnerware around the massive table. Some guests are already comfortably chatting amongst their neighbors when their attention is grabbed, and they all turn as we walk through the doors. The group stands, bowing their heads.

"Isn't this supposed to be a secret location?"

Again, no one answers me.

"Ladies and gentlemen," my grandfather proudly announces, "my granddaughter, Princess Wyndreana Storm, House of Storm." Again, I wince at the name.

He pauses, giving a proud smile, and bows as he gestures for me to be seated, saying, "And the future Queen of Ladorielle and its Realm."

The guests raise their glasses and say, "Cheers, long live the princess."

My face flushes as one servant pulls my chair next to Grandfather at the head of the table. On the other side of his seat is Grandmother Eleena. Giving a wink, she says, "Good to see you again, my dear."

My mind struggles with the logic, thinking that we shouldn't be sitting here, eating and enjoying ourselves, when so many are now fighting to the death to save the kingdom. We should be out there fighting, too.

The rest of my escorting troops trail behind Dad and take their place around the table.

Before all are seated, Grandfather raises his goblet. "May we have strength, courage, and wisdom to bring an end to our dark past...where peace will once again flow throughout our world." He veers to my grandmother and smiles.

"Hear, hear," all say, raising their drinks and taking a sip.

Grandfather nods. "Please be seated." The guests wait for him to take his seat first before following suit. "Shall we get started?" he commands.

My grandfather looks at me. "We have it on good authority that the mole among us hides well and isn't easily detected. The Underworld knows you're here, Wynter."

"But how?" I grab my necklace. "We had the locket infused. Doctor Brekker assured us it would be repaired and not to worry about being followed."

"Ah, yes. I suppose that is, indeed, true. However, once a tracker catches your scent, it's nearly impossible to lose them. Unless they're killed, of course."

"You're saying they followed me here, and yet you still bring me to this fortress, risking everyone else?"

"Not entirely, true, sir," Dad interrupts. "We did lose the trackers off Dragonscale Island. I killed them myself."

Grandfather's facial expression shows anger rather than being pleased with what my dad just said. Which continues to raise my suspicion. I look at Dad and he makes eye contact with me. He gives a silent nod that he, too, knows something is off.

"We should be fighting, you know..." I stand and hit the table. "I'm not one to be kept as your precious prize! We should be out there fighting right now. Not feasting."

"Settle down, Wynter," my grandmother says. "We have magical forces surrounding the Island and Storm Castle as we speak. Rest assured we are all safe, and the war is nearly over. Besides you must complete your trial before the blood moon ends."

I look around the massive table. The other guests avoid eye contact, looking down at the plates in front of them. "Tell me, Grandfather...can you see them?"

"See what?"

"The Wraiths."

He smiles. "I don't need to see wraiths to know who the mole is. He's a dragon shifter. A Trek ally."

Whispers begin around the table.

"That means—" I look at Dad and Garrick.

"They know she's here!" A man bursts through the doors.

"Impossible." Dad stands.

"How did they find her?" Grandfather asks, appearing genuinely stunned. "We are hidden by the Elementals' magic."

"Dark dragons are circling above our invisible island headquarters as we speak," the man adds.

I'm startled by this news, and I'm beginning to feel a little fatigued with all the running. Will it ever stop?

"Why are they still chasing me? It should be over by now." My memory stamp is gone. Not to mention, I'm eighteen, so I have gained my power already, so they can't steal that from me.

"You're not fully rested yet," Dad says. "And that little stunt you pulled back in the grotto depleted some of your energy."

"Not to mention you healed Garrick and your dad," Duncan says.

"Healed, you say?" Grandfather asks.

"Yes, Grandfather, you know that."

He looks stunned by my answer. "Yes, I know, I was merely thinking that perhaps it's why we're in the position we're in now."

That doesn't make any sense.

"Remember you can't leave Ashengale until you're at a hundred percent. Prematurely leaving will result in either your gifts being stripped forever or not functioning to their complete capacity," my grandfather reiterates.

"So, I'm a cell phone battery?"

Some of the people around the table chuckle at my remark.

"It's not funny!" My anger boils. I try to force down the tension and begin to develop a headache. *Something isn't right.*

"Never thought of it that way, but sure. Like a cell phone," Dad says. "Your grandfather is right. You need to be at full charge for an optimum result."

Grandfather clears his throat. "Let's not rile up everyone, shall we? Let's think this through rationally. We'll put the soldiers on double duty and keep Wynter hidden. She'll be safe until her full rest is complete. Then tomorrow, she can begin the journey to her ascension."

"It still doesn't answer one question," I say, annoyed by my grandfather's evasiveness.

"Which is?" Grandfather takes a swig of his ale.

"I thought nobody could get past the outer Island."

"Aye, that is true, yes," he agrees.

"Yet were under attack. And that would leave only one other way in." I look at Geneviève across from me, sitting next to Dad.

"Wrong again, my child. While that, too, is true, Geneviève is a trusty druid she hasn't left this palace since yesterday," Grandfather says.

"Are you saying Geneviève is the mole?" I ask.

"No, but it does raise the question of why suddenly we're under attack, doesn't it?" Grandfather narrows his eyes.

Geneviève stands. "Excuse me, I'm not the mole!"

"Sir, I can second that," Dad says.

I realize he's hiding something. "Right, you, the all-knowing Dragonscale can see all, yet you can't see the coming attack? Tell me, if you can see all, then why not stop it?"

"How quickly you forget, my student. Free will, will always take precedence. I cannot interfere with that. I can only guide one into making the right decision."

His answer doesn't satisfy me.

He eyes Geneviève. "The most likely option: this mole is a dragon of the dark with a Trek rider."

Geneviève sits. "Yes, you already mentioned that." Her tone is acrid.

"He has markings of Ashengale and can easily slip through. As a shifter, he, too, can withstand the heat of the surface. I know what your next question is going to be, my friends." He smiles. "Why are we not being bombarded with an army of dark dragons, right now?"

"The thought did cross my mind," I say.

The rest take note.

"Because if a dragon of the dark tries to penetrate our barrier and gets caught, it's immediate death. Should they get caught with this hide and go seek, their skin is forever marked as a trespasser with a price on their head, and they will be hunted until death comes calling. So, you see, once a dragon has chosen a side, they are to remain with their faction for eternity. This mole, whoever they are, has been branded under the skin much like when a druid receives a rune. When they fly through our cave, their branding lights up like a Christmas tree."

Or you're the mole, and you're the reason the dark dragons haven't attacked. It's what I want to say out loud, but I won't. If he is truly my grandfather, he would be able to read my mind. "Then how did they get inside Ashengale?" I ask, fishing for information.

Dad looks at me and nods. Good, we're on the same page. He grabs Geneviève's attention, as though sending her a secret message she understands. Aunt Fran stands back by the fireplace, smiles, and nods. I'm onto something here.

"A possible distraction, like the attack we had?" one guest remarks.

"Folks, calm yourselves. We will find them. Most of the dark shifters are either captured or dead."

I glare at my grandfather. "Except the mole."

"We will find the intruder." He smiles and takes his mug, lifting it in the air. "To victory!"

The rest of the party raises their mugs, except us—Dad and Geneviève. "Are you saying I'm not safe...yet? I'm still having to run from the madness?"

"Not yet. It is part of your process. You're not branded if you choose good, but should you choose the dark path, you will be."

The silence around the table speaks loud and clear. "I see."

"Now, it's more important than ever to wear that necklace," Dad says. "Namari will be by your side twenty-four-seven. He's going to take up residence in your room until it's safe again."

My head droops down, looking at the table as the headache increases. "Does anyone have a muscle relaxer to kill this pain?" I lay two fingers against my right temple.

Grandfather waves his hand up to one of the servants. "Find something for my granddaughter, will you please, Margaret?"

"Yes, sire," she says.

"Wynter, love. I'm sorry you have been put through so much. It will be over soon. I promise you," my grandmother says.

I huff. "Promises." I look up at her and glare. "I've been filled with so many promises, but nobody keeps their word anymore. Everywhere I turn, it seems something ends up standing in the way."

"We could bounce her back to Earth," Geneviève remarks. "To Jeff's cabin in the mountains. Is it still safe?"

"No, she can't leave the Island, yet," Dad says.

"What is Dad doing, Aunt Fran?"

"It's a distraction," she answers. *"He knows. Play along in the conversation."*

"However," Grandfather interjects, "that's not a bad idea after she's ready."

"So, wait. Are you saying I'm stuck here?" I ask.

"Not for long, dear," Grandmother says. "Like your grandfather said, the Trek can't get in here. Only the bloodline of a Dragon can, unless they have a Druid. And the only one left is Geneviève." She looks at Geneviève and smiles as she takes a sip of red wine.

"One big happy family," I mutter.

"Look, it won't be so bad," Geneviève counters. "There is so much to learn while you're here." She looks over at my grandfather. "Besides, Dragonscale has your schedule packed with tasks to accomplish."

"I was under the impression that I wasn't going to be here that long. I mean, don't we have a villain to kill? Several actually," I say.

Light laughter flits around the table.

"Precisely why you must remain here until you have gained your full power," Grandfather says.

"You make it sound so simple. Like this will take days rather than months. We don't have months to waste. The first full moon has arrived, and we have already been under attack."

"Yes, well, that's why we have Aoes to turn back time."

"Right. It's going to take me a little time to wrap my head around that. More déjà vu episodes. I seem to have them frequently."

Grandfather smiles. "Aoes will tamper with time when he performs a time jump, and no one will be the wiser. It will all work out in the end. Try not to think about it too much, or your head will hurt more working out the logistics." One of the servants comes back with something on a silver tray with a glass of water. "Speaking of a headache, here. Take this for your pain." He gives a nod to the servant, gesturing for them to set the items in front of my plate.

The pill looks exactly like the headache medicine I had back home. *Home.* Now, that seems to alter my definition a bit, since I know the truth.

As soon as I take the pill, I feel nauseous. "What's going on?"

"Sorry," my grandfather says, "I forgot to mention, it will also knock you out for a while."

"But why?"

"Another lesson to learn, my dear. Don't trust anyone. Didn't your father teach you anything?"

It's the last thing I remember before my eyes shut.

17
THE MOLE

A HIGH-PITCH SOUND IMPALES my thoughts with voices blending simultaneously together as I drift back into consciousness, abruptly pulled from the depths of darkness. The ringing is intrusive, making my brain ache as shouts and screams stab my mind. The deep nightmare and reality merge together. My eyes jolt open as I find myself waking on the floor in a blunder of chaos. Debris falls on my head, without warning, slicing my cheek. Instinctively I touch the gash, smearing the blood. The pain is minimal. I'll heal, it's only a flesh wound.

The sound of metal clashing together grabs my attention. Two soldiers are locked in battle, prompting me to roll out of the way and under the table. The same table where we all sat around eating before I was knocked out. *Knocked out.* My memory skims the past.

He gave me a pill saying, *"Another lesson to learn, my dear. Don't trust anyone. Didn't your father teach you anything?"*

Where is he? I look around, crawling from one end of the table to the other, surveying his whereabouts. This small combat that started in the war room is his doing, I have no doubt. But why? Why would he betray us? I think further back when we first arrived, and I knew then something was off. I should have caught on to him sooner. The memories churn my stomach.

Familiar looking feet tap around the floor with a second pair, matching the movement. It's Dad fighting my grandfather in a dance of swords. I focus on them clashing. The scrape of metal, their grunts, a fight to the death. My grandfather—*the traitor*—looks to be enjoying himself. Anger builds as the battle plays out. *Is he the mole? This doesn't make any sense.*

The last time I saw my grandfather before this afternoon he was said to have a meeting at Ashengale castle. What meeting? Was it a trap? Maybe this man fighting my father isn't really my grandfather at all. I mean, if it's him, he'd have the power to end this charade. He would shift into a dragon.

A woman's shouts grabbing my attention. To the right my grandmother Eleena spars with Geneviève. *Is she a mole, too?* A fireball grows in her hand, and she aims it at her opponent, but Gen vanishes, appearing behind my grandmother, and kicks her forward. *Nice move.* They play cat and mouse gracefully. *What's going on? Why is my grandmother fighting Geneviève?*

A loud bursting roar calls out, and an enemy stretches forward with a sword in the air, coming straight for my neck. I dip out of the way as the blade hits the stone floor with a loud ping.

Garrick acrobats over to the random foe who attempted to sever my neck, and slices him in half, then turns in time to stop another blade aiming for his throat. He and his opponent push off and circle.

My instincts kick in, and I blast the guy Garrick is fighting with fire, burning him to a crisp as he goes up in flames and disappears into ash. Garrick nods, taking off to engage his next opponent. It's an all-out battle in the war room.

Eleena prepares another ball of fire, getting ready to hurl it toward Geneviève's back.

Time to move. In that instant, I roll out from under the table and without hesitation form a fireball of my own, blasting my grandmother from behind. The surge startles her, and she turns, focusing her anger on me.

She smiles. "Well, it looks like we woke the beast." She throws her flame at me instead, allowing Geneviève to take cover. "You should be dead!"

Guess the ring worked. I dart out of the way, using the skills I'd forgotten I had. I'm not a vampire, but a dragon shifter, and my power grows. I can feel it. How can I stop this battle without allowing my anger and rage to take over? Shifting is not an option. *Think, Wynter, think.*

Eleena releases another fireball and misses, destroying a column a few feet away from me, which lands on our allies. My rage escalates. Fear no longer triggers the icy blast of my past. *I know what to do.*

The adrenaline intensifies and in one fell swoop, I cast ice at everyone's feet, which grows over their ankles, traveling up their legs and stopping at their necks, halting the surge.

Geneviève, Garrick, and my dad relax, along with the guards protecting the attempted coup. Sounds of fallen debris scatter in bits and pieces across the floor as the room begins to settle in stillness.

"Well done, my niece," Aunt Fran says. *"Glad to see you're awake."*

"What happened?"

"It seems we found the moles."

I glare at the man I'm supposed to call Grandfather and then to Eleena. They both appear stunned.

Eleena's eyes glow green with rage and not the blue I'm used to seeing from the Storms—although she's not from that bloodline, anyway. "I thought you killed her!" she seethes, stretching her neck, as the ice grows tighter around her.

"So, my first assumption is true, then...You are not who you appear to be," I reply, pacing forward.

"Surprise, surprise," the faux Dragonscale interrupts. "I should have known Iknes Shaw poison wouldn't work with you." He glances to Eleena. "See, I told you."

Really? That's something I didn't expect. I file that away for later. Question is: why? Why would they think Iknes Shaw would kill me? Anyone in their right mind knows a Deagon can't be killed any other way but through the heart. Thoughts of Aunt Fran being poisoned as a little girl come to mind. Unless that's what happens if the poison is allowed to reach the heart.

His grin angers me more and I straighten. "Who sent you?"

He ignores me, and I twist my palm in the air as though I have a doorknob in my hand, tightening the ice around him.

He laughs. "You think that is going to make me talk?"

"Who wants me dead, besides Sarmira?" I ask. My eyes burn with rage.

"Do not shift. It's what he wants," Aunt Fran says. *"If you shift it will bring more dark dragons."*

"Don't worry. I won't."

"Wynter," Geneviève says, nudging my arm. "Your eyes are glowing."

I'm taken aback by her comment and release the pressure around the impostor's neck, allowing him to speak. *"They* don't want you dead. You would be of no use to *them* otherwise."

Eleena looks a little surprised by his confession.

"Who is he referring to?"

"I don't know," Aunt Fran answers. *"The question is...why?"*

"What does she want with me now?" I demand. "She's nowhere near me."

His sly grin grows. "Oh, I see, we're on the subject of Sarmira still."

I tilt my head in confusion. "Who else would 'they' be? Yes, of course, I'm referring to Sarmira and her demon puppets."

"Oh, you didn't know?" He cackles out an annoying laugh.

Eleena, too, looks annoyed and narrows her brows at him. "Have you gone completely mad?" She tries to squirm, pulling her head upward. "What are you doing? Stick to the plan."

"Oh, my dear," he boasts, looking over at her, "I haven't told you the entire arrangement yet. *He* made sure not to clue you in it, that somehow you would mess things up… again."

"When were you going to let me in on your little secret, Miles?" Eleena looks angry.

Miles? I know that name but where? I need to think. "Okay, enough," I say. "I'll ask again, if it wasn't Sarmira, then who sent you?"

"I do say, I quite enjoy you stewing in rage and uncertainty. *He* was right about that, at least."

My hand grows hot, pushing flames to my fingertips, before forming a ball of fire. "Start talking or I start barbecuing."

"Wynter stop," Dad interrupts. "He's egging you on." Dad brings me down from my fury, sort of the way Cory did, only with outspoken words, rather than soothing pacification.

Miles, who still looks like my grandfather, squeals in a creepy, wicked way. "Oh no, please go on. Throw it!"

"Do you have a death wish?" my dad asks, his eyes glowing blue.

Is he going to try and compel this guy?

Glancing at Eleena, she struggles to break free, and I enforce the ice around her neck. Miles notices, and his conniving grin fades.

"Now that I've got your attention…speak. Who are you, Miles?" I glance at him, then back to her, trying to remember where I've heard his name. He hasn't revealed his identity yet. Faces I remember, names not so much.

He appears surprised by my question. "What? Are you blind? I'm your grandfather, of course." He grins again. "Now, let me go, and I won't punish you for holding me against my will."

I'm reminded of Cory. He always told me my power comes from my emotions. This time, I'm in control. I click my cheek at his answer. "You're not my grandfather. You and I both know it. You may look like him, but he would never try to kill me. I'll ask again. Who. Are. You?"

He glances to Eleena, and her eyes narrow at him, once more. I've seen that look before. My stomach churns with bile. *No, it can't be...*

My eyes flit between them, and I raise my chin. "We've met before, haven't we?" I turn my head to look at Dad, and he furrows his brow. Then I look at Geneviève. It doesn't matter if they don't catch on yet, because both these masqueraders will be dead before anyone reacts.

Lifting my chin, I say, "I know who you two really are, hiding behind the faces of my grandparents. Very clever, indeed and you didn't think I would catch on?" My hand again ignites in fire.

Miles grins. "You weren't supposed to wake up." He turns to Eleena. "She's stronger than she looks. A minor detail that can be adjusted, I'm sure he will be pleased to hear this."

My voice grows loud. "Who sent you?" I blast a warning shot to the wall behind him, and Miles cackles more, unmoved by my theatrics."

"Wynter?" I hear the unease in Dad's voice. The flames in my hand flicker.

Miles's eyes widen. "Doesn't matter. You're going to kill us anyway."

I nod. "Yes, you're right." I stroll closer. "What have you done with them?" I demand. The blaze in my hand grows.

I sense Geneviève, Garrick, and Dad tense, and recognize the uncertainty in their eyes.

"Oh," he says, in a snide tone. "Are we negotiating now?" Miles's eye twitches and his mouth firms.

"Wynter, you'll melt the ice," Geneviève whispers, standing behind me.

"I'm counting on it." My lips curve into an evil smile. "It's been a couple days since I've had Trek flesh and bone."

I hear a loud gulp come from Miles.

"Trek?" Geneviève looks at the frozen goons. I can see a glare of anger in her eyes, as well.

"Impossible. I would have smelled them," Dad says. The tension in his voice thickens.

"Me, too," Garrick concurs.

"I've not a clue as to how, but they've masked their odor well. Only a Trek can pull off such a feat...Though I'm guessing, in order to get past the gates of Ashengale, they needed some pretty heavy salve to cover the scent. They're Trek all right, Dad. Well, at least this one is." I pierce a stare at Miles, waiting to see if either of them fidget at my words. If I'm right, they will change to their true form in defeat.

Miles quivers. "I don't care if you drink my blood, go for it. Better yet, take my essence. I'd like to see you try."

"Oh, I won't drink your blood. I'm not a Nytemire like my father." I turn my head to Dad and he looks confused. *Come on, Dad, catch up.* Only a select few know Dad's true identity is that of a shifter. His cover has always been to hide behind the façade of a Nytemire.

Tilting my neck to the side, I glance back to Miles. "First, I'll cook you until the meat is tender—raw meat gives me heartburn." I lick my lips. "Then when your flesh is ready to fall off the bone, I will consume you like a delicacy."

I have a surge of temptation rising within me to shift, and I realize I'm not as stable as I thought. The dragon side of me will take over if I don't stay in control of my feelings. I begin to undergo the emotions I had when I devoured the last Trek who'd posed as Rory's mom. I feel my veins burn as the black lines appear down my arms.

Miles shivers. I'm not sure if it's the ice he's encased in, my words, or both, but I definitely have this fraud's attention. His façade fades, revealing his true form.

My body cools just in time. Nothing like playing chicken at the last second. But for family, I would have done it if it meant saving them.

I give a slight nod, squinting. "I remember you now. You and Lira staged a ruse in the Grengore Mines." I turn my head. "Miles impersonated you, Dad."

I hear a growl deep in Dad's throat, and Geneviève puts out her arm to hold him back.

I clench my fists in anger. "One more time. Where are they?" My voice is loud, the words concise.

Miles laughs again and his eyes roll in the back of his head.

"No," I hear Dad yell and he lunges forward.

"He's going to warn the others,'" Geneviève says.

I grin. "Not if I can help it." I blast the man, charring him to a crunchy delicacy. "Dinner anyone?" I grin wider, turning to the other fake. "Your turn." Fire begins to grow in my palm once more.

"Wait," she pleads.

The flames in my fingers dissipate. "I'm listening."

"Release me and I'll show you."

"Nuh-uh...tell me where Dragonscale is, or you suffer the same fate as Miles...Lira."

She swallows hard, transforming back to her original state. "He...he's..."

"Spit it out!"

"Dead."

Gasps are heard from many who survived the battle in the war room.

"You're lying."

"Am I?"

"Yes, because otherwise I would have inherited his powers." The flames in my hand return.

She squirms, as though she didn't know that piece of information. "How do you know that?"

I straighten my shoulders. "Why am I answering to this con artist?"

I look back at Dad. He grins, saying, "Answer my daughter. Where are they, Lira?"

Lira gasps for air as more pressure from the ice creeps up her neck. "The dark witches can't find Eleena—"

"The dark witches? What do they want with her?" I release some of the tension from the ice.

Lira firms her lips before curving a snide smile. "You don't know?"

I shift my chin upward and scowl. "Know what?"

She looks to Dad, as if for approval. I veer his direction. "Dad, what are you not telling me?"

"I'm not sure myself." He folds his arms and circles around her. "Yes, Lira, do tell. What do you know?"

"Eleena comes from old blood, like me." She stares at Dad. "You of all people should know that."

He doesn't take her bait, and so she continues, "She and I used to be friends, until..."

"Until what?" I demand.

She raises her eyes at me. "Until she married Ian. Before he became Dragonscale."

"What does that have to do with anything?"

"You really don't know, do you?" She glances to Dad, and Geneviève, then Garrick. "My, my, such secrets this family ho lds..."

"What's that supposed to mean?" My patience is running thin.

"Your grandmother may consider herself a Light Witch, but she was born to the House of Shadow-Raven."

"You're lying," I press. "I've never heard of such a coven. House of Ashburn is on the council board. They represent all witches, whether light or dark."

I can tell she's observing our reaction. "Let me put it to you this way. She isn't just an old friend." She smiles, as though she's enjoying holding us in suspense.

"Go on," Dad presses. He unsheathes his sword. "I've had just about enough of your manipulation. I'm losing patience."

She sneers. "I'm quite surprised Eleena has kept this sneaky little secret to herself." Lira pauses to gain a reaction, but no one moves. "She's my younger sister."

"I don't believe you. Besides, you haven't proof," Dad scoffs. He swirls his sword and circles her.

Lira ignores his threats and directs her attention to me. "Perhaps not, but what if I told you that your grandparents' marriage was arranged? Ask your great-grandmother Sara if you don't believe me."

Her words sink in. Why would my great-grandmother keep this from us? *"Aunt Fran, is this true?"*

"I honestly don't know. I've only seen my parents madly in love with each other. If it was arranged, they're definitely great actors."

I bite down on my tongue to avoid saying too much. "I'll ask again, where are my grandparents?"

Lira firms her lips and doesn't say a word.

"Garrick, when was the last time you saw Ian in the form of Dragonscale?" Dad asks.

"Not since he flew through the caverns with Wynter."

"They have them, Dad."

He nods. "I know. I'm beginning to see that. Take her to the dungeon and let her stew." He brings forth chains a guard has been holding. "Perhaps dispelling your magic will keep you secure. We don't want you getting away again," he adds.

She laughs. "You can't possibly think valiancium steel will work on me."

"By itself, no," he says. He supplies a choker to accompany the valiancium chain fused with liquid onyx. "But this will." Dad gives a gratifying grin.

Lira's eyes grow big, and she struggles. Without warning, the ice cracks and Lira springs free. She's quick, and before I have time to react, Lira gathers strength, blasting us with powerful magic, reminding me of the same magic Moyer cast back at the mansion.

I'm flung backward, smashing into the wall behind me. My body aches and my head throbs. I feel something wet behind my skull. Blood. The pressure is painful as I cover my head with my hands. Lira is nowhere to be found.

Most everyone is lying on the ground, either hurt or dead. Geneviève stirs, but Dad isn't moving. "Dad?" No answer.

I crawl to him. "Dad?" I look for my aunt, too. "Aunt Fran?"

Geneviève struggles to reach my dad, stretching out her hand to help.

I hear some of the others slowly regain consciousness, moaning in pain. A few ghostly spirits pass by, but not Dad. This is a good sign, and I hold onto that. I still can't see where Aunt Fran went off to.

"My Lord," Garrick calls. He slowly gets up and comes to Dad's aid.

Geneviève puts her two fingers to his neck. Her breath is heavy, and she, too, is severely injured.

"He's breathing," Geneviève says. Relief fills her face. "He's still alive. Wynter, can you heal him?"

"Yes, of course." I bring my hand over his head but nothing comes. "What's going on? Where are my powers?" I look at my hands. "They're not glowing."

"Wynter?" Geneviève calls again. She looks at me with a questionable expression. But she isn't looking at me, but through me. I turn around to see my body lying unconscious on the floor.

18

AM I DEAD?

THIS ISN'T POSSIBLE. "No," I whisper. I put a hand to my mouth as the blood seeps beneath my body. "But I have the immortality ring on my finger."

Geneviève shouts, "Wynter!" She shimmies over to hold my head, ignoring her own pain. Her leg is bent at the knee at an awkward angle—it's broken.

Dad stirs, grunting in discomfort. "What was that?" he asks as he puts a hand to his head.

"Powerful magic from a very powerful witch," Garrick says. He puts a hand forward for Dad to grab.

"How are you?" Dad asks, looking up at Garrick.

He's dazed like everyone else but appears to be unharmed. Garrick locks eyes on my body, and Dad follows his gaze. Dad struggles to get up and Garrick helps him.

"Wynter?" Panic coats Dad's face. "No, this can't be. She's a Deagon. She's wearing the immortality ring I gave her. She can't be dead."

"Wynter hasn't completed her trials, My Lord, so she hasn't the magical protection infused within her soul yet," Garrick says. "She's just as vulnerable as any other mortal."

So, that's why I'm unconscious because I'm not at full power? I thought turning eighteen automatically made me immortal.

Geneviève looks up at Dad. "She's not healing."

Is it because I lay near death that my body doesn't have the capacity to heal? Oh, this is bad...very, very bad. Panic begins to flow through my mind. *Think.*

"We have to stop the bleeding," Garrick says as he moves forward and kneels near my head. He takes the initiative, grabbing a table linen, ripping it in strips, and begins wrapping my skull with the cloth. "We don't have a healer."

Dad looks like he's going into shock.

Garrick looks at him. "Head wounds always look worse than they really are, My Lord."

"Yeah, but that's a lot of blood," Geneviève says.

Garrick doesn't say anything.

I feel sick, yet I still have my five senses. I put my head between my knees. I'm still solid looking, and not at all appearing like a ghost, yet none of them can see me. *"Aunt Fran, where are you?"*

"Geneviève, do you have enough strength to get us out of here?" Dad asks. "We need to find Nyta."

She nods. "Perhaps the druid circle near Ashengale City? It's probably the securest place to port. At this point, I don't have much faith anywhere else is safer."

My soul begins to lift from the ground. "No, no, no, I'm not ready to go," I cry. "I'm not dead!"

As though someone can hear me, a whisper calls out, "Wynter, come, it's time."

I ignore the voice. Geneviève prepares to teleport out as my spirit rises higher and higher.

Fear grips me. "I can't be dead. This isn't how it's supposed to end." I shut my eyes, willing myself back to my body.

When I open them, I find myself still with Dad and the others, but this time we're outside the druid circle of Ashengale, like Geneviève mentioned.

My broken body lies on the grassy hill above the outskirts of the city. Smoke can be seen trailing from ruined structures, as screams of panic, agony, and fear are heard across the hills. The waterfall that was once a crystal-clear blue is now dyed cherry-red from the blood of the fallen. This once luscious green, beautiful, and hidden oasis is now a warzone of death and destruction. Above, I watch in horror as Ashengale's dragon armies fight the dark dragon riders with fiery fury. It's still a war in Ashengale, or it's round two, from the enemy."

"Where are we to go?" Geneviève asks.

I sense her fear.

A bright light forms within the druid circle, drawing attention, and within moments, Rory, Chad, Blair, and the others appear.

Rory looks around at her group anxiously. "Where is Cory?" she asks. Her attention is drawn to us, and she runs to Geneviève. "Mom?" She kneels beside her, along with my dying body. "What happened?"

"What do you mean where's Cory?" I say as loud as I can, but no one hears me.

I feel Rory's worry. The bandage Garrick wrapped my head in is still bound, but the dressing is soaked in blood. There's so much going on it's hard for me to focus.

Rory's heart quickens. I sense her panic. "Is she—"

"No," Geneviève interrupts, "but her pulse is faint."

I float above, trying my hardest to reach back into my damaged body. Everyone is flustered. How can I show everyone I'm right here?

"Mom, you're hurt, too," Rory says.

A woman with long, wavy red hair covered in a dark-colored cloak comes to Geneviève's side and kneels to touch my forehead. My body is still in her arms.

"Redmae, is that really you?" Geneviève asks as tears begin to flow down her cheeks, and she reaches out for her other daughter.

"Yes, Mom, it's really me."

"We're not sure if the medicine worked," Rory says. "She only took half the dose Aoes gave me. It's supposed to suppress the curse."

Confusion grazes across Geneviève's face. I'm confused, too.

Redmae smiles. "Long story, Mom. Right now, we need to figure a way out of here." She glances over to the hills that are covered in ash.

"What about Wynter?" Rory asks.

The dressing around my head has darkened. Geneviève looks up at Blair. "Her head won't stop bleeding."

"I can try and slow the hemorrhaging, but that's all I can do. She's much stronger than I, and because she has her own healing abilities, it may not work." Blair kneels, placing both palms around my skull, and her hands glow. She shakes her head. "I can't feel any improvement. We need to get her to Nyta. If her heart stops and has a chance to grow cold, she's as good as dead...forever."

"We don't know where the priestess is," Dad says.

His comment prompts everyone to look again at the chaos erupting onto Ashengale City.

"This region has been breached," Garrick says. "We barely got out alive. Does anyone know where else to go?" Garrick's eyes widen. He turns a full circle. "Where's Fran?"

Both Dad and Geneviève shake their heads. "She's a ghost, Rick. The blast wouldn't have hurt her," Geneviève says trying to reassure him.

"Then where is she?"

"Don't worry. We'll find her," Dad says. "Besides, knowing my sister-in-law, she went after Lira."

"That's quite plausible," Garrick says. He huffs in slight relief, but still his face shows concern.

"Right now, we should probably find a more ideal place to go. A safe place Nyta may be," Geneviève suggests, "but my leg it needs—"

"Let me help, Gen," Blair says, and her hands glow, again, like before. "This is going to hurt. Can someone brace Geneviève so she doesn't move?"

Garrick and Dad hold her down. Blair sets the break, followed by a scream of agony. She wraps her glowing hand over Gen's broken joint. "It won't heal very fast, but it will do for now, I think."

"Thank you," Geneviève says, gasping for breath.

Cole, who has been silent for much of the time, begins to call out, "W—wraiths...Wraiths, wr—wra- wraiths," he murmurs over and over as he sways back and forth.

Shock trails over Blair's face. "These are the first words he's said since—"

"Since what?" Dad presses.

Several voices invade my thoughts, keeping me from hearing Blair's reply.

My attention is diverted to the sound of a waterfall a few feet away and seeing the crimson-dyed stream distracts me. I swear the river is speaking. *"Wynter this way."*

"Wynter, please wake up," Dad implores, redirecting my attention from the whisper. I feel his cold hands brush across my face. My spirit form is still connected to my physical body. It wants me back, but something is stopping me from crossing over.

"Did you see that?" Rory asks. "Wynter felt your touch, Jeff."

"She can hear us," Redmae says. "Of that, I am sure."

"Can you get inside her mind, Red?" Rory asks.

"No, not as a human. I would have to change back to a wolf."

The rushing sounds of water float through my veins, as though it calls to me. I hear other spiritual voices around me call my name, too. I ignore it. I don't want to go. How can I get back to my body? "No, I won't go with you, whoever you are."

"We better get Cole out of here before his voice carries," Dad says. "Gen, do you have the strength to port us out of here, now? I don't think we want to draw attention with him shouting."

She looks at Rory. "We can combine our magic and do this together."

Rory nods.

Cole continues to repeat the word "wraith" over and over.

"What about her trials?" Blair asks. "Isn't she supposed to stay here on Dragonscale Island?"

"There won't be any trials if she dies," Dad replies.

"No, don't go yet. Dad, please, help me get back." My pleas go unanswered.

Cole's voice grows louder. "Wraiths, wraiths!"

"We need to go now," Chad says.

"Quick, everyone link hands. I feel more energy now that Blair has healed me." Geneviève holds me in her right arm, while casting a portal stone with her left hand.

They fade away, taking my body but leaving my spirit form alone.

A gust of wind blows across my soul, pulling me higher into the sky. "No, not again." I was so close. I look up. "I'm not ready," I scream.

My life essence glides freely across the land, and I feel like I've no control over my movement. I need to wake up. My family needs me. I panic. This isn't how it's supposed to end.

19
IT'S ONLY A DREAM

MY BODY FLOATS THROUGH the air, weightless. When I look at my hands, I see right through them.

"Come with me," I hear a familiar voice say.

"Aunt Fran, is that you?" The sky is dark, but the stars are bright. *"Where are you taking me?"* My question goes unanswered.

The wind kicks up and I find myself spiraling downward, landing in a forest. My feet gently touch blades of grass. The soft bristles tickle my toes. I look down. *I'm barefoot? And I'm dressed in a white nightgown.*

The rushing water of a stream nearby distracts me, and I look up. There in the distance a figure appears and puts out a beckoning hand.

At first, I don't recognize her. She looks different. *"Aunt Fran, do you know what's happening to me?"*

"This way, I'll show you," she answers and turns toward the woods behind her.

I float like a spirit, following her, weaving between the trees. *"Where are we going?"*

"You will see. It's not far now."

An uneasy feeling tells me something isn't right.

Dad's words spring through my thoughts, reminding me to listen to my gut, and my gut is telling me to run. In the opposite direction. I stop. *"Aunt Fran, where are you taking me?"*

"Wynter, what's wrong? Don't you trust me?"

I tilt my head. *"You're not my aunt. You look like her, but it isn't you."*

"What are you talking about? Of course, it's me. You're a ghost. I'm taking you to the place where all dead people go."

"Dead?"

You've passed on, my dear. She smiles, putting out her hand. *"Your feelings are valid, and I understand the hesitation, but I assure you, all your questions will be answered soon. Now, come with me, and I'll show you the eternity gate."*

"I don't believe you." I take a step backward. *"I just saw my body. They said I was alive."*

"Honey, you didn't make it through Rory's port. You didn't have enough strength." She reaches for me again. *"Now, come with me if you wish not to be caught by the demon shadows of Scarlet Hollow. Besides, there is someone who has been waiting to meet you."*

"What is Scarlet Hollow?"

"Don't you know? Scarlet Hollow is the in between world, where supernatural spirits go before being called to the eternal gates."

"Then why are you here?"

"I'm the gatekeeper of this world. It's my spiritual duty to guide the souls to their rightful places."

I think through the logic, and I know something is off. I don't trust any of it. This ghost-like image before me looks like my aunt but something tells me, it's not really her.

"Leave, now," a voice calls out through my thoughts.

"Cory, is that you?" I turn a complete circle, only to see the thick trees and brush on all sides, and the ghostly image in front of me. Her features change to concern.

I take a step back. *"You're not my aunt. She would fight for me. She would help me get back."*

The spectral being moves forward. *"Yes, I am your Aunt Fran. Now, come with me."*

"No." I turn to run, but I can't move. My feet adhere to the ground as the soft blades of grass that once tickled my toes, grip them and spread slowly over the top of my skin, until they reach my ankles.

The illusion of my aunt fades, and in her place a woman I've never seen before appears. She has the face of a beauty queen. Her hair is black and wavy, with eyes green as emeralds. She wears a matching green gown, and a golden crown with diamonds set in facets which rests upon her head. Her high cheekbones, full red lips, and elevated neckline accentuates her oval face. She gives an evil grin.

"Sarmira," I whisper, taking a wild guess. I know it's her, even though I've never set eyes with her face before. It's the only thing that makes sense. Why else would anyone lure me away from my body? "You don't fool me. You placed me in a dream stamp, didn't you?"

She doesn't answer. Her malevolent laugh sends chills down my spine. "I would say my plan is working out perfectly. Wouldn't you agree?" Her body turns to a solid form. She circles me like a cat watching a mouse struggle in a trap.

"So, you have somehow sent me back to your sick undead world again, am I right." I strain to be free from her grasp. Ironically, this reminds me of when Aunt Fran was restrained at the hands of my grandmother Eleena when we tried to explain our circumstances in her personal library. Is this a dark witch trait... this immobilization spell she has on me? Lira mentioned my grandmother had dark witch blood running through her veins. Is Sarmira an extension of that? Is she a dead, scorned, dark witch in disguise?

Sarmira seethes. "Iknes Shaw venom takes time to run its course. I imagine soon you will finally be mine." Her eyes narrow and the curve of her smile sends loud and clear, her wicked intent. "This will be fun indeed."

"So, you set this all up..." I struggle to free myself.

"Me? Oh, hardly. My dear, I do wish I could take all the credit for this, but no." Sarmira hums an evil happy tune, adding under her breath, "*He* did say it would work, but I didn't believe him. Lira's never followed through with any task I've handed her, but she and Miles pulled off the impossible."

"Who are you referring to?" I demand. Miles mentioned someone other than Sarmira being behind this charade. I want to know who it is.

She ignores me. "And now, I have you so far away from your body it will be next to impossible to find it." She threads her fingers together and covers her smiling lips. "Very clever, indeed."

Cory calls me, again. *"Wynter, break free. Remember fear fuels her power. You have the same magic within you, too. The grass is an illusion brought on by the poison. This is a dream like before, back when you were at the Manor, jailed in the cell block below, and you appeared at the cabin. Remember?"*

"Yes, I do. Cory, where are you?"

"Honestly, I don't know, but we're apparently on the same dimensional plane. You must break free."

"Wait, why is this Sarmira and not Moyer. Cory something isn't right. I can feel it in my gut. Are you implying Sarmira has been freed?"

"No time to explain, Wynter. Trust me. Remember what I've taught you. Reach deep within your soul and break the bonds holding you there."

The silence between Sarmira and myself must have alerted her that something was amiss because I feel an ice-cold sensation crawl up my body. "Why are you so quiet?" The sounds of the waterfall in the background fades and soon the area fills with fog. "Answer me!"

Fear. Cory said fear fuels her. I need to remember that. "Is this, some sick trick, Sarmira?" I glare at her as she comes around to face me. Her body language and the expression on her face shows surprise, as though I've challenged her somehow. "You seriously think I'm going to fall for your games? I know you can't hurt me otherwise you would have done it already."

She appears annoyed and gathers her composure. Her eyes glow green as though she's about to challenge my claim, but disappears instead, and I'm released from her twisted grasp for the time being. Freedom is short lived. The ground I stand on disappears and I fall into a bottomless hole of darkness and even though I feel as weightless as a ghost, my body is heavy, which makes it more terrifying as I plummet downward.

I flail for a moment, spinning like a toy top, before grasping control and tethering my way into murky nothingness. I still feel the icy sensations crawling through me from when Sarmira cast her immobilization spell, but something else has grabbed my attention. I feel something dark...sinister...an evil aura in my presence. Why do I get the feeling I'm not going to a place of white fluffy clouds with unicorns and rainbows, but rather the opposite direction, where a demon lurks in the shadows waiting on its prey? I feel constricted which is going to send me in a panic if I don't start controlling this demonic awful dream. I stop fighting the outside noise and close my eyes. *Just breathe.* I visualize my body floating, weightless, hanging in suspension as my body dangles in midair.

A cold chill runs through my veins, and Cory calls to me again, telepathically. *"Wynter, you must wake up and find me so the three can be one."*

I jerk in response to the sound of his voice. "Cory?" My voice echoes through the black hole of nothingness.

The sensation of evil lingers, giving me goosebumps followed by many other voices calling out my name. Their whispers come from all different directions. *"Cory, how do I get out of here?"* Whispers and shouts plead for help, and it toys with my emotions. My ears ring and my head fills with agonizing pain. The pressure is so intense, I scream.

A familiar venomous laugh calls out. It's her. "Soon oh very soon. It won't be long now."

"Where am I?"

"Your own personal hell," Sarmira says, laughing. "I finally have you where I want you. You think you're so clever, don't you?"

The pressure inside my head eases, as though she released a tension strap, leaving my mind to twitch slightly. My temples pulsate as the blood pumps my veins. It burns like fire for a moment, until all sensation is gone. I feel nothing except for a faint pulse of pain. My brain says it's supposed to hurt, yet my nerves don't respond.

Faint whispers of many different voices start up again. None of the words make any sense. They all speak at once, each saying something different. Some warning me to stay away, some pulling me to them, eager to grab onto me, while others laugh.

Worry enters the depths of my core. Has *she* finally captured me? No, not possible. I try to think. There must be a way to escape, knowing deep within my soul, it's the evil witch herself that has put me in this pit of darkness. "What do you want with me, Sarmira?"

"You're so amusing, my child." Her condescending tone makes me want to rip her throat out. "Haven't you figured it out yet?" She laughs. "Why it's you I want: your soul, your mind, your body. I've waited so long for this. Finally, I have the Child of Darkness within my grasp. What's a few more minutes?"

My heart sinks. *Child of Darkness?* I ball my palms into fists. My rage festers, but it does nothing for me. "I will never allow you to take my soul."

She continues to heckle. "I hold the cards now. You're in my world, and I'm going to make you suffer before I take hold of your very soul."

Her words try to penetrate my mind, and the pressure from earlier begins to throb beneath my skull once more. I scream in agony. The pulsating cries of souls lost and wanting to be free, pull at my psyche. I resist her invasion.

The pressure releases again. She's toying with me. Seeing how far I'll go before I give in. My breathing is heavy. It feels like ten thousand bricks are on my chest.

"See, I told you. I have the power now," Sarmira's voice echoes.

"Wynter you're in control," Cory says. *"This is your dream. You create the narrative, remember?"*

I smile inwardly. He's right. I need to get back to my body. "Is that all you've got, Sarmira?" I shout. "I told you my soul isn't for you to take."

I resist and the darkness clears immediately. I find myself in a different place, now, but it isn't a pleasant one. I panic. *No, please no, not here.* The songbirds sing. Their melody plays like a sweet lullaby while circling the sky. I'm in Songbird Meadow. *This isn't real. It's all in my head.*

A tempered laugh comes from the clouds. "Go, my feathered pets," she says. "Food awaits you."

"No!" The birds focus on me, and sail in my direction.

"Leave me alone!" I attempt to run but my legs are wrapped in blades of grass yet again. The more I struggle the tighter my ankles bind.

"No, please, no." The birds reach me and peck my flesh as though it's the most delicious they've ever had. My arms burn with pain and my skin peels. I fight through the agony of being torn apart.

"It's all in your mind, Wynter," Cory says.

Loud rumbling thunder roars, and rain pours from the sky, drenching the ground. It's cold, and my bones feel like they will break. I cry out in anguish to make Sarmira call off the birds, but they keep pecking at me. It's her sick demented way to have me cry out for mercy. I won't give in. I close my eyes again to drive the dream to my narrative and not hers. Silence follows and the birds release me.

I take a few seconds to breathe in the quiet, listen to the crashing waves and open my eyes. I wipe the hair from my face to find a dead body next to me.

The dead body's soulless eyes open, saying, "Trust your instincts."

I push the corpse away. "You're not real!" *It's only a dream.* I keep repeating the words over and over. This is Sarmira's way of gaining control. I stop fighting and relax my body a third time. *Think, Wynter, think.* I lie down in the shallow waters, hoping it will ground my soul. I need to focus. I must remind myself I'm in a dream stamp. But how? Maybe I'm not dead after all.

"Wynter, wake up. It's only a dream," Cory whispers. It sounds like he's next to me. I turn my head to see him smile. I reach for him, and he disappears.

20

SCARLET HOLLOW

I FIND MYSELF LYING on a shoreline. Wet hair and clothes cling to my limbs. This illusion is different. This time I'm wearing the clothes I had on my body before I fell unconscious in the physical world. I shiver as the cold sea breeze grazes the surface of my skin. This feels like reality, yet somehow I know it isn't. When will the nightmare end?

My muscles are weak, and I struggle to stand. Waves of pain travel down my lower back sending dull pulsating aches through my entire body, like I have a bad case of the flu. My skull feels like my brain is about to explode. I touch my temples to discover a bandage wrapped around my head. Is this some kind of sick prank? Is this supposed to mimic the bandage Garrick wrapped up my head within the physical world? I look around feeling a little disoriented. Or did Sarmira give up and release me allowing me to push through her torment and I'm finally awake? It doesn't make sense. How did I get here?

I feel alive and well, not at all like I've died, roaming the planet as a spirit.

The ocean waves beat against the shore, pulling the sand beneath the arch of my feet and the sun beats down on my skin, warming my cold frame. I shiver again, craving the sun's rays. My body feels like it's been stuck in a freezer for an eternity.

"Where am I now?" I whisper.

"You're in Scarlet Hollow." A glowing green wisp whisks by, giggling playfully.

A second wisp of blue appears and buzzes back and forth in my face. This one is not as friendly. Annoyed, I swat at it and the wisp becomes more aggressive. A third wisp comes to the aid of its buzzing buddies, saying, "Who are you, and what are you doing here?" This one glows a fierce yellow.

"I don't know." I recoil, folding my arms and cup my elbows. I walk toward dry land, ignoring the flying wisps about my head.

"Be careful. Stay away from the shadows," the yellow wisp says with an ominous tone.

"The shadows?" I look up to see blood orange clouds form slowly in front of the sun. Seagulls make their presence known a short distance away as more water rushes around my ankles. The icy sensation of salt water enters my veins waking me more to the reality that I'm in uncharted territories and nothing I see can be assumed real. A heavy fog rolls in. I try to make out what lies beyond, but I can't see through it. The wisps seem agitated and then they all streak away, buzzing with fear. Something is awry.

Moving away from the water, I keep my thoughts focused. I've learned enough to know when my gut is telling me to be watchful. *Wait... my abilities.* I can make a fire. Extending my palm, I focus my energy to the tips of my fingers. Nothing happens. My heart quickens. "Where's my magic?" If this truly is my dream, then I should be able to control what I want.

I look toward the rumbling clouds, again barely seeing through the fog. My anger builds, and I can feel the pressure of frustration increase. Thunder roars overhead, followed by drops of rain that splatter upon the sand, and strong gusts of wind pick up, kicking strands of hair over my face. Wicked laughter calls out from the clouds. *Sarmira.* I'm still trapped in a nightmare that won't end.

The wind howls. An image appears in front of me but it's translucent and unrecognizable. The image takes shape. It's a male figure. "Cory?" I step closer. "Cory, is that you?"

He reaches for my hand. "She's coming for me." His voice is muffled, like he's speaking under water.

Thunder continues to roar. "You will never find him," Sarmira says.

"What have you done with him?" I shout.

She cackles another annoying laugh.

"Cory, please tell me where you are." My heart aches. I can see through his shadowed image. He gestures with his hand for me to come forward.

"You dare show yourself, Cory," Sarmira howls. "I will find your soul before Wynter does, and when I do, nothing will stand between me and the power that is rightfully mine." She throws something sharp at him and he disappears, but I can still hear his voice.

"Wynter, run. She's trying to confuse you. Use your instincts," he warns.

"Tell me where you are."

"I'm in The Veil, where souls are protected from the evil demons that plague the lands of Scarlet Hollow. You must find a way to reach me. I cannot show you the way as I don't know myself."

Sarmira starts the mental assault again, bringing on more pain within my mind. She is stuffing as many soulless entities' minds as she can into my brain. There's a multitude of voices to distinguish between and it makes my head throb.

More haunting laughs echo. The seagulls become noisier, and a black specter-like image approaches hovering above the sandy shoreline, which then divides into two wraiths. More phantoms appear behind them, coming through the fog. It gives me an uneasy feeling and my impulse is to move, but I can't. I want to, but the horror of seeing so many wraiths stuns me in fear.

"Run!" Cory says again.

My feet don't move. I'm terrified.

"I said, run... now, before they capture you," he presses.

I stare at the black images moving forward as they multiply.

"Snap out of it," he pleads.

I step backward, not paying attention to where my feet are and tumble, keeping my eyes on the shadows coming forward. I scramble to get up. The images grow larger as they draw closer. *Is this Sarmira's army?*

"Listen to your heart, trust your instincts. Your gut will never steer you wrong, but hurry. There isn't much time," Cory says, his voice echoing. *"She's looking, hunting, but I'm hiding, holding onto hope. She can't find me as long as you're alive."*

"Alive?" That's the hope I needed. *"I'm alive? You mean physically?"*

"Yes."

I look up at the sky and see lightning strike, illuminating the dark clouds. The black wraiths before me come closer, bringing with them more friends. They attempt to encircle me.

"Run! Move! Don't let them touch you or it's over," Cory calls. *"Wynter, run, get out of there now!"*

I look around seeing nothing but the grey mists growing darker.

"How?" I ask. *"They are closing in too fast, Cory."* I haven't a clue what direction to escape. *"How do I get out of here?"* I panic. The crashing waves hit my feet, again.

"Along the water line," he says out loud, no longer speaking in my mind. "This way." Cory appears, and grabbing my hand, he pulls me back toward the depths of the deep ocean. His touch feels real, but I know physically it isn't him.

"They will not come near the water," he says. "Now jump!"

I plunge into the sea. Rising to the surface, I turn my head and witness the wraiths waiting on the edge of the shoreline, but they do not pursue me. They stand there like they're waiting for orders to attack, lingering, their numbers growing by the dozen. "So many of them. Why don't they follow?" I ask.

"Because they can't. The water will dissolve them into nothing," he says. "Don't stop, keep going."

I pick up the pace and wade farther out until my body aches and my feet no longer touch the sand.

"Keep swimming," Cory urges.

"I'm so tired."

A large wave rushes in like rumbling thunder, drenching me. It's cold, and my bones feel like they will break. I wipe the hair from my face. Struggling with the current, I try to swim, but my ankles are wrapped in kelp. The more I struggle the tighter the kelp grips me.

This isn't real. It's only a dream. I stop fighting and relax my body.

Something grabs my ankle and I'm pulled under water. *"This way,"* an unfamiliar voice says. Opening my eyes, I see a human-like fish. I'm hesitant and instantly think it's another ploy.

"Come," it says with a smile, trying to lure me.

I've read about sirens but never seen them with my own eyes. It hums, and I feel it trying to lull me, but I'm stronger. I'm not fooled.

Pushing from the siren's grasp, I come to the surface gasping for air. Land is a short distance away. I'm not as far offshore as I thought. The wraiths have disappeared.

Trudging in the ocean, I turn to check if anyone is behind me. It's as though Sarmira switched off a light, and a sunset glows on the horizon. I swim toward the beach that glistens in the twilight. It isn't the same landscape. A lighthouse overlooks a large cliff, and the loud sound of a foghorn shakes my senses.

So, another illusion? Her dream stamp scenes are giving me whiplash. I'm skeptical at this point. I feel like I'm in a never-ending time loop.

The last seconds of sunlight bleed through the haze, and I take this opportunity to head in the direction of the shoreline.

The rain pounds down again as I swim closer. I'm exhausted, but I use whatever strength I have left until my feet reach land. I see smoke trailing from the lighthouse chimney. By the time I reach the sandy beach, the sun has disappeared, the rains have stopped, and a full moon begins to crest.

Of course, I've been pulled into Sarmira's insane world, and nothing can be taken for granted. Everything I see around me I need to remember is an illusion. If I'm under Sarmira's influence, it means my body is in the physical world somewhere, and I need to find it—if I'm ever to wake up. Cory said I'm alive.

Ocean droplets spray my face and the taste of salt on my lips brings this dream into reality. The atmosphere, although creepy, smells refreshing. This experience feels different than the last one.

I plant my feet on the ground, digging my toes into the wet sand and although my muscles feel weak, I press on. I must find a place to rest, get out of the open. I fear *she* will send her wraiths after me again or throw me into yet another scene of her torturous liking. Hiding from her is impossible.

Stumbling, I push forward, making my way up the cliff right below the lighthouse with overhanging vines that look like washed up kelp. Fatigued and out of breath, I rest my back against the crag and fall backward into a dark opening.

21
UNEXPECTED VISITORS

"**O**w." I LAND ON my rear. "An invisible wall, how clever." My voice echoes. I stand and notice water drips from the walls that surround me. The musty smell has me assuming I'm in a cavern of some sort. The lighting is dim, but my nocturnal eyes adjust easily. Guess that's one advantage of having my magical abilities. Still annoyed, I can't seem to find my other powers yet.

The dark cave feels cool but not like outside. There's a flickering light in the distance. Reflective shadows spread across the sides and ceiling indicating ahead is a room with a crackling fire. I feel like I'm not alone, too.

Across from me and easing closer, a shadow moves in my direction. I flinch. "Who's there?" It stops and lingers for a moment, looking at me, with its eyes staring. I can't make out the face.

The urge to go to the warmth of the fire set in the center of the room like a small firepit, pulls heavier on me than finding out who or what is in the shadows. My fingers are numb and my body yearns for warmth. The smell of burning cedar and hearing it crackle brings fond memories of camping days with Dad and Aunt Fran. Something tells me that whoever is hiding in the dark corner isn't threatening.

"Who are you?"

Putting my hands out toward the warmth of the fire in front of me, I look around and notice the walls are etched in drawings that appear to tell ancient stories. It reminds me of the time I explored the painted rocks and dwellings of Arizona.

A raven is perched high on a ledge that juts from the rocky ceiling. It stares at me, making a series of ear-piercing squawks along with its companion. Giant roots grow out between the gaps where a large nest rests, and the birds flap their wings in discontent. A howl from outside the cave responds to them, followed by the rustling of leaves. *Wolves?*

"I see you made it," the shadow finally says and comes into view. The woman's voice is calming. "I was beginning to worry Sarmira had gotten to you." She wears a black cloak about her shoulders and a cowl covers her head.

I shiver hearing the wicked witch's name.

She steps closer. "I do believe this is good news." Hidden shadows reveal half her face inside the hood.

I step back, not knowing if I'm moving into yet another trap of Sarmira's mind games. "I'll ask again, who are you?"

She smiles. "An old family friend." Turning around, she gestures with her hands extending her arms wide in explanation. "I have created this for you. I'm one of the few that can penetrate the mind of one under a dream stamp. I'm hunted daily by the Underworld because of my talents. You're protected from Sarmira here. Once you leave, though, the shield will fade."

Her reference to Sarmira has me on edge. "You know her?"

"Not by choice, I assure you."

"And you created this for me?" I briefly glance at the raw stone covered walls and painted artwork etched into it, again. "Do you mean this cave? I'm so confused. I've been battling the nightmare from—"

"The dream stamp is her doing, yes, I know. The cave is mine. I was informed of your accident—"

"Accident?"

She takes a deep breath. "Your untimely situation with Lira. You do remember, do you not?"

I nod. "Yes." The blast of her power plays back in my mind. "Sorry, but you still haven't said who you are." I cross my arms, covering my shoulders to warm myself better by the fire.

She paces closer, edging to the opposite side of the firepit. "I am many things to many people."

"And yet, you still haven't told me your name."

She drops her hood, revealing long white hair adorned with a silver circlet interlocking with branches and leaves that loop around the piece. Three purple crystals, two on the side and one in the center, are set within the coils. "Petra."

Why does that name sound so familiar?

The birds in the corner scaffolding, squawk and flap their wings. "I do suppose you're right, Meeka," Petra says. One bird flies to the woman's shoulder. "Artan?" The second bird in the rafters protests his concern. "Oh, I assure you, she will not harm you. Not all witches are the same."

"Witches? But I'm not a witch." I furrow my brows thinking back to being in my grandmother's library. *Or am I?*

Petra smiles, looking as though she's waiting for me to discover some long-lost truth about myself. The other bird flies down to her opposite shoulder.

"Can you tell me why I'm here?" I ask.

"In this cave? I think I've answered that."

"No. I mean, why haven't I woken up yet. I know I'm dreaming. I know for some weird reason this is an 'out of body' experience. I watched myself lift from my physical body and I know in reality I'm trying to heal from a traumatic encounter."

"Impressive."

"You're just an illusion."

"Am I?" The birds caw in response, too.

"Well, if you're not in my imagination, then explain to me why I can't do this." I try to summon the fire power I once had, only to discover the flames shoot from my fingers. I gasp.

Petra grunts with satisfaction. "She's ready."

A second figure comes from behind her with fire engine red hair and golden amber eyes, wearing a black leather vest and pants with red boots laced to the knees and matching cloak. She has a quiver set behind her back. "I will warn the others to prepare." She turns to leave.

"Wait."

The woman stops to face me.

"I've seen you before. You're Redmae."

Surprised, she raises one brow. "Excellent observation, but I don't think we've officially met."

I look down, thinking how to respond. Glancing to Petra and then back to Redmae, I say, "I saw you at the druid circle."

She lifts her chin and stiffens as though not expecting to hear my admission. "I see." She looks at Petra.

"I saw you all there," I say. "Rory, your mother, Geneviève, my dad, Aunt Fran..." My mind drifts. "And Cole. I tried to let you know, but my words went unheard."

Redmae hesitates at first, and says, "Wynter, we've come to take you home."

"Home." I huff. "You sound like you know how to bring me back from the dead? Buzzing wisps said I'm in Scarlet Hollow, is that true?"

"You're in The Veil of Scarlet Hollow, yes," Petra answers. She points to the entrance. "Through there is your way to freedom from this place, but before you can go, we must brief you and inform the others from the outside world so that you can cross unharmed."

"Unharmed?" I don't like where this conversation is going.

"Don't be frightened," Redmae says. "We have been trying to reach you for a few days, now."

"A few days?" I look at Petra for assurance. "Forgive me, but I'm not exactly the trusting type. How do I know this isn't just another one of Sarmira's tricks?"

Petra sighs. "I imagine it's difficult to trust what is real and what is not but fear not, what Redmae says is true. Sarmira has you bouncing around like a ragdoll. I imagine it's hard to find the truth right now."

Redmae nods in agreement. "You're imprisoned within your own body. Sarmira keeps resetting scenes within your mind in a continuous time loop. It's why you haven't been able to wake up."

Her confession has me worried. "And so what's different this time?"

"The fever from your physical body finally broke," Redmae answers. "I think it allowed you to finally focus. The ocean shore outside is the entrance to Scarlet Hollow's Veil. Somehow, some-way, you managed to break free from Sarmira's grasp."

"Cory."

"What?" Redmae sounds stunned. "Have you seen Cory?"

Redmae's eyes show concern. "Yes," I say. "I mean sort of. He's been following me through my nightmare from the beginning." I don't want to ask what my heart fears, but I do anyway. "Is Cory dead?"

The silence between them both is deafening.

Redmae looks to the side walls of the cave, then to the blazing fire, as if trying to find the right words, then stares at me, answering, "Honestly, we don't know."

My heart sinks. "What happened to him?"

"I don't know, I wasn't there. I mean I was there, but I have no memory of what happened to Cory. All I know, is when my sister Rory ported us all out of Storm River Manor, Cory did not come with us."

"Hold up. Rory went to Storm River Manor without me?"

"Wynter, I'm sorry, I don't have the answers you seek because I was still in my wolf form, and many of those memories have been wiped. I wish I could help you."

I look at Petra. She shakes her head in agreement with Redmae.

"He's alive," I say. "He has to be. He said something about trapped in The Veil."

"If he's truly in The Veil, then yes, it's highly possible he's still alive. Listen carefully. We haven't much time. I've cast a spell, but it will wear off soon. The Super Blue Blood Moon is still approaching. You must find your way to your body before Sarmira does," Petra says.

"Cory said the same thing. I mean, about his body."

"Yes, it appears you're both under the same dream stamp and in a continuous time loop," Petra answers.

"How are either of you able to reach me?"

"I'm a seer." She smiles looking over at Redmae. "She is a dire; a bloodline that can penetrate any mind they wish to, in wolf form."

I smile. "I'm glad you're here. And I'm glad to see that Rory pulled off the impossible. She brought you back from Madame Moyer's grasp."

Redmae firms her lips. "As much as she could, anyway."

"What do you mean by that?"

"Rory gave me an antidote for the curse but only half, the other half—well let's just say others needed the medicine as well. A slight hiccup but we're handling it. For now, we need to find out why you're not waking up." She turns and stares at the fire. "I used to have these dreams where if I stared at the flames long enough, I could see the answer I was looking for." She turns back to look at me. "Not sure if it will work in this dream, though."

"Why not?"

She smiles. "It isn't my dream." Redmae stares a few seconds more. "I'm a silver dire wolf, a descendant from the direct bloodline of the first dire wolf. Only that line can cross over in the dream world of the unconscious. I can only connect when you sleep."

"Here," Petra says and put out her hand, revealing a necklace. Instinctively I reach out to grab my locket around my neck and it isn't there. "My necklace. I've forgotten all about it." My heart races as I stare in wonder at the locket threaded between Petra's fingers. She holds it out for me to grab.

"It was lost, but I do believe it appears its rightful owner has come to claim it, once again," she says.

Taking the necklace, I fasten it around my neck. "How is it possible? I mean, I never take it off."

Petra grunts. "Sarmira has ways of removing items in her made-up dreamworld, making one believe something isn't there when it is. I merely reminded you it was missing. Your subconscious has done the rest. Now perhaps we can work on getting you out of this nightmare."

Redmae gestures behind me and I turn. Someone is lying on a bed. The shadows within the cave are dark, so I move closer to take a look.

I don't recognize the face and turn back to both Petra and Redmae. "I'm confused."

"Wynter, think. Look closer, who do you see?" Redmae asks. She points to the person lying on the cot without a face.

"I can't see who they are."

"Petra, it didn't work," Redmae says.

"What didn't work?" I ask.

They both don't answer.

"What didn't work?" I ask again. "Are you suggesting this is me?"

Petra nods. "But if you cannot see your face, then it means something is wrong. We guided you to your body, but clearly it isn't working."

"What do you propose we do next, Petra?" Redmae asks.

"Take her to the lighthouse. We need to jog her memory some more." Petra's face shows signs of worry.

"I want to wake up just as much as you two do."

"Yes, we know. We do, too. So much has changed in the real world, we can't defeat *her* without you."

"*Her?* You mean Sarmira. Right?"

Petra narrows her eyes at Redmae. "She needs to go to the lighthouse. Go tell the others what we've found out."

"What did you find out, what do you mean?"

Redmae bows her head. "You have to find out what's holding you back before your spirit will release you."

"And how do I do that? Like I said before, I've already tried to get back to my body."

"Until you can figure out which door will lead you home, you will continue on the same endless path. You need to find out what is keeping you here—it's the only way."

Redmae bows and walks out of the cave, leaving us alone.

I huff in frustration. "So, what do I need to do?"

"I don't know, you tell me. It's your dream."

Petra points to the same doorway that Redmae exited. "Through there is your way out of here. Stick to the path and do not veer off it, no matter how much you want to. Allow the compass on your locket, to guide you, Wynter."

"Wait, what's beyond the doorway?"

"There are steps leading to a lighthouse. There you will find what you seek."

"What's so special about it?"

Petra begins to fade. "The spell has expired."

"Where are you going? Please, wait. What are you trying to tell me?"

"The lighthouse is a hub of The Veil." Petra fades in and out again. "Where the subconscious and conscious meet. My physical body is waking up."

Physical body? I cover my mouth in surprise. "I know who you are."

She smiles. "I knew you would figure it out." She disappears in a cloud of white smoke that quickly fades away leaving me alone in a never-ending nightmare.

22

THE LIGHTHOUSE

"**A**ND JUST LIKE THAT, she's gone," I say, annoyed.

My necklace begins to glow. Wait. This is different. I didn't have my necklace with me in all the other nightmares. I'd forgotten all about it. I hold the locket, balancing it on my fingers. The white rose glitters from the firelight. Beneath the filigree design the blue light from the stone permeates through the silver inlay.

"What are you trying to tell me?" I open the locket. The compass points in the same direction as Petra did earlier. "Guess this is my way home." It has me wondering if the Elementals knew this would happen, and the compass was part of the plan the whole time.

I follow the jagged steps up as my mind drifts to the past, to the basement stairwell at Storm River Manor.

My fingertips guide me around the spiral passageway as I recall the torturous things Moyer did to young children and teens. "Shake it off, Wynter, this isn't Storm River Manor." My footsteps echo with every step I take, and my knees become weak. There must be a hundred steps or more. "You can do it. Keep pushing. Clear your mind."

The whispers come back and flit through my brain. Although I can't see anyone, I feel like I'm not alone. "Red, Petra, is that you? Have you come back?"

My question goes unanswered. The stone inside my necklace continues to glow blue guiding me up the steps. It feels like forever, but soon I see a glint of light in the darkness ahead. Seagulls make their presence known in the skies above that reverberate through the chamber. Petra said to stay on the path and I'll be safe. Still, I'm on guard. Every time I think things are going my way, Sarmira plays her games, plucking me into another area. I hope what Petra said is true, that The Veil will protect me from that evil witch. I wonder if she knows where I am right now. Can she see me?

My locket continues to glow, and the compass needle keeps pointing forward. Even my compass has me a little suspicious whether the direction I'm going is toward freedom or a trap. All I know is I need to get back to my body. I have so many unanswered questions.

I don't know whether Cory being in Scarlet Hollow is a good thing or bad thing. He's probably trapped like me. Something inside me knows, the voice of Cory was real. I must find him. First, I need to wake up.

My thoughts go to Cole. Seeing him with the others at the Druid circle was confusing. I want to know what happened. He kept murmuring the word *wraith*. Why? Can he see ghosts like me? And Lira, the thought of her makes my blood boil. Her disappearing act came as a complete surprise. I won't be fooled again. That magical surge of power was no accident. I should have seen it coming. I can't help but think Moyer's magic and Lira's are connected somehow. And Miles... What did he mean by '*They* don't want you dead. You would be of no use to *them* otherwise.' He wasn't referring to Sarmira. There is someone else. No, I'm missing something.

I draw closer to the top and as I do, the sounds of the ocean become clearer, and the gulls cry out searching for food. Crickets sing, and the grass rustles in the air. A cold breeze brushes across my arms. Is that the wind or another lost spirit? I don't see ghosts in this world like I do in the physical one; they're all solid looking, like they're still alive. Here, those wraiths that tried to surround me and lined the shore before I escaped, they were a different kind of creepy.

If what Miles and Lira said is true—and I can't bank on anything those two say—then who exactly staged the coup back in the war room?

I suppose my biggest surprise is finding out Eleena, my grandmother, is Lira's younger sister. A part of me says Lira is lying, but another part thinks she isn't. Are all these circumstances preventing me from waking? The truth lies here in Scarlet Hollow. I feel it. Somehow my subconscious knows this. Or is it something else that's hanging on? All these emotions I have are building into an overwhelming fear.

The last step of the stairwell leads me to the edge of the cliff, and I overlook the ocean below. This area isn't familiar except for the familiar beach I remember I walked along to reach the cave.

Looking down at my feet, I see a faint cobblestone trail leading to the house entrance. I'm much closer to the lighthouse tower. Smoke escapes the chimney. *Someone's home.* It reminds me of when I came upon the cottage at Storm River Manor, except this house is overhanging on a cliff and not hidden by trees.

My compass glows brighter, pointing at the front door. I go to it, still on guard that Sarmira will scoop me up at any moment and I knock. "Hello? Is anybody home?"

Silence follows.

I knock again, and the door creaks open, welcoming me to the crackling of a fire and the sounds of faint folklore music in the background.

I push the entrance fully open. "Hello, anyone home?" I ask again.

The fire is inviting, and I go to it, warming my body. I'm still freezing. The warm flames heat my fingers as a soothing sensation travels up my arms and throughout my body. Slowly, I begin to thaw again; I hope for good this time.

I take a second to look around. The music playing comes from an old record player in the corner. Fresh flowers sit next to the box. *Someone lives here.* Suddenly I feel like I've broken into someone's home. I'm sure Petra said this was where I was to go.

The kitchen and living room are connected as one big space, and to the right between them is a hallway along the back wall.

A small envelope falls to the floor. I pick it up and turn it over to see it's addressed to me. *How odd.*

I attempt to open it, but I'm interrupted.

"I see you found your way," Redmae says, popping behind me.

I jump. "Really?"

"Sorry, I should have been a bit more sensitive."

"Ya think? Was there something you needed to tell me? I didn't expect you to come back. Petra said I must find my body."

"I'm here to help."

Still fumbling with the envelope in my hands, I hold it up.

"What's that?" she asks.

"I don't know. I was about to open it when you scared my soul from my body."

Redmae grins. "Your soul has already left your body."

"Not funny, Red."

She focuses on the item in my hand. "What do you think it is?"

"Only one way to find out." I tear into the envelope and pull out a long black feather. "What is this, some kind of joke?"

"It means something otherwise she wouldn't have left it for you."

"By she, you mean Petra."

"Of course." Redmae looks around. "This is her home."

I tuck the feather back in the envelope and slide it to the inside pocket of my jacket. "So, did you find anything out while you were away?"

"Yes. Seems we have problems in the real world. It appears that Sarmira has tipped the balance of power, and the magical realm is fading."

"What do you mean, like disappearing?"

"Her evil demons have begun to possess the people in our world, as well as the humans on earth, and we have no clue how to stop it."

"Demon possession is how Sarmira went years undetected using Moyer as a vessel. That shouldn't have any relevance on why the magic is fading," I say.

"You would think that, yes. But there is something else you should know.... Everyone is aging. Except Rory and me."

"What do you suppose the common thread is?"

"I can only guess it's the dire bloodline."

I look at my hands. "That means I'm aging, too?"

"No, oddly that has us also perplexed. This magical aging curse doesn't seem to be affecting you. Nyta thinks there is a connection between you and the magic."

"Any idea how to stop it?"

"Not yet, but she's working on it. The more important issue is getting your spiritual self, back into your physical body."

"Show me how."

"Wynter if I knew how to do that, don't you think I would have shown you by now?"

I glance down the hallway. "Do you know what's down there?"

"Only one way to find out," Redmae says. "This is your world, remember?"

Together we walk down the dark hallway with my glowing blue eyes lighting the way. The floor creaks with each step we take. At the end of the hall three doors reveal themselves. A red one, a green one, and a blue one.

The wind outside howls. I smile. "You think Sarmira notices I've disappeared off her radar?"

"Definitely. Let her get angry. It's your dream. She can't reach you in The Veil, remember?"

Even though I know this is my dream, I still feel like Sarmira is in control. I don't trust anything in this fantasy nightmare, even if Redmae says I'm safe. "Don't you find it odd that each door is a different color?"

"So open one of them and we can find out why," Redmae encourages.

My shaky hand tries the knob of the green door, first. I peek in. "It's a simple bathroom."

"Okay, so try the next one."

A sign hangs on the red door, stating 'private.'

Staring at Redmae, I say, "Let me guess, my thoughts, right?"

She shrugs. "I don't know, Wynter. Only one way to find out."

I try to turn the nob. "It's locked. A door I can't open, and I'm betting this is the door to freedom." There are private memories buried deep inside my mind. I mean after all, if I'm locked in my own dream, what else can it be?

"Try the other one, Wynter."

I reach for the knob of the blue door when a loud knock comes from the front entrance of the cottage, startling both of us.

Redmae's eyes grow wide like mine.

We walk back to the living room and stare at the front door. "Who can that be?" I ask.

Redmae rolls her eyes. "It's your dream. I keep telling you that."

The knock from the other side becomes louder and more urgent, jolting us. "Whatever it is wants in." The storm brews outside, and the whistling increases with raging winds. More banging surges with intensity. "I'm scared to open it."

"There's only one way to find out who it is." Redmae changes to a wolf.

"Wait, you can do that?"

"Why not? Dreamworld, physical world, either way I'm a dire, remember?"

I huff. "Right." I pause, not knowing what to think.

"Well, go on, answer it."

I turn the knob, open the door, and find myself astounded by who's standing there.

23

THE THREE DOORS

"Cole!" My mind clouds in anger. "What are you doing here?"

Redmae moves next to me and growls. *"I'd like to know the same thing."*

"The last thing I remember, you tried to turn me into your own personal vampire. How are *you* in my nightmare?" My thoughts travel back to when I last saw Cole at the druid circle. *"Isn't he supposed to be locked away in his own mind in the physical world?"*

"Yes, but how did you know that?" Drool drips from her jaws and sizzles on the wood floor, leaving a mark.

The searing sounds remind me of the first time I met Redmae in the barn at Storm River Manor and almost died. I smirk at the memories and the irony of my current situation. *"I was there, hovering over my body, when I heard him calling out 'wraiths.'"*

"Wynter, relax, I'm here to help." Cole glances at my growling protector. "I could use a little help, Red."

She stops growling and sits. Her glowing silver eyes fade.

I tilt my head and squint at Cole. "Moyer has you possessed by a demon. I never would let you in my world. So, how are you here right now?"

Redmae stays in wolf form, giving a vibrating grumble.

"What, you think because it's your dream you're in control?" He laughs. "Wait, how do you know my body is possessed by a demon?"

"Um, hello, mansion, Moyer, vampire…"

He raises a brow, ignoring my taunts. "I know how to find Cory."

That grabs my attention. "Where is he?"

He winks.

"I don't have time for your games, Cole."

"It's got to be a trick, Wynter. Don't give in to his ploys."

"Don't worry, I'm onto him."

Annoyed by his mind games, I ask, "Why are you, really here, Cole?"

He looks up and down at the doorframe, giving a slight sheepish grin. "May I come in?"

I smirk. "Oh, I get it. You need my permission to enter, don't you? How ludicrous. Even in dreams, a vampire must have consent."

He scowls and furrows his brows. "I'm glad I can amuse you, cousin." He presses his hands against the open-air doorway, as though glass separates us, trying his best to push through the invisible barrier. "Enough of the games Wynter, please. Kindly let me in."

Redmae gives a low warning growl.

"What are you thinking, Red?"

"That no one can reach him in the physical world. He's locked up within his own mind. Anytime someone tries to communicate, he attempts to burn them with his glowing blue eyes. Nyta has covered his eyes with metal plates and placed valiancium cuffs around his wrists. In the real world, he's just as lethal as Sarmira."

"That's comforting." I look at Cole, unsettled by Redmae's comment.

"You've never seen a raging necromancer, bound, and left at the mercy of others, I take it?"

"Necromancy?"

"Wynter, where have you been? That's the Storm bloodline. Why do you think they have glowing blue eyes?"

"Right. Well, I'm a Storm and I can't do that with my eyes." I raise a brow thinking of the possibilities. *"Not yet, at least."*

Cole appears impatient. "Um, hello?" He props one arm up along the doorframe. The rain outside pounds away, and he's getting wet.

"I should let you rot. It's not every day I get to have the upper hand on a vampire." I back away another step, contemplating my next move.

Cole's smirk fades. "Oh, come one! Seriously, I've come to help."

"I assumed the glowing eyes were from being a Nytemire."

"Nytemires are the result of a necromancer turned vampire. Wynter, I thought you already knew this."

"I did, sort of. I'm a Storm, he's a Storm, the thought of me having that skill repulses me."

"Well, you're not a vampire, so I think you're safe."

I huff, looking at Cole. *"Not yet anyway."*

"Honestly, he can't hurt you in your dream. You're in control, remember?"

I pace the floor in thought. "Who's to say you won't attack me again, Cole, like last time? I mean, after all, I may be in my own personal dream, but it appears Sarmira controls my nightmares." I stab a glare at him and point. "Your words, not mine."

Cole alternates to the other arm now, leaning up against the opposite side of the doorframe. "You know, I swear you two are having a private conversation and leaving me out of it."

I give a grin. "Is it that obvious?"

"Are those trust issues bearing down on you again, Wynter?" He tries to push in again, as though he's forgotten about the invisible wall, and smashes his face.

I giggle slightly at his frustration. I'm enjoying this.

"I've come to warn you… and help. I swear it. Trust me, you are going to want to know what I have to say."

Thunder rolls outside. Sarmira is close by. The expression on Cole's face is not only amusing it's also terrifying. He's utterly vulnerable. Something is different about him. He might be a vampire, but there isn't any evil emotion that I can detect. It's like the good side of him is here in Scarlet Hollow and the evil side of him is still in the physical world. Wait...is that possible?

Cole stops banging against the invisible glass and turns his head to the side as if to listen. A cackle, rumbles through the clouds, followed by a screeching sound not far behind him. His desperate pleas reveal pure fear in his eyes as he turns back to me, saying, "Come on, let me in, please. If she finds out I'm here, in your thoughts, she won't hesitate to eliminate me from the picture in the real world, and then you can forget ever finding Cory."

I shiver. "So, you know where he is?"

Cole nods. "Yes."

"Careful, Wynter. He could be lying."

"Possibly. But there's fear in his eyes."

"It's no different than the fear she sent across the lands of Storm River Manor when Moyer unearthed her shadow walkers, her personal guards. They obeyed her or it was death. How do we know she didn't send him here, and it is death for him now, in the physical world, despite what we do?"

"Good point, Red. But what if he's not lying?" I hesitate. "How do we know you're not sending us into a trap?"

The roars of thunder booms more forcefully. Lightning strikes a tree overhead in the distance, and the branches quickly go up in flames.

"Please, Wynter, let me in before she finds me, or you will never know whether I tell the truth or not." He stares at me in fear. "It's true, she could be up to another one of her tricks, and I understand why you're hesitant, but you're in The Veil within Scarlet Hollow, and it's the only way someone can reach an unconscious soul."

I turn to Redmae for validation.

"He tells the truth. That's why Petra needed my help to guide you to the lighthouse. Dire bloodlines are the only exception, other than a ghost, that can pass the barrier of The Veil and into Scarlet Hollow. Or in his case, a trapped, possessed soul."

"And I'm supposed to believe you? Like I said, Cole, you are possessed by a demon in the physical world."

He nods. "True, but that's just it. Something happened when I stabbed Cory—"

"Wait, what?" My rage builds hearing this news.

Cole gulps. "This is the complicated part."

"Oh boy, here we go."

"Wait, you knew about this, Red?" My anger turns to rage, and the fact I don't have the powers in this dream world is the only thing that prevents me from blasting them both into nothingness on the spot.

"Wynter, you've missed a lot."

"Apparently. Is this why Cory is missing?"

"We think it's part of the reason, yes. Let Cole in. If he does anything, I'll tear him to shreds." She growls, revealing her large, jagged teeth.

"Cole, I see you!" Sarmira's voice rings loud through the thunder. Her laugh echoes, and the sheer terror in Cole's eyes sends chills down my spine.

Where is a truth serum when you need one? I'm annoyed that this dream stamp has been full of lies at every turn. I don't know who to trust anymore. It can't be worse than the wrath of Sarmira outside. I cave. "Fine, come in."

He dashes into the house, and I shut the door.

Cole cups his hands together and blows into them. He looks at the fireplace. "May I?"

"Be my guest. Although, you may have to ask Red if she wants to share."

Redmae's amber eyes turn crimson and begin to glow.

"Interesting. A vampire isn't one to need warmth, let alone a demon. What do you make of that, Red?"

"It means something is off. But like I said before, the magic is fading. It's affecting Cole like the rest of the Storms in the physical world."

"Are you aware that the Undead Plane and Scarlet Hollow are the same place?" Cole asks as he goes to the fire, warming his hands as though he has human senses.

I stare at his odd behavior, answering, "Are you referring to where we are right now verses Scarlet Hollow, or The Veil in general?"

"Sort of, yes. There are two sections within Scarlet Hollow—well, three actually." He glances around the room. He appears nervous. "There's this one we are in, commonly called The Veil. Those you find here are all asleep in one form or another. Whether we're off to a normal rest from the daily grind..." He looks at Redmae. "Or, in a deep coma from where one cannot wake up..." He glances at me. "Or in my case, locked in the mind of a body I cannot escape, we're considered to be in The Veil."

"What are you saying, Cole?" I squint and fold my arms across my chest.

Cole continues to warm his hands and body. "The Veil is where a soul is protected, for a time."

I remember my grandmother mentioning something like this, and why my mother doesn't like to travel to Scarlet Hollow too often. Noticing Cole warming himself at the fire I ask, "I thought Nytemires didn't need the heat? They already have cold blood running through their veins."

Cole grunts in irritation. "Yes, well, we don't have the same supernatural powers when we're imprisoned within our own mind while our bodies fight for life in the physical world."

I swallow hard. I didn't expect that answer. "So, maybe you can tell me exactly what's going on? You mentioned three sections of this world. What are the other two?"

He clears his throat. "Well, each soul that is brought to Scarlet Hollow has their own version of the world. The Veil, and this cottage, and the dream it appears in, is yours."

"I gathered that. But what are the other sections, Cole. Why are you being so cryptic?"

"It's not my intensions, believe me. I'm still trying to figure out how I arrived in your version of The Veil in the first place. At any rate the second section is the largest area. It's where the demons roam and where lost souls flee from the soulless armies."

Flashbacks of my arrival come to mind and as Cole continues his explanation, I start to put the pieces together. "Are you saying Cory is in The Veil, too?"

"Yes, and I know where he is. But you cannot reach him from here. You will need to go to Scarlet Hollow through the physical world, instead."

"What do you mean in the physical world?"

"The House of Bloodbane are the keepers of the Crimson Moors. It's the physical representation of Scarlet Hollow."

I look at Redmae, and she relaxes a bit, lying down in front of the warm fire, remaining in wolf form. *I sense the brothers are connected somehow, like they're magically bonded.*

"The residents of the place you know as Scarlet Hollow are here either by death or a deathless, out-of-body experience, such as a deep coma. The souls trapped between these worlds must seek The Veil before the soulless armies find them. I'm able to reach you because our bodies are in close proximity to each other—in the physical world. At least that's my theory."

"I've never read about the Crimson Moors in any of my great grandmother Sara's journals."

"I can't answer why you never read about the Crimson Moors, but what I can answer is my brother and I are connected mentally. I can feel his pain, I can read his thoughts, and I can see his body..."

"Body?" I take a deep breath and narrow my eyes menacingly at him. "Yes, you did mention you stabbed Cory. Care to elaborate?"

He puts up his index finger. "I'm getting to that. First, I need to explain the situation, please."

I raise an eyebrow. "Go on."

Cole takes a breath and sits in a chair next to the fireplace. "Finding you was the easy part, getting you to this safe house wasn't."

"Safe house?" I look at Red, then back to Cole.

"You're in a world Sarmira sent you to, through a dream stamp."

"Yes, I know."

"Then you know she's put in all these nightmares."

"I am beginning to gather that, yes. Once I arrived in a cave below this house, and Petra came to me, explaining it, I was able to understand more."

"Then you know you have the power to change the outcome."

"Outcome of what, exactly? This nightmare? Waking up? Finding Cory? You're not answering my question, Cole."

Redmae grunts. *"He's stalling, but why?"*

"You see it, too, huh?"

"Wynter, that's it. I know how we can bring the twins back and you, too. I must warn the others."

Before I have time to respond, she fades away.

"Where did she go?" Cole asks.

"Redmae does that from time to time." I smile at his uncertainty. "So, tell me, Cole, why are you really here?"

"I told you. I know where Cory is."

"I see. And you expect me to believe that? You're dead, aren't you?" I ask. "I mean, why else are you here?"

"No, I'm not dead, and neither are you or Cory. We're all under Sarmira's dream stamp. She wants it that way."

"Yes, to bend us to her dark will, I know."

"No. I mean, yes, but no. Don't you see? We're the three to be one."

"How do you know about that?"

He grins. "I may not have the insight or power from my physical body, but I still have my spiritual one. We all do."

"We?"

He's silent for a few seconds. "Madame Moyer."

I tilt my head. "She's here?"

"The *real* Maura Moyer, somewhere here, yes. I've bumped into her a time or two."

"Her spirit is alive, is that what you're saying? That she is trapped like you, Cory...and me?" My heart pounds at the thought of being possessed. "You're saying we're all trapped here?"

"The only way to break the curse is to find our bodies in the real world. Except, unlike us... our bodies are with the Storms. We have a chance to get out of here."

I look down at my necklace and notice Cole can see it.

"Your necklace protects you and the watch protects Cory."

I look at Cole's wrist to see it's bare. "How can you see my necklace?"

"I told you. I'm the real Cole before Sarmira got her claws in me. At that point, Sarmira had my body possessed by a demon. The day I attacked you at Storm River Manor, while yes I'm still a vampire, it was the demon controlling me. I've been here, trapped in this world of Scarlet Hollow, escaping shadow demons at every turn, experiencing every level of anger, pain, and frustration my physical body would feel if I were awake. I haven't any control over what the demon possessing me does, because of this…" He looks around, frustrated. "This place!"

"So, how do you know for sure you're not dead or something?"

"Because I don't have my powers… a key to knowing whether you're dead or alive."

I think back to when I tried to use mine to warm up by starting a fire.

"So, if you're not possessed by Sarmira and not trapped within your own body, then why aren't you waking up? I'm confused."

"There was a battle on the grounds of Storm River Manor. Many souls were lost," he says.

I gasp, fearing the worst. My heart pounds as I wait to hear more.

Cole's eyes show regret, as though he dreads what he is about to reveal. "Per Moyer's instructions, I stabbed Derek… The evil me, I mean."

"You did what?" If it wasn't for my lack of magical powers, I would have knocked Cole out cold.

"I know none of this is making any sense, but please hear me out."

I nod. "Okay." I take a seat on a chair next to one of the cabin windows.

He fills me in on how he and his brother fought, and what he did. It makes sense, now, why Cory is missing, and the demon is trapped inside Cole's body.

I snicker at the visual. "Ironic that after you stab your brother in the heart; in that same instance, your own mind freezes, freeing you from Sarmira's grasp. No wonder Sarmira's after you. You're the fish that got away."

"I guess you could say that. She knows the physical side of me is trapped. She wants that part of me back."

"Do you think my grandmother Moyer has witnessed the same horrors as you? I mean trapped within her own mind, watching helplessly as Sarmira inflicted pain onto others?"

"Most definitely."

A tear sheds, and I wonder if the physical me is really crying. I'm losing my family one by one and I feel powerless to stop it. "You said we're not dead, at least not in The Veil."

"No, not yet."

"Yet?"

"You were close, but you managed to fight your way here," he says. "I wouldn't be standing in front of you if you weren't in The Veil.

"So, was it you who guided me here?" I ponder the fact that Cole and Cory are identical twins. Cole managed to fool me once before.

"All of us, really. Redmae, Petra, and myself. We were among the many voices you heard."

I frown, seeing the puzzle pieces come together. "And you're certain Cory is in The Veil, too?"

Cole nods. "He is, yes. But far away, in his own version. I've come across him a time or two."

Cole hesitates and I see concern in his eyes.

"What is it? What are you not telling me?"

"The only way to be released from Sarmira's grasp is for you to find your body and wake up."

"Yes, I know, but I can't figure out why I can't find it."

"I can help you, Wynter, but I also need your help to find, me."

"Huh? I don't understand. Didn't you just say we're near each other in the physical world?"

"What I mean is, I need to be released from the demon that possesses my soul. Only then can I lead you to my brother."

A loud thud distracts us. "What was that?" I ask. The hallway glows bright blue.

"I think I've overstayed my welcome," Cole says. The crack in his voice concerns me.

"You said so yourself—or maybe it was Redmae—it's my dream and I control it in this cabin." I stand, pulling at Cole's hand. "Come on. Let's check this out."

At the end of the hallway the three doors I saw earlier with Redmae, light up. "What do you suppose this means?"

"Perhaps a breakthrough?" Cole answers.

We walk side-by-side down the hallway until we reach the doors. "Which one do I choose?"

The lights flicker. I turn the knob to the door that says, 'Private.' "It's still locked."

"Try the other one."

My attention is thwarted when I look at Cole. "You're fading."

His eyes grow wide. "No, not yet. I'm not ready to go."

"Something tells me you have more to say."

"Once you wake" —he fades in and out— "intended to give me."

"Give you what?"

"The—"

Cole disappears and the locked private door opens.

24

THE RAVEN

I PUSH THE DOOR open further, and it makes a creaking sound that echoes through the hallway. The space in front of me is pitch black, like the cave, and there is no light to give me comfort.

A chilling sensation surges through my body—a sensation I've felt before. The labradorite tucked within the filigree of the silver wires of my necklace glows, prompting me to open the locket. Inside, the compass spins wildly. *I don't know what to do.*

Thinking I'm on the precipice of both worlds, I take one step over the threshold, and instead of entering what I expected to be a room there is a stairwell leading downward. *Great, another basement.*

Instinctively my eyes glow blue before I brave the unknown and take my first step into the pit of darkness. The walls light up revealing cobwebs and cracked plaster as I pass down each step. The whistling winds add to the creepy vibes. Flashbacks of the manor pulsate through my thoughts. The wooden planks beneath my feet creak with each step. My breath is heavy, and I swear I can hear my own heartbeat. I push the fear aside. Cole's last words keep playing over in my mind. What do I need to give him? I have nothing of his... that I know of.

The journey downward takes a few minutes and I reach the bottom only to find a whole lot of nothingness despite my newly acquired night vision. It feels empty and smells like a dank and dreary basement.

Memories pull me in, playing with my emotions, reminding me of the time when Moyer tortured my mind right before I woke in the basement cell, and she made me watch the innocent boy be tortured while she stole his very essence of magic. I feel that same presence in this room.

"I wondered when you would finally arrive," a voice calls out in the darkness.

"Who's there?" It doesn't sound like Sarmira or anyone else familiar.

A bright green orb appears in the blackness, and it illuminates the room. I glance briefly at my surroundings to see that I am indeed in a dark, empty, cemented space of a basement.

The light comes closer. "Don't be afraid. I'm here to help. To guide you out of this hellhole Sarmira has put you in."

"Who are you?"

"I'm the caretaker of the Tower of Light and the gatekeeper to other dimensions. I'm sure you've discovered you're in the in between. Your consciousness is in the spirit world, but your body is still in the real one. I'm here to help you get back to it. There is more work to be done. You're not ready for this world yet."

I squint. "How can I trust you? How do I know this isn't another one of Sarmira's ploys? Petra tried. So did Red. Even Cole. What makes you so sure you can help?"

The orb vanishes, and in its place a woman no older than me appears. "You don't, but from the reaction on your face, I trust you can see I tell the truth."

"How is this possible? I'm staring at—me? I mean you look like me except for the hair and green eyes."

She smiles. "Because I'm in your head, I look like you. In the real world, I take on many different forms. Nobody knows what I really look like. If they did, they would hunt me down." She paces closer. "When you wake from this nightmare, you will only remember my name."

"Which is?"

"The Raven, but my name is different in the real world." She looks up at the ceiling. "Pay no attention to the surroundings. No magic can penetrate the walls of this cottage."

I raise an eyebrow. "I saw Petra. Was she real?"

The Raven hums a laugh. "Illusions can be tricky, but alas I can say it was her spirit coming to your aid in the cave."

"Spirit? She isn't—"

"Oh, my dear, no. Neither am I, or you, rest assured."

"Then how are you here?"

"My magic comes from the Oracle's Coven."

"Oracle's Coven?"

"We are the gatekeepers to all the worlds in the galaxy, as I mentioned."

"Kind of like the Hall of Secrets?" I ask.

She laughs. "I think you're getting it. No one can penetrate our power."

"Wait a minute." My mind turns with theories. "That means there is a gatekeeper for the Hall of Secrets?"

She hesitates. "The short answer: yes." She lights a candle for more brightness. "Remember what this house looks like from the outside. You will need that imprint to find me in the real world."

She moves to another area in the basement, and a light beams from the ceiling, revealing a body lying on what looks like a dais. I collect my emotions, trying hard not to be too excited. I am, after all, in Sarmira's world, and nothing can surprise me at this point.

I turn to see that it's Cory's body, lying on the cot with a dagger stabbed in his heart. My eyes glisten. "No, I won't believe he's dead. Cole said as much." I look back at The Raven. "Please tell me this is just another illusion?"

She nods toward Cory and shows me a glimpse of where he's located. I can see red trees, with sap that resembles blood oozing down the trunks. The blades of grass are the same scarlet shades. "What are you showing me?"

"This is where Cory waits. You must wake up and find him."

A tear slides down my cheek. My eyes sting, and my body shakes with fury.

"It's an illusion. You know in your heart he isn't dead. He's a vampire, remember?" The Raven says in a soothing voice. "You must wake up, Wynter."

I wipe my tears. "Nothing seems real anymore. Everywhere I turn, change happens in a matter of seconds."

"That's what dreams do. Wynter, it is time." The Raven holds out her hand for me to take. "Are you ready to awaken?"

She stands next to the body lying on the altar, only it's no longer Cory. I see long white-blonde hair trailing over a girl's arm. Her hands are clasped atop her abdomen, and there is a sense of peace. I come closer to view her face. "That can't be."

"Why can't it?"

"Because Cory was just here."

The girl's hair glistens from the light of The Raven's aura. "How is this possible that I'm looking at... me?"

Nyta suddenly appears, standing beside us. "Wynter, I'm here to bring you back."

"Tell me... what do I need to do?"

The Raven turns to Nyta and says, "She's ready to listen." She moves to stand next to me gazing upon my cloned body, adding, "Wynter, you're in a unique situation. Remember, once you wake, everywhere you go, there will be a mirror image of yourself in this domain and the natural one. But be careful, Sarmira is hunting you. This means, she will see you... in both the physical and spiritual worlds."

"How can I protect myself?" I look down at my necklace. "It's all beginning to make sense now. This was why my father told me never to take this off."

"Yes," The Raven confirms. "You also have gained a new ability. You can spirit jump."

"Spirit jump? What do you mean?"

"Remember your skills with projection?" Nyta asks.

I nod.

"The reason no one could figure out how to save you is because you projected out of your body. It was never your spirit. It was an astral projection. It's why you couldn't heal yourself. All your energy is going into projecting."

The Raven steps in and adds, "It's similar to how Sarmira controls the dream stamp for anyone under her spell. She meditates. That's how she can find you in a dream stamp... but you can do the same."

"What are you both saying? That I can travel to Scarlet Hollow while in the physical world?"

"Yes," The Raven affirms. "When Lira threw her formidable power upon you and the others in the war room, she inadvertently triggered your projection. Something I don't think Sarmira even knows about. But because you had no control at the time with the spiritual power of projection, it put your mind into a tailspin, leaving you with no sense of direction, forcing you to find your way. Be mindful, this meditation is draining and will leave you completely vulnerable."

"Wait a second. That means she knows where I am in the physical world, too." My heart begins to race. "All she has to do is meditate."

The Raven nods. "But because you have the necklace on, your physical body is shielded. All she sees is what you see now. Your body lying on a dais."

Nyta smiles. "You're forgetting one very crucial aspect of what we're trying to tell you—if meditation will make you weak, then—"

"Then that means it also makes Sarmira weak when she meditates." My eyes widen with excitement.

The Raven flashes a smile full of sneaky joy. "Precisely. I do believe for the first time since pursuing a solution to defeat Sarmira, you have found it." She folds her arms, teasing, "Please tell me again. What is keeping you here?"

I grin. "Nothing."

"Wynter," Nyta says, "we all need you to help us win this fight. People are counting on you to end this evil with Sarmira. Are you ready?"

I nod. "Yes."

"Take my hand, and I'll pull you from this hellhole. Now, concentrate. Picture in your mind all the memories of your past and present," she says.

I visualize the thunder outside dissipating, with the clouds parting, and the sun poking through the haze. I see Nyta turns translucent.

"She's coming through. Nyta, be prepared," The Raven warns.

"Take my hand," Nyta says. "Please, before I fade away."

I hesitate. "How do I know this isn't another trick?"

The Raven passes in between Nyta and me. "Close your eyes. Reach down deep within your soul, Wynter. Do you feel it?"

"Yes."

"Bring your focus in. Concentrate. What do you see?"

"I see a room, a person lying on a bed."

"Look around. Feel your surroundings," The Raven goes on. "Let your mind clear and stay focused. Where are you?"

"A place I don't recognize."

"Look closer. What do you see?" she asks again.

My feet land on the floor. "I'm in a room, not like where I am now. This place isn't familiar." I move closer to the person lying on the bed. In the corner, I see a white wolf. The animal is sleeping. I smile. "Red."

"Go on, Wynter. What else do you see?" she coaxes.

"I don't know. I've never been here before." I pace forward to the foot of the bed and see a face. She looks familiar. I have an uneasy feeling that something isn't right. Sarmira is going to pluck me out of this scene again.

"It's okay. Go to her."

My heart is pounding. I'm so confused. "I can't breathe." I choke on my own saliva. Feeling a little dizzy, I motion toward the bed for fear of losing my balance. Both Nyta and The Raven try and reach for my hand to keep me from falling before they fade away. They cry out my name together. A hand reaches for me, and I go to grab it but miss.

My body plummets as though I'm falling through the air. My eyes focus on them as I plunge farther and farther down the hole of nothingness.

"Wynter, wake up," Cory says.

My eyes bolt open, and I sit upright on a bed.

25
AWAKE

THE SMELL OF BURNING cedar crackles, hitting my senses and wakes me from the pit of darkness. My head throbs and my thoughts jumble around, wondering if I'm finally waking from a long-drawn-out nightmare. Every one of my five senses is amplified. I fight through the discomfort, but it feels different this time. The pain feels real—not that it didn't feel real before, but this time something has changed. *Am I really awake?*

It feels like déjà vu. I'm in the same cave I was in earlier with Redmae and Petra, in the same hollow cavity with the same painted cave etchings and the same blazing fire in the middle of the room as before, except this time a black cauldron hangs on a hook atop the flames, with steam escaping the rim.

I'm hesitant to get my hopes up that this time my soul has found my body. Bouncing from one dream to the next in Sarmira's devious skit has me cautious that I'm still in her playful nightmare.

A squawk distracts my focus, piercing my eardrums, as though to alert anyone who will listen that I'm awake. I look up to see the same two birds in my dream perched atop the rafters. It feels like I've looped back around and awoken from my dream state only to be back in another dream. I don't trust it.

How is it possible that a dream can be an exact replica of the real world? Unless—I turn to see if I'm in the exact spot of the body that was lying here earlier, the one I couldn't recognize, the one without a face. The body is gone. I look down and see I'm lying on a cot—well more like a twin mattress. It's a bed without a fancy frame, but it's sitting on a solid slab of rock.

One of the large birds' screeches. "Shoo, go, shoo," I say. I throw a pillow at them, miss badly, and they remain perched high above my head in defiance.

"You're a stubborn couple of birds, aren't you." I glare at them.

I pull away the covers to reveal bare feet and I'm dressed in a nightgown. I curl my toes and swirl my ankles. Hearing them crackle and pop from the stiffness of being immobile for so long makes me wonder if I'll be able to stand, I swing my legs over the edge. The cold stone floor sends shivers up my spine. A tingling sensation runs down my thighs to my knees as I stand and attempt to walk. My legs feel weak when I put weight on them, like I've been to the gym and worked out for hours. I take one step and fall to the floor. "Ouch."

A growl from behind me, followed by a concerned whine, prompts me to look over my shoulder. A large ball of white fur comes to my side. "Redmae?"

Her crimson eyes peer back at me with worry. She pushes with her nose under one of my elbows. *"Let's get you back in bed."*

"You're in my thoughts. I must still be in a dream state." I wrap my arms around her neck to pull myself back up and plop back onto the cot.

"No, my friend. This time, you're...awake."

"How can that be?"

"You have managed to break through Sarmira's dream stamp...finally."

"Why are you still a wolf? What's happened?"

"As long as I remain a wolf, I can speak to you telepathically. However, something odd has happened in the physical world that has us all perplexed. I cannot change back to being a human. But I can still help you through your new-found thought process."

"Hang on a second...'New-found.'"

"Like my sister Rory, who nearly lost her sight from the arrow that struck her at Geneviève's Ranch, you too, now have the same insight."

"The Waxlily. You used the Waxlily to cure whatever I had that poisoned me."

"Nyta did, yes. She figured it out. Wait, how do you know you were poisoned?"

I smirk. *"In the war room, my grandfather—"* It's all coming back. I sit up. *"Ian—"*

"Yes, we discovered you had Iknes Shaw poison in your veins—"

"And Lira tried to finish me off with her spell blasting powers."

"I wasn't there, but yes, that fits with the story your dad and Geneviève told."

My thoughts jumble around trying to think back to my last moments of when I was truly awake. *"I was told I wasn't to leave the Island."*

"You haven't left," Redmae answers. *"You're under Ashengale city. Deeply hidden from the outside world."*

"I see you are alert." From the shadows underneath the perching birds, a woman dressed in a purple robe hobbles toward my bed. She uses a cane—a staff more precisely— to help her walk. The top of it has a circular purple stone that glows. It's Nyta.

"You've been out for quite a while, my dear." Her bluish hands with long pointy nails reach out from beneath her long sleeves and touch my forehead. Her hands are cold as she pats above my eyes, my temples, and cheeks. "The fever appears to have broken. This is good news." She scruffs the top of Redmae's head. "Your legs are much too weak to walk yet."

"When is this dream loop going to end?" I slam my fists against the side of the bed in frustration. "Ouch!"

Nyta chuckles at my childish temper tantrum. "My dear, you're conscious, I assure you. It took some creative thinking, but we managed to bring you back to your body with the help of Petra."

I think back to the events of my fading nightmare. "I remember her giving me a warning." I place a hand over my forehead. "Wait, no... There was someone else in my dream besides Petra. She called herself The Raven."

"You mean...the Eye of the Raven?"

I squint. "That doesn't sound familiar."

Nyta raises a brow.

"Why? What do you know?"

Redmae nestles beside my bed while Nyta roams to the back of the room where a large dresser sits. "It could be nothing. Let's focus on your health first, shall we?"

She dips a dry cloth into the basin that sits atop the dresser and squeezes out the liquid. "How do you feel?"

"Like I've been hit by a semi-truck."

"That would be the poison still running its course." She waddles back to me and places the clean cloth on my head. "You had us really nervous." She presses my shoulders down. "Lie back and allow the medicine to work its magic."

I huff. "Magic." A foul smell resonates. "What is that gawd awful odor?"

"It's grimmroot, basilore, and lily dust soaked in swamp water."

"Sounds disgusting and smells repulsive."

"I know, but it will help you heal. You've been out a long time. Longer than any of the other charges I've trained in the past." Nyta grunts and looks over at Redmae.

"How long have I been out?"

"Three days."

"So much time has passed. We're behind. That means—"

"Relax, Aoes has managed to manipulate time. We're safe here."

"How is that possible?"

She huffs. "How is anything possible? Thank the stars above you found your way with the help of what little magic is left."

"So, it's true. The magic is fading?" I look over at Redmae, remembering her warning.

Nyta soaks the cloth again in a bowl of liquid, wrings it out, and then places the damp rag back on my forehead. "A lot has changed since you have been…" She pauses as if to find the right words. "Asleep."

"That's an understatement. I've been trying to communicate with everyone here. Even Rory can't connect with me. And she's supposed to be a wolf whisperer." I hear annoyance in Redmae's tone. *"Except Nyta."*

"What do you mean?"

"It's like playing charades. She has to guess what it is I'm trying to say. I can understand every person that walks this planet, but it's one way. They cannot understand me. Nyta is more open than the others. Like I mentioned in your dreams, I can interconnect while others sleep, so, I also visit Nyta."

"Is that normal?"

I can feel Redmae's frustration. *"No, it isn't normal. As I've mentioned before, something is seriously off. The balance of power has been tipped, and many people are concerned."*

Nyta pats my forehead a bit more with the cloth. "Now, tell me. What is the last thing you remember before drifting off into dreamland."

I huff at Nyta's dry sense of humor. The war room comes to mind. "I took a pill to alleviate a headache—I have a similar pain now." I press my hand against the back of my head. "Ian— er, I mean my grandfather…" I stop for a second to collect my thoughts. "He gave me something other than a pain pill." I look up at Nyta as the puzzle pieces come together, realizing the severity of what's happened. "I'd woken up. Dad, Geneviève, Garrick, my grandmother, and grandfather—they were all fighting each other." I dig deeper, remembering the battle in the war room, finding out Miles was the mole... "Except it wasn't my grandfather who gave me the poisonous pill—"

"Miles." Nyta has a sour expression. "Your dad filled us in on what transpired." Her tone takes an angry turn.

More memories come, and I take a deep breath. "Cory is missing."

Nyta nods. "Yes, but tell me how you know that?"

My heart falls to the pit of my stomach. "Because he was there with me. I saw Cole, too. I need to find them."

Nyta furrows her brows. "You saw Cole?" She looks over at Redmae who grunts at Nyta's stare.

"Yes. He was warning me about something, but I can't remember what it was." I sit up. "I know dreams have a way of sending relief to people once they wake up, but what I experienced isn't any ordinary dream."

"No, I suppose not." Nyta presses me back down. "You need to lie still until the toxins leave your body."

I swallow hard and feel pain in my throat.

"Are you thirsty?"

I nod and cough.

"Blood or water?" Nyta grins.

I laugh. "Ow." My head starts pounding. "Guess my brain isn't ready for jokes." I glance at the water pitcher.

Nyta smirks. "I don't think blood will stay down like water. A good sign, nevertheless." She wobbles over to the fire where a pot is brewing. Using a ladle, she scoops up some liquid into a bowl and brings it over to me. "Here, drink this first. It will settle your stomach, then we'll try water or Trek blood."

"No offense, Nyta, but this smells revolting." My nostrils burn from the aroma.

She chuckles. "It is edible, I assure you of that."

"I don't have cravings for blood. Besides, haven't you heard? I'm a dragon shifter."

"Yes, I did hear those rumors." She grins.

"You already knew?" I look into Nyta's eyes. "Can you see what I see?"

She nods. "Of course, Princess. What kind of priestess do you take me for?"

"Right," I say, drinking the liquid. "Call me Wynter, please. I'm no princess."

She looks surprised. "All right. But sooner or later, you're going to have to come to terms with your position and title."

"I know." I pinch my fingers against my nose. "I don't want to be queen." Nyta spoons another portion of soup into my mouth.

"In time, perhaps you will come to understand. We don't have to discuss it right now." She takes the cloth and wrings it out again into the liquid beside her. "You haven't eaten for days, and you need the medicine. The Iknes Shaw poison needs to dilute out of your system. I've stopped it from killing you; however, there's a side effect from doing that. It will accelerate your transformation, and if you haven't already experienced it, you will begin to communicate within the thoughts of others. More so than before."

I look at Redmae and smile. "Like dire wolves."

Nyta smiles, too, looking in my direction. "Yes, as well as other animals. You will need to learn how to protect yourself from intrusive thoughts."

"I've heard that before."

"Yes, well, this will be much more stressful than just the thoughts of dragons. I've contacted a channeler to teach you how to block out those unwanted voices, but we can talk about that later. Right now, we are more concerned about your transformation."

"Are you saying I won't have any control in changing?" Worry sets in. Throbbing pain pounds against my skull, as the anxiety intensifies. "I feel odd. Like I'm not myself." Bringing my hands to my head, I notice scales begin to form around my wrists.

Nyta sees my arms, too, and the look on her face tells me all I need to know. "The poison is—"

"No. You'll be fine. You've already transformed once. Plus, shifting won't hurt anything that we know of, but with the uncertainty of the weakened magic in our realm it's best we keep you from shifting for now. We don't want to take any chances of Sarmira and her ghouls from finding you."

My body gets cold. "Unless it's already too late...that's why my skin is changing, right?" I look over at Redmae.

She lets out a soft howl, grunts, and yawns as if my anxiety with the transformation isn't a big deal. *"Like Nyta said, you'll be fine."*

Nyta gets up and waddles to the brewing kettle, brings out another cloth, dips it into the liquid, wrings it out, and comes back pressing the rag down onto my forearm. "Your transformation doesn't stop just because you sleep for a few days. I told your father this might happen. That the Iknes Shaw poison could provoke you to shift because you were in the middle of your ascension trials. The soup I gave you is supposed to help."

"Do you mean, like suppressing it?"

"Something like that, yes." She goes back to her small kitchen and pours the remaining liquid from her pot of stew into crystal jars.

"What are you doing now?"

"Fixing you a few bottles of medicine to curb your body from shifting. Of course, if you need to shift as a last resort, please do. Keep in mind, if you do, it will send a message to the dark dragons as to where you are. Your necklace is supposed to help cloak you, but as we all know, that strategy hasn't been working very well. It will all be explained this evening." She finishes and brings a couple of vials to my leather jacket hanging on the wall, tucking them inside the pocket.

She turns to me and hobbles back to my side. "Take one sip twice a day. If you miss a dose, those scales will appear."

I breathe in deep, trying to collect my thoughts. "Tell me more about Miles, please."

"The pill he gave you was laced with Iknes Shaw poison. I don't think that he and Lira intended to have it work out the way it did, but it almost acted in their favor. Her blast forced you to project out of your body because you had the poison still in your system, and your antibodies were already fighting the toxins, and, well, we know that the only way to kill a dragon shifter is through the heart—you my dear, haven't completed your trials, which made this event a million to one."

"I somehow remember hearing this before in my dream." Realizing how close to death I really came fills my veins with anger.

"I'm not telling you this to bring out your rage. I'm telling you this so you can use it to your advantage. Wynter, you must—and I stress the word must—keep your emotions in check, or…. You. Will. Fail."

She pauses and turns back around to fill more vials. "I know this must be difficult for you. For your full power to take effect you must learn control: mentally, physically, and emotionally. The power of a dragon shifter, if not properly taught, can be disastrous. Not to mention, being vulnerable allows the darkness to take hold of you."

"Are you saying my transformation back at Ashengale Castle is why my body wants to transform now? Are you saying I can't control it?" My heart sinks and I sit up.

Again, Nyta presses me to lie back down. "Not now. You need your rest and strength if you're to finish the trials successfully. Just relax."

"The trials." My head hits the pillow in frustration.

She takes the bowl of medicine sitting beside me, pours it down the drain, refills it, and comes back to repeat rinsing the cloth. She presses it back on my arm where the scales have nearly disappeared.

I close my eyes. "All I remember is chaos."

"You're still in the most vulnerable time for a shifter and you're much more powerful than you give yourself credit for, Wynter. The trials are there to teach you what is needed to defeat her… And control your magic. Only then will you be able to handle the Sword of Valor."

I open my eyes. "Handle? I haven't a clue where the Sword of Valor is, let alone wield it."

Nyta grins, looking down at my necklace. "Something tells me you shouldn't have any problems with that."

My necklace glows, triggering a locked memory from my dream.

"The Iknes Shaw poison is how the dream stamp was placed into your mind."

I realize three days isn't that much, but it feels like we've wasted time. The Super Blue Blood Moon is still approaching.

Nyta turns to the Ravens that have stayed quiet, and she slips something in one of their claws. "Go tell them we're ready," she whispers.

"I heard that," I say. The birds fly off together through the mouth of a dark tunnel. If I listen, I can hear the faint sounds of crashing waves on an ocean shore.

"I was counting on it," Nyta says. "Your body is improving. Do you have the strength to tell me more of what you remember?" She smiles. "Your dream, perhaps?"

"Dream?" I pause. "Right, my dream."

She turns to me and places the rag back on my head. "Yes, the nightmare you had right before you woke up. You kept calling for Cole."

"Cole?"

She flashes a playful smile. "Yes, is there something you're not telling us, Wynter?"

"No. Cole is a ruthless vampire that takes what he wants regardless of what anyone feels." *At least the old Cole did, anyway.*

Nyta snickers. "I was just teasing. I know where your heart belongs. But it does beg the question of why you were calling out Cole's name."

"It's fuzzy." I work hard to think back. "I'm supposed to do something. It's all jumbled together, though. You were there too."

"Me?" She chuckles. "Try harder, Wynter," she presses. "It's important. You mentioned The Raven."

I close my eyes again, trying to remember anything useful. "Yes. I think I was in her home. She was ominous and didn't tell me her name. Only that she went by the name The Raven. She said she was the gatekeeper to the sister planet Elleirodal."

"Interesting," Nyta says. "Go on, tell us more. Dreams can be a bit tricky. It's true, I did pass through and was there. It's remarkable you remember that." She presses her hand over the cloth that's against my forehead. "Now, think. What else can you see?"

"I remember The Raven saying that over and over again, too—asking what else I can see." I reach deep, but nothing comes. "I don't know. I can't seem to retain much."

"I'm confident that in time you will remember."

My stomach churns, and I sit up again. A rush of dread begins to fill my head with thoughts of death and destruction. "Is everyone okay?"

"Fine, fine," Nyta says. "I think we should focus on you getting your strength back for now."

I can tell she's holding something back, but I don't press the issue.

Another flash of my nightmare comes to mind. "I remember a dead body appeared beside me." I look at Nyta for an answer. "Why would I dream something like that?"

"I don't know, child. It must mean something. I'm sure we'll figure it all out soon enough."

She checks on the cloth still stuck to my arm. "You almost died, remember, or do I need to keep reminding you of that?" She smirks. "You're not invincible, Wynter." She takes the rag and soaks it again in the bowl of putrid smelling water. "Like I said, the trials will teach you how to defeat her."

"But how? I can't even shift according to you."

"Doesn't mean you still can't use your magic. Did you forget you still have light witch abilities running through your veins?" Nyta looks down at my necklace. "Something tells me you shouldn't have any problems with that, either."

I take the locket and open it. The compass inside points in the same direction where the birds flew through earlier. One of the flecks of embedded gems inside glows.

Nyta smiles. "Now I think we're getting somewhere. Trust your instincts. You'll need that when you become queen."

"I don't want to be queen."

"I know." She pats my shoulder.

"How do we know if someone isn't doing the same to us, invading our private conversation?"

She looks to my neck, and I grab the chain, looping it around my finger. "Oh."

"The Amulet of Protection should shield you now that Doctor Brekker has managed to dispel the dark magic that was growing within the locket." She brings me my jacket. "It's time to find Cory."

"Cory," I whisper. "He's missing and I hate that I can't remember parts of my dream. But Nyta, Cory isn't the only one. If Miles and Lira impersonated my grandparents, then that begs the question: where are they?" I look up at her. "Do you know where we should start looking?"

She takes the bowl of medicine and washes it out. "No one knows where Cory is, except maybe his brother. As for your grandparents, your father has already formed a crew in search of them."

"Cole." Thinking back to our encounter at the lighthouse, I ask, "Wait, Cole had a message."

Nyta chuckles. "Fortunately for us, you talk in your sleep." She grabs her walking stick and puts on a cloak. "I already have an idea what that message is, but first I need to run an errand. I won't be long. Perhaps you and Redmae can catch up." She departs through the dark tunnel.

Redmae sits up and yawns as though she had been sleeping this entire time.

I shake my head and huff. *"Did you have a nice nap?"*

26
SECRETS BETWEEN SISTERS

REDMAE GRUNTS AS THOUGH she's been put on the spot with Nyta's abrupt departure. I swear if Redmae were human right now, I'd see her eyes roll. *"So, tell me, Red, what did I miss while I was off in dreamland?"*

She nudges my hand.

It's quite unreal seeing her as a wolf but still able to talk to me. *"I still feel like I'm going to get plucked from here and land in some other odd place in Sarmira's universe."*

"Trust me, you're not in a dream state anymore."

I laugh at the irony of her saying "trust." *"Was Cole real? I mean, was that reality in my dream or imagination?"*

"You've officially met Cole in your dreams." She laughs.

"Red, that sounded so wrong, in so many ways."

She grunts. *"No pun intended, My Lady. But it's still funny."*

I try to sit up and get a shooting pain down my spine. "Ow."

"It might be better to stay lying down for a bit, like Nyta said."

"Noted." I breathe in deep brought on by the frustration of doing nothing but resting. *"So, Rory managed to bring you back."* I pause a minute to collect my memory of what Rory was tasked to do. *"I thought the goal was to break the curse, Red. I take it that didn't happen?"*

"Long story."

"Isn't it always? So, give me the short version."

Redmae gives a small growl. *"I'll enlighten you later."*

"Red, come on. Apparently I'm not going anywhere, and I could use a little briefing."

I look down to see my necklace glow a new color. *"Something is wrong. If we're still on Dragonscale Island—"* I feel my throat go dry. *"Truthfully, where are we, Redmae?"*

"Just like we said earlier, under Ashengale city, deep in the caverns away from the war still going on above us."

"The war is still engaged?"

"Unfortunately, yes. Severe casualties from both sides, too."

"Tell me what you know."

"You should rest. Giving you too much information may not be good right now. Especially since your body is fighting change."

"I'm done resting. I want to find Cory—and the others." Another memory flashes across my mind. *"Hang on a second, I think I know what Cole was trying to say to me."*

"I know."

"You know? But how?"

"When you were asleep, I mean when I visited your mind while you were unconscious and Cole came to visit, I read his mind. We already accomplished what that task involved."

"Well, what was it?"

Before Redmae answers, we hear footsteps tracing down the dark tunnel, from where Nyta left earlier. Redmae growls at first and then whimpers. *"It's okay. It's my sister."*

"Rory. Is it really you?" She walks out from the shadows, alone.

"Hey, there. I heard you were awake," she says. "They're all worried about you."

"Word travels fast. Where are the others?"

"Waiting where it's safe. Queen Sara sent me to get you. There are spies everywhere. Nyta will be back soon, and when she gets here, I'll take you to where they're all hiding."

"You mean the spies?" I tease.

"Hah! Calling me out for not being specific." She laughs. "I'll take you to family and friends."

Flashes of memory flit across my mind of how I arrived here, then I remember once again, the blast of Lira's powerful magic. She killed so many people in the war room. "How are they? I mean, Dad, Geneviève, and Garrick."

"Recovering better than you," Rory says.

"Nothing like keeping it real, Rory."

"I'm sorry, I don't know what to say. Forgive me. I feel like you've risen from the dead. Nyta said she would bring you back, but none of us believed her."

"I see. Well, here I am. Alive and kicking." My heart races.

"Wynter, you died. You had no pulse, but something brought you back."

"Yeah, I gathered that. I think this is what saved me, honestly." I hold up my finger revealing the ring that Dad gave me made of Lapis Lazuli. I feel the heat rise beneath my skin, but not from anger, more from the thought that I might have cheated death somehow. I think back to the dead body in my nightmare. "I'm here now."

"How did you get this?" Rory asks.

"My father handed them out to his men before we headed to the war room."

"That must be why most of your dad's army survived the attempted coup, "Rory says."

My thoughts ramp up thinking of the others. "How are Zak, Blair, Chad—"

Rory tilts her head. "They're fine. Wait, I'm confused. How do you know about them being here?"

"Because I was there."

"Where?"

"At the Druid circle before my body took me to Scarlet Hollow."

"So, you saw everything."

"Yes. Powerless to help."

"Hang on a second. Does that mean you remember what happened in the war room?"

"Yes. I'm assuming you've been briefed, too."

She grins, giving that mischievous eye like when she's ready to fight. She looks at Redmae, then back to me. "I'm looking forward to returning the favor to our enemies." She comes closer. "So, hurry up and get well, will you?"

"Nyta said Lira's blast forced me to project out of my body."

"Guess that explains why you didn't die, I suppose."

"No. It's why my body wouldn't heal. I don't think anybody knows why I didn't die. Even the enemy doesn't know.

"Then it's a miracle."

I chuckle.

Redmae is quiet, so I say, *"Perhaps now is a good time to tell Rory."*

"What, about us communicating telepathically?" Redmae grunts. *"I'm not sure now is the time for that.*

"It's perfect timing. Get it out of the way. She needs to know." I grin, looking at Redmae. *"If you don't, I will."*

Rory interrupts, "Why do I get the distinct feeling I'm suddenly the third wheel around here?"

Redmae grunts again, yawns as she stands on all fours and follows to the side of my bed. *"It appears my sister is smarter than I thought."*

I silently laugh on the inside. *"You don't know your sister very well, do you."*

Rory pokes a stare looking at me confused. "Wynter what's going on?"

I send Rory a sizable grin. "Ask your sister." I glance at Redmae, again giving a frowning tease. And she doesn't look pleased.

I feel an intense look from Rory, and it's so dramatic that her heart begins to race. She presses the issue. "You make that look when communicating telepathically. I've been around you and Cory long enough to know that. What's wrong?" Her eyes grow big and she glares. "You can hear my sister, can't you," she guesses and folds her arms in frustration.

"Cat's out of the bag now," I say, glancing to Redmae.

Rory turns to look at her sister, and Redmae lets out an annoying howl.

Rory looks back at me. "When were you going to tell me?" Her face flushes. "I have been trying to communicate with my sister for over a week. At first, I thought it had something to do with only giving her half the dose, but seeing you two transfer thoughts together, I'm beginning to think there's something wrong with me."

"It's not like that, Rory. When I woke, Redmae was in my head. She's been trying to link with you since she changed back to a wolf."

She takes a deep breath. "Guess that explains a lot."

"Please don't hate me. It just happened."

"I don't hate you, Wynter. It's just frustrating not being able to hear my sister."

"Rory, we will figure it out." I can see she's having a difficult time with this.

"I'm fine." She moves closer to my side. "But how are you? I mean, you must have a lot of questions right now."

"I have a few And apparently I'm immortal."

"That's just it, you're not." Rory hesitates and looks at Redmae for assurance, but she stays quiet. "The poison reached your heart, but something remarkable happened. We can't explain it. According to your dad, you must finish your trials before the transformation is complete. Until then you're a mortal."

I hold up the ring again. "Like I said, I think this kept me alive. It must've worked."

"We should have more of these rings made," Rory says.

A rush of fear washes over me, hearing Rory talk about past events. "Something tells me this was in Sarmira's plans all along. She couldn't get to me by possessing Moyer, so she's getting creative."

Rory grins. "Well, we're smarter."

I raise an eyebrow. "I know that look. Rory Fernshadow, what do you have up your sleeve?"

She looks down at her arms, stretching them outward. "Do you not notice? I'm wearing a sleeveless tunic." She grins more.

I laugh at her cheesy joke, but I still feel like Rory has some animosity hidden deep inside. "Something tells me both you and Redmae have some declarations of your own to bear."

Rory glances at her sister. "Red blames me for the reason she's still a wolf."

"Still a wolf?" I look at Redmae and she nudges Rory's hand.

"I don't blame you, Rory," Redmae says, knowing Rory can't hear her.

"Redmae says she doesn't blame you."

Rory closes her eyes a minute to collect her thoughts before answering. "The serum Aoes gave me to save Redmae didn't completely work out the way we all had hoped." Rory pets her sister's head.

Redmae's eyes look to be sulking like when a domestic dog has done something wrong.

"Are you talking about the antidote or the curse, Rory? I mean, you have to know, none of those events were your fault," I say.

She paces. "I know, I keep telling myself that, but—"

"You feel guilty somehow. But why?"

Rory comes to sit next to my bed. "That night, when the first full moon of January rose, my sister turned back to an elf." She wipes a falling tear. "Anyway, I gave her the antidote, but it wasn't enough. The next day she turned back into a wolf. Aoes said to give her the full dose, and I didn't do that."

"Because I bit Akira. He was protecting my sister. I was the threat at the time, and I tried to kill Rory. He was only doing what was right. If anyone should feel guilty, it's me."

"I'm so sorry, Red. I thought you said you could transform into a human."

"I thought so too, but as I said before, when I left you the first time in your dream in order to tell the others, and transformed to a wolf in your nightmare, I woke up as a wolf and haven't been able to change back since." She slumps down to the floor, grunting in frustration.

I smile at Rory. "So, we keep searching for a cure. When all of this is over, I'll be there to help. We won't stop until we find it."

Rory half smiles. "There's more."

"There always is, isn't there?"

"I can't change at will anymore, either." She huffs. "I finally find out I'm a silver dire, like my sister, but I can't transform like I should be able to."

I frown. "Come again?"

"Oh, right, you didn't know that either. Like I said. A lot has changed since you have been sleeping. I can change—rather could change into wolf form but can't anymore." She, too, slouches in frustration. "And my porting abilities are unpredictable."

"Sarmira is the common denominator here. Like I said, we will figure this out, Rory. I promise you."

She grunts. "Says the princess who hates promises."

I jab her in the gut.

"Ow." She giggles.

"I'm still not ready to be queen, but if it means protecting the people that I love, I'll do whatever it takes to heal, to defend them."

Redmae comes over and brushing up against my bed, lifts up both paws, lays them across my body and proceeds to lick my face.

"Really?"

"Well, I'm still an animal. We lick things. I cannot help it."

Rory snickers. "Guess my sister agrees."

I glare at Redmae, saying aloud, "You're lucky I like you."

Redmae gives a small rolling howl.

"Okay, Rover, stand down."

"Who's Rover? My name is Redmae, Wynter."

I shake my head. *"Never mind. Now get down, you're crushing me."*

She licks my face a second time. *"Sorry,"* she says, lying down next to my bed.

"While you were out, all Redmae did was whimper and howl. We knew something was wrong," Rory says.

"Well, I'm back in the land of the living, and it sounds like we have work to do."

"So, you think there is a connection to what's going on out there?" Rory turns toward the entrance. "I mean, we get our magic from the moon, not Dragonscale."

I gasp. "That's it, Rory, I could kiss you!"

"What?" She appears confused.

"The reason magic is dying is because Sarmira must have done something with Dragonscale's power." I look over at Redmae. She, too, is focused on me. "That's my theory, anyway." I clasp my hands together and think. "Tell me, what happened while I was asleep, as much as you can remember."

Nyta comes back with a basket of items before Rory can answer. "I take it you three have been briefed?"

"Not everything, no," I say. "But the look on your face tells me that will have to wait."

"Very observant of you. And you're right." She prepares herbs as she speaks. "I've made a request to the council, and they voted unanimously."

"That's what that message you sent earlier was, wasn't it?" I ask, realizing that the situation is much more severe than I first thought.

She doesn't answer, grabbing a coffer above the shelf.

"How am I to continue with these trials if Sarmira is on the loose, hunting me down?"

Nyta smiles. "Very carefully, my dear."

"Is that what I think it is?"

Nyta opens the top. The heart beats all on its own. "There is one-way to defeat her..." She turns to me as she closes the lid, tucking it into her large bag. "I'll fill you in later, once we have spoken to the others."

"Others?"

She smiles, looking at Rory and Redmae and then back at me. "Your dad, great-grandmother Sara, Geneviève..."

I glance at Rory and she shrugs.

"It's time we go. I can see your strength has returned. You need to go change." Nyta points to a room off to the side. "Your clothes are in there."

Once I'm changed back into jeans and a T-shirt, Nyta picks up my leather jacket resting across the end of the bed and encourages me to put it on, and then grabs her cloak. "Are you two ready?" She glances at the sisters.

Redmae, stretches, sits up, and yawns.

"I'll take that as a yes," Nyta says.

"What, no portals to bounce us from one end of the land to the other?" I joke, looking at Rory.

"It's not far, Wynter," Rory answers.

"I'm sorry, bad joke."

"Use your compass, Wynter," Nyta says. "You try leading the way instead. It will be good practice for you. It'll give you the knowledge you need for the journey you're about to take."

My necklace glows a bright sapphire. I take the locket and open it. The compass inside points to the entrance of the cave. One of the embedded gems inside glows; however, the precious rocks seem to play like dot-to -dots, leading the way. "Nyta, it's a map?"

She smiles. "Now I believe we're getting somewhere. When the Elementals charmed your necklace—"

"Wait, you know about that?"

"I'm a Seer, Wynter, remember? I may be a healer, but I still have the gift of sight, when fate allows it." She puts out the fire before heading out. "Perhaps someday I'll tell you the story of how that came to be." Nyta nods to my necklace. "That shows you the pathway to the destination it wishes you to seek."

"It wishes?"

"The magic within the Elemental compass tells you where to go and you follow it."

"Can I ask it to take me to other places? Like, can I ask it where the Sword of Valor is?"

"It's like an achievement compass. It will light up when you have accomplished a task, and then shows you the way to the next obstacle blocking your path."

"That sounds complicated."

"Does it? Seems it's telling you where to go now, is it not?" She grabs her wooden staff from the corner. "Shall we follow its blue glow?"

"I'm up for the adventure, if you are."

Redmae comes to my side. "Hop onto my back. Save your strength."

I look back at Rory and she nods.

My eyes quickly adjust to complete darkness as the glowing compass leads us through the passageway out of Nyta's cave and I see a light at the end of the tunnel.

27
UNDERGROUND CITY

AN AMAZING SIGHT OVERWHELMS my eyes with beauty as I leave the dark dwelling of Nyta's cave. I turn around and look back to see her home is a small hut carved into the side of a rocky hill with flowers lining the edge of her house. The entrance is a grand fir tree and at the base of the trunk is her door. The tree has grown right through to the top of the hillside where branches of pine needles spread throughout the magnificent evergreen. A well-tended garden surrounds the tree and the entire hillside, and a walkway divides her home from the overlooking cliff where a ravine reveals more greenery.

"What's down there?" I ask.

"Dragons," Rory answers with a devilish grin.

"More dragons? How far down do these caverns go under the city?"

"For miles and miles," she says.

The gems on my locket light up like stars, and I look up to see a deep blue sky. "I was told I wasn't to leave the Island."

"And you haven't," Nyta says. "This is the underground city deep underneath Ashengale known as Crystal Cove. I assure you, we're still on Dragonscale Island. You've been sleeping for a week, which also has given you ample time to charge."

"That's a relief. This is such an unusual place, Nyta. I remember the dark riders reaching Doctor Brekker's office. How do we know they won't try again?"

"None of the dark riders made it out alive," she assures me. "This world underneath the chaotic city of Ashengale is still safe from the war...for the time being, anyway." She presses forward down the path, using her staff as a walking stick.

Dragonscale's words come to mind. "I was told nothing can breach the walls of Ashengale, yet it still happened."

"Yes, well, we intend to remedy that."

I sigh. "Please tell me more about this Underground City. I only know that it hides many creatures thought to be extinct. Is it part of Crystal Cove?"

Nyta gives me a stern eye. "You're near the core of Ladorielle."

"You mean like a world within a world?" I question.

"Something like that, yes." Nyta's staff digs in the dirt with every step she takes as Rory, Red, and I follow behind her. "This city is so large one might call it a country. The underground city is a community, and its name isn't known by many. People on the surface think it's a mythical place. The residents keep to themselves, and most don't travel from beyond this world. Doctor Brekker is their mayor.

I look around to see the vast hills and valleys as we trek along the pathway. Birds fly above, and I hear the faint sounds of an ocean. I'm in awe because this place looks like a whole new world. There's a blue sky, and as I attempt to look beyond what my eyes can see, it appears there is a horizon line. "Is that an ocean beyond those hills?" I point.

Nyta nods. "Before my time, long ago, both planets lived in harmony, prior to the underworld destroying our sun. When the world of Ladorielle came under attack, my people fled the chaos from the sister planet of Elleirodal."

"Yes, I remember Dad mentioned that there was an alliance to save both planets, which is why the eyes of both Ladorielle and Elleirodal share the same molten light."

Nyta grunts. "This is true. And the core of this city operates its power. Thankfully, this world was discovered beneath Ladorielle. It allowed our ancestors to create a new way to protect our dying sun. Of course, they thought if Ladorielle had such a place like this, perhaps Elleirodal might, too."

"And I'm guessing they were right, since the sister planet has an identical eye," Rory adds.

Nyta points in the direction of the ocean. "That opening, is this planet's eye. It gives light to Elleirodal, and their eye is the same, and gives its light to us here on Ladorielle. Beneath the ground we walk is the molten light.

"Many don't reach beyond Ashengale City. And if they do, the only way to reach this country is to be vigorously vetted from the kingdom of Dragonscale Island."

"Dragonscale Island is made of lava and volcanos," I say.

"Yes," Nyta agrees. "And beneath those fissures, valleys of ash, volcanoes, and lava flows, lies Ashengale's caverns, and dwellings. Below that, hundreds of miles deep beneath the surface, is this hidden world." She smiles as though what she said has enlightened my mind, which it most certainly did.

The path we follow winds down along the cliff and the more we travel downward the wider the path becomes. It isn't long before we come to the end and reach a small village.

"This is Nuknir, my village within the community of Crystal Cove, and it's protected by magic. We were fortunate enough to have the molten lava from the 'eye' to cloak our location.

"After the war, the new Dragonscale knew he needed to create a hidden location, a safe haven for all. The underworld was after their own people who had decided to defect. Many had risked their lives to save the people of Ladorielle in the name of peace, so when the Council of Twelve was formed, this place wasn't on their radar. All the council knows is Ashengale is in Dragonscale's Kingdom, and Dragonscale Island is his territory."

I glance toward Rory. "Did you know this area existed?"

"Yes," Rory confesses. "I've known since the day I woke at the Lake of No Return, cured of the Sea Spike poison."

"This was the secret you said you saw."

"Yes, and I saw you here in a vision, but I wasn't sure what that meant until now," Rory says.

Not far off the beaten path, a blacksmith with features similar to Nyta's, hammers out horseshoes when he stops and notices us approach. "How are you this fine day, Rufluk?" Nyta says.

"Priestess Nyta. Good to see you." He comes to greet her. "What brings you by?" He makes eye contact with me. "Who do we have here?" Wiping his hands after taking off his gloves, he comes forward to shake my hand.

"This is a friend's daughter and her pet," she says.

"Pet? I'll show you pet!" Redmae lets out an ominous growl and shows her many teeth.

He steps backward unsure of the large beast, and eyes Rory, attempting to appear calm. "Good to see you again, Huntress."

"My wolf means no harm," Rory says.

"Yes," he replies. "Rumor has it you're a wolf whisperer."

Rory grins. "Something like that, I guess."

"Just stay calm," Redmae says. *"We're still in dangerous territory. As long as no one knows who you really are, we're safe."*

I begin to feel nervous. *"What do you mean by that?"*

"There's a price on your head, and we can't be too cautious."

"Well, that's comforting," I say.

"Nice to meet you," he says, taking my hand. "I'm Rufluk De' Lorikous, but people here just call me Lucky."

"Rufluk. Are the horses ready?" Nyta interrupts.

"Indeed, madame. I'll call for the stable boy to fetch him." His eyes search mine, as if he sees a ghost and proceeds to look inside my head. He snaps his fingers, grabbing the young boy's attention, who is not much older than thirteen.

"What is he doing?" I ask.

"Scanning your brainwaves to make sure you're not an enemy."

"And how can they detect that? Who is to say, he isn't an enemy?"

"Remember Rosie?"

"Yes, she can detect lies and deceit."

"They're also known as angels of truth."

"But if he knows who I am, are we not risking my location?"

"Most will not know who you are in these parts, anyway."

"Tristian," Rufluk begins, "go grab Priestess Nyta's horse in the pasture, will you, as well as two more?"

"Yes, sir. Right away, sir." The youngster nods and runs off.

He drops my gaze. "My Lady, please forgive me, if I had known it was you—"

"Please, no need to apologize," I interrupt, trying hard not to gape at what Redmae revealed. "Did I pass your test?" I ask.

He blushes. "With flying colors." He glances at Nyta. "You know there are spies everywhere looking for her."

"Which is why we need your cloaking horses."

Rufluk nods, looking up at me. "My horses can definitely do that, Priestess Nyta."

"Good. We need to get her to the Hall of Preparation."

"The Hall of what?" I whisper.

Nyta shakes her head and smiles. "You will see."

The boy brings back Nyta's horse, along with two others. "Here is Ghost, Priestess Nyta," the boy says, and hands the reins to her. The white horse greets Nyta with a warming neigh.

Nyta flips the boy a coin.

"Thanks!" He runs off, celebrating.

Rufluk hands me the reins of the second horse. "You can ride, yes?" he asks.

"Of course." I smile, remembering my white mare Eluna.

"His name is Shadow." His coat lives up to the name, with a dark grey hide and dirty white mane and tail. Rory's horse is white with grey spots on its rear. "This is Ash."

Nyta mounts her horse with ease. "Thank you again, Rufluk. We'll be in touch."

He nods, stepping back, allowing the four of us to pass.

Once we reach the outskirts of Nuknir, Nyta says, "I was worried how that might have played out."

"Redmae filled me in," I say.

"Hmm, I suspected as much."

"Well, I'd like to be filled in..." Rory says, sounding annoyed.

"He's an Aerial," Nyta says.

Rory raises a brow. "Really? What's he doing this far under Ashengale?"

"I've never asked. But there are many here, hiding, undetected." Nyta smiles.

"What's an Aerial?" I ask.

"An angel guardian," Rory answers. "They're everywhere but usually never show themselves to those in the physical world." The surprise in Rory's tone makes me more curious.

Nyta quickly changes the subject. "How much do you know about the Hall of Secrets, Wynter?"

"Not much, only that it is a hub to many doors to different worlds," I say.

Nyta stays quiet.

"Wait a minute. Is that where you're taking me?" I ask.

She doesn't answer, but her silence tells me what I need to know. After about an hour, we come to an archway, with cypress trees as a fence. I spy labradorite gems dangling above an arched trellis along with other stones such as amethyst, Lapis Lazuli, and quartz.

"The stones are protection against negative energies. Once we pass through the gate, anything negative will be left behind," Nyta says.

"What's beyond it?"

"A portal to Wisteria Keep, and the Hall of Secrets. This is the gate between both Ladorielle and Elleirodal."

The distracting play of light on the crystals brings back some memories. I remember the story my dad told me about what these beautiful rocks do; how they protect those of good hearts. It shelters those from evil and allows healing energies to do their magic. Prompted by the thought, I look down at my necklace. It isn't glowing blue, but when I open it up, the compass is pointing in this direction through the gate.

"The gate leads to freedom. It's where those who wish to escape the suppression of Elleirodal can safely live, hidden here, by the magic from Ladorielle. The labradorite protects it, and the other crystals work together to support the barrier each having a unique power, so that Wisteria Keep can remain the neutral zone between our worlds."

"How do you know we were not followed?" I ask.

"That's easy. Redmae can sense anyone near a ten-mile radius. Even someone using invisibility can't hide from her power."

"What is she talking about?"

"I'm a dire bloodline. It will all make sense soon."

"Is that why Moyer kept you around?"

"For the most part, I believe so. For years, she tried to clone me, but never quite got it right."

"What about the beast that turned you?"

"He didn't turn me, I mean, yes, I have the werewolf gene now because he bit me and without the antidote, I'll remain a wolf forever and never see my human life again, but before I knew I was a dire wolf, Moyer had already tried to replicate my power. I happened to fall right into her lap, so to speak. The difference is she made werewolves, and that species I am not."

"Care to elaborate?"

"Nyta has told me the story of my bloodline this past week, which makes sense, and I finally know who I am, and why I'm important to the prophecy. The fascinating part is I can read all minds, whereas a werewolf can only stick to the pack's frequency waves. The day I was released from her grasp it severed my ties to the werewolf pack."

"Shall we pass through, Redmae?" Nyta asks. "Is it safe?"

Redmae dips her head in gesture, and we continue on through the arched crystal gate.

People are selling goods on the side of the cobblestone walkway, leading to a huge castle estate ahead. "Are we going there?" I point.

"Yes, the home of our queen," Nyta affirms. "Dragonscale appointed her ruler of this territory as a reward for helping defeat the Underworld thousands of years ago."

"Is she Nuknir, like you?"

"Yes. Her second in command rules the House of Dhalri."

"Which is where?"

"They are all from Elleirodal, hidden from the eyes of the Underworld. You see, The Council of Twelve do not know that House of Dhalri still exists. Legends told over the centuries, say that it collapsed under the attack by the House of Zhir when Princess Petra escaped from her kingdom. She sought refuge with the fae folk, and the Eye of the Raven took Petra under her wing. Much remains a mystery regarding what happened. All we know is that Petra is a direct link to your bloodline."

My heart feels like it's rising to the back of my throat. "Are you saying I'm a descendant of the House of Zhir?" A wave of icy cold panic grips me.

"There is still much we do not know Wynter, and many books that speak of that time were lost. I'm sorry I don't have all the answers. It is believed that your great grandmother Petra and the Princess Petra of history are one and the same, but there isn't any proof."

"That would mean she was over a thousand years old. That would be impossible."

"Aye, very true," Nyta confirms. "Immortals have been known to live longer than a thousand years, however it still doesn't answer the question as to why Sarmira would want her dead..."

"Unless she knew." I think back to Dad's story of when Bryce slashed Sarmira with the Sword of Valor, shattering her into a million shards.

"Because House of Dhalri aligned themselves with the people of Ladorielle, we were allowed to relocate and rebuild, here, under the protection of Dragonscale. We've been hiding from the Underworld ever since."

We continue down the cobblestone path, and for once I feel safe. Nobody appears to pay us a bit of attention. It's kind of nice. I don't feel like I'm being watched.

"Wynter," I hear a whisper.

I turn, and no one is near us. Just a bunch of vendors talking with customers. "Did you hear that?"

"Hear what? The market with people shouting?" Nyta asks.

"Never mind," I say. *"Red, did you hear it?"*

"Just your thoughts and everyone else's."

"So, you didn't hear someone call my name?"

"Nope, why?"

"Nothing. Must be my imagination." I look behind me and nothing stands out of the ordinary.

We pass through an enchanted-looking garden. Trails curve every which way like a maze. "Where to now?" I ask.

"What does your compass tell you?"

"It's turned slightly to the right."

"Then we go right."

Down this path, there are many willow trees paving the way. Their branches drape over the walkway and some of the leaves have fallen, sprinkling over the cobblestone in a green carpet of foliage. It isn't long before we come to a dead end forcing us to go left or right. I look down at my compass. "It says to go left."

"Then we shall go left," Nyta says.

"Why are we putting our faith into this compass when you surely already know the way?"

Nyta chuckles. "I need to be confident enough to know you will use the compass properly. There will come a time that we will go our separate ways."

I nod, leading Shadow down a path with a slight decline and through beautiful knotty pines and luscious oak trees. A giant hill reveals itself in the distance. And at the top is a giant tree. It glows a magnificent blue. "What is that?"

Nyta smiles. "That, my dear, is the legendary blue oak tree, the Tree of Tranquility. It is protected by the fae."

"The fae really exist?" I ask, stunned.

"Of course. The fae are very powerful creatures. You will understand once we arrive at the top of the hill.

We incline, and soon we reach the peak. At the base of the tree is a path winding up and around the enormous trunk. Giant roots weave in and out rising from the ground at the base of the tree. It's like a winding catwalk trailing around the trunk. My brain doesn't comprehend its massive size. It's so big that it would be comparable in size, in human terms to a skyscraper. "The compass is telling me we need to keep going up, to the top of that tree."

Nyta smiles. She dismounts Ghost and leads her to an enclosed pasture to the right of the grand tree to graze. "We will let the horses rest here while we venture up the trunk."

I nod and slide off Shadow, while Rory dismounts Ash.

We take the horses to the stable house where caretakers give the horses their due rest.

"The door to our destination is at the top." Nyta points, looking upward. "There we will meet the others waiting for us."

"I'm confused. Are you saying my father and Aunt Fran are up there in the tree?" *Aunt Fran.* I haven't heard from her since before the fight in the war room. She's a ghost, so I shouldn't be worried. Yet she hasn't come to check on me since I'd woken.

"You'll find out who is there soon enough," Nyta says, encouraging me to press forward.

I step onto the first plank at the base of the magnificent tree trunk and a wood path spirals its way around the tree. Large roots entangle around each beam forming a strong guardrail, with lights dangling. I stare up in awe. "So weird."

Rory puts a hand on my shoulder. "Wait until you get to the top." She passes me by and takes the steps two at a time with ease.

"Showoff. Are you in some sort of a hurry?" I ask.

"Aren't we all? We're almost there."

"Do you think you have the strength to walk?" Nyta asks.

"I can do this. Maybe not as fast as Rory but I can do this."

The compass is true to its reputation, and as I wind around the grand trunk, the compass's needle continues to readjust upward with my every step.

We reach the halfway point and I need to take a break. "Can we sit? My legs feel weak. And this compass is now pointing at the trunk. Is something wrong?"

"Touch the bark in front of you," Nyta says.

Uncertain of Nyta's motive, I do as she asks, and a door appears that wasn't there before. "Uh huh."

Nyta laughs. "It's Ladorielle magic, my dear." She turns a knob on the side which opens it and we walk inside.

It's like looking at a grand hall, similar to Storm River Manor, except the inside is made of wood, and the setup is slightly different. Spiral stairs hug the interior walls of the hollow tree. I look up to see the stairs appear to go upward for miles.

"Hop onto my back. Save your strength," Redmae urges.

I do as Redmae suggests and hop on. *"Have you been here before?"*

"Yes, many times. I mean, back and forth when visiting you and returning to update your family. This tree is the secret gateway between worlds and the Underground.

"Are you saying what I think you're saying…That at the top is the portal to the Hall of Secrets?"

"Yes."

Redmae follows Nyta up the spiral steps with Rory trailing behind us. I feel dizzy as we wind around and around. *"Close your eyes. It will keep you from getting lightheaded."*

I lay my head down on Redmae's neck. *"How much longer?"*

"Not long now."

We approach a door and Nyta opens it. "Here we are. The town's library."

I smile. "Let me guess, you have a Hall of History that leads to the Hall of Secrets." I scruff Redmae's neck.

Nyta clicks her tongue. "Not bad, you're catching on quickly."

"Not really. Redmae spilled the beans earlier."

"Spilled the what?" Nyta looks confused.

"Beans. You know. Little tiny... Oh, never mind."

Like all the other libraries I've seen, this is an exact copy of all the others.

"This is our version of the Hall of History. Here we call it Hall of Preparation," Nyta says.

I slide off Redmae's back and look around in awe at all the identical features.

Nyta leads us to the Hall of Secrets iron door. "I don't have the key," I say.

"You still don't get it, do you?" She glances at my throat.

I touch my locket, and I'm reminded of the attached key my aunt suggested I link my chain to. "How very clever. My aunt said it would open many doors. I guess this is what she meant."

Nyta smiles, gesturing to the lock on the door. "Lead the way, Princess," Nyta encourages.

The iron door opens with ease, and like the Hall of History at Storm River Manor, this too, is narrow, tight, and has a corner we go around before standing in front of a familiar door—that looks just like the green door I'd been to many times before.

"Go on, open it," Nyta says.

In all the times I'd seen Cory do in the past, I insert the key, the doorframe lights up, and the secret door unlocks.

28

NEW PORTAL DOOR

T HE HALL IS AS I remember. A circular room with doors to different dimensions set a few feet apart all the way around the space. It still amazes me that this one portal hub syncs all other worlds together. As I pass the threshold, I notice many familiar faces conversing, but they all cease as one when they see me.

Their stares make me feel uncomfortable. Some people stand while others sit around the oval meeting table. I'm aghast, and I don't know what to say. Everyone is here, and it's as though I never left for Ashengale in search of the Sword of Valor. But as Nyta warned, their solemn faces are an open book; all of them have aged twenty years or more. Clearly something terrible has happened.

"Well, look who the cat dragged in," Blair huffs. She sits next to her brother Chad.

"I see you have escaped the hellhole of Storm River Manor, too," I shoot back.

"Blair, be nice." Chad gets up and greets me with a hug. "Please, come sit." He looks gaunt, and his cheekbones are sunk in. His lips are grey, and his eyes are about to pop from his sockets.

"Are you ill, Uncle?" I ask. I can feel the tension, and the air is heavy.

"We all are," Blair answers. She, too, has similar features. She doesn't meet my eyes and stares down at her hands.

"Redmae, what's going on?"

"This is what I meant when I said the magic is fading."

"Wynter, there is so much to tell you and I—we..." Blair looks at each one seated around the table. "I have no idea where to start."

I raise my brow. "Perhaps from the beginning?" My hungry eyes wander, settling on the assortment of food across the table. "What's the celebration?"

"We are preparing for battle," Chad says as he takes his seat. "It's our last supper before the great battle ahead. There's a lot to cover, and everyone needs their strength. This room is the only place we are protected from Sarmira, it appears."

"I hear it's already begun, Uncle." They all look frail. "Forgive me, but none of you appear to be in any shape for war."

Our attention is diverted as servants push through the room with trays of food.

"Halle?" I whisper.

She looks up. "Good to see you, again, Wynter."

"I didn't expect to see you, here."

"You two have met?" Nyta asks.

"Yes, Scale Café."

Halle smiles as Rosie follows shortly behind her, carrying a water pitcher. "Are you going to have a seat, Wynter?" she asks.

"Rosie?" I murmur.

"Good to see you, dear." Her eyes look swollen, like she's been crying. She pours a glass of water at an empty chair near Chad. "Come sit down."

"Are you okay?"

"I'll be fine." She continues around the table with her water jug.

The room grows quieter. All the attention is focused on me. My eyes drift again across all the faces. "There are so many more of you here than when I left the hall a week ago."

Stepping farther into the room, my gaze wanders, soaking in the appearance of the desiccated supernatural life filling the portal hub. Their aging features have me stunned. I see Thom and Dom, the dwarven twins, along with Zak, Nora's brother, next to them. Zak appears cold, but then again Iknes Shaw always look that way.

"Anyone care to enlighten me as to this horrific scene I'm witnessing right now?"

The room stays quiet. No one answers me. I wait patiently for someone to start talking, but nothing happens, so I go on. "Would someone please say something? The suspense is killing me. I feel like I'm in some sort of alternate reality."

Rosie sets the pitcher of water down on the buffet table, and walks up to me, breaking the silence. Putting her arms around my shoulders, she says, "Wynter, please have a seat." She pulls an empty chair next to Chad. "There is much to discuss."

Stepping forward, I look beyond them and spot Akira, which prompts me to see Arryn standing guard at the Ladorielle passageway where Storm Castle is beyond.

Other things stand out, too, like Garrick, who looks really old, and appears to be on edge, holding a position next to the door to Dragonscale Island, and not showing the calm cool nature I'm used to seeing.

"Nyta mentioned something's happened to all of you, but I didn't picture how bad, until now. Do you think it's Moyer's doing?"

"No, this couldn't possibly be her doing," Chad says. "It's a curse. Dark witch magic. I saw this once before, years ago. Before Moyer fell victim to the possession of Sarmira. I was only a boy, then. We were playing in the garden when something called to us both—"

"Don't, brother." Blair crouches in a chair opposite of Uncle Chad.

He scoffs. "What? Do you think we're safe now, dear sister? It's time to tell them." My uncle coughs.

I know he's of dragon descent. So is my father, Garrick, Aunt Fran, and many others in this room. The only way to kill a Deagon is through the heart. Whatever this curse is if it doesn't affect the heart then they're all safe. But what about the others? An odd sensation comes over me, and instinctively I realize whatever it is that befell them leaves me feeling helpless.

"There is so much to tell and we're not sure where to begin," Rosie says. "The magic is dying, and soon, Ladorielle will be no more."

"Nyta, Red, and I couldn't bring ourselves to tell you. You needed to see for yourself," Rory adds.

My eyes cloud with tears as I glance at all the familiar faces, looking cold, pale, and deathly ill, until I land on the last one, and I stop.

"Cory? Why didn't you tell me you found him?" I cry, and I move toward him in joy, but a hand grabs my wrist to hold me back. It's Blair. "What are you doing? Let go."

"It isn't Cory, Wynter," she blurts.

"What do you mean it's not Cory?" My heart sinks, not wanting to believe her.

"It's Cole." Her eyes glisten as she fights with the words. Black veins appear beneath her skin, then fade. She twitches in her chair, looking at Rory. Her demeanor clearly has changed since the last time I saw her. I can see vengeance in her eyes, but she's holding back her rage.

The person that Blair claims is Cole, rocks back and forth, looking down at his empty plate. His aura has no color. Nothing is there. Normally, a person has some kind of color for me to detect. Grey is the sign of either an undead or someone invisible. Most people have bright auras surrounding them, and on rare occasions, I can see black, which gives me the sense that the person is evil. But Cole has no color, at all.

When dreaming, everything makes sense, then we wake up not making sense of any of it. Cole had a message for me. I wish I could remember. I step closer and stare at him, hoping he will give me a clue that the good side of him is still in there. He looks exactly like his brother, incredibly handsome, but there is a clear indication that Cole has changed. I see within his bright blue eyes nothing but a blank gaze. To see Cole as he is now, and not the predator he once was, ironically terrifies me. I wave my hand in front of his face, but he simply doesn't see it.

Blair swallows hard. I can feel her fear, anger, and sorrow all rolled into one. She adjusts in her seat before answering, "The boys did it to themselves. I watched it all happen in slow motion—" Blair shifts in her seat more, and I can tell the memory is uncomfortable to recall.

This thick-skinned, hot-headed vampire relative of mine chokes on her words. "Cole and Cory were fighting it out, and the next thing I see, Cole stabs Cory in the heart, freezing him in an instant. And in that precise moment, I watch Cole's eyes glaze over in an empty stare, all his emotions evaporated. He, too, was affected by his own actions. Cole is awake physically but intellectually his mind is gone. Although Cory has been petrified physically by the actions of his brother, I know he's alive. I feel it. They're connected somehow, and we haven't quite figured out how to release either of them from this curse."

"Curse? You mean there is more than one?"

I turn my attention back to Cory's brother. "Cole, can you hear me?" He stares into space, as though he's blind. I move near him, and he doesn't budge, doesn't even recognize my presence until I touch his cheek. He flinches. His ears ignore me, but I know his psyche doesn't. I feel his heart quicken to the sound of my voice. He can hear voices; I sense that much. Although he can hear, he does not react. It's like he's sleepwalking, yet when I touched his cheek a moment ago, he felt it. "What did she do to you?" I whisper.

"He can't understand you," Blair says.

"Oh, on the contrary, Blair, he's in there listening. He may not be able to communicate back, but he can comprehend everything that is going on. I can feel it. It's almost as though he's frozen as a statue but can still walk and listen. Moyer's done a number on him, that's for sure—rather I would say Sarmira." I look at Blair. "You're right. The brothers are connected. Of that, I am sure.

Cole's gaze stays focused on the wall in front of him and he begins to hum. I can't take my eyes off him. *"What's really wrong with you?"* I ask, hoping Redmae can give me some answers, but she stays silent.

I take my seat. A part of me becomes confused. I feel a tinge of anger begin to build, aside from the fact that we have established that this is Cole. Deep inside, I crave for the beast to come out so I can use my power, but I know it won't do any good. Until my training is complete, I won't have the ability to find someone with a mere thought. I can remember knowing everything, past, present, and future—Dragonscale showed me when I first transformed—but like a fading dream, those moments don't come to me anymore. It wasn't meant for me to remember.

People stare while Rosie pours me a glass of water. "You all act like you've not seen me before. What is it?"

Dom mutters something under his breath, clanging his fork to his plate for another bite of food.

Dishes from the others start clinking together again, as though it's business as usual. The staring stops, and people begin having small conversations among themselves.

Servants pop in and out of the room from the Storm Castle portal as though it's just another ordinary day. Which reminds me, *"Where is my great grandmother Sara?"*

"She should be arriving soon," Redmae says.

Nyta settles next to me, placing her bag on the floor. A servant takes her cloak and staff and hangs them both in the closet behind us.

Halle pours a glass of water for her mother Nyta, and sets one additional place setting, then leaves. My gaze follows her out the entrance with the rest of the servants.

"I want her close to me. Call it a motherly gesture," Nyta says. "The cruelty happening in our world right now...the shadow walkers won't hesitate to take Halle, like they did Nora, if they found her."

"Like Nora?" I look over at Rosie. "Oh, you mean, holding her at Storm River Manor. I understand. I just didn't expect her to be here is all." I pull at the back of my neck and rub the tension.

"Headache?" Nyta gestures to the pocket of my jacket. "You might need another dose."

I reach in and grab the bottle taking a swig. "Amazing how much things can change in such a short period of time." Sliding the bottle back in my pocket, I plate my food from the array of delicious dishes centered on the table and try to calm my nerves.

Noticing not everyone is here, I ask, "I imagine we're waiting on the queen?"

"Geneviève and your dad. They were tasked with an errand," Nyta says.

Seeing Cole in this state of mind makes me wonder if the real Cole can hear thoughts. Doubtful, I don't trust that with the demon possessing his body, he'd probably hear them, too. Cory used to be able to hear my thoughts; I wonder if he still can. I wonder if I meditate long enough perhaps, I might find him that way. "If this is Cole sitting across the table from me, then that begs the question: where is Cory? Is he still alive?" Each person that was directed to seek out and rescue Redmae at Storm River Manor isn't talking. I pound a fist on the table, and everyone jumps. "Stop treating me like a child." I raise my brow. "Rory?" She stays quiet.

"Fine then I'll talk." I chug down a bunch of water. "I was there, outside my body when Lira cast her blast spell and disappeared. I saw how injured Geneviève was, and that Dad was down, too. I saw Garrick wrap my injured head. And then Geneviève ported us all out to the Druid circle." I look over at Rory. "I saw you and the others—" I stare at Zak, Chad, Blair, the dwarven twins and Arryn. "All of you were there, except Cory." I look over at Cole and point. "He was yelling out 'wraiths'..."

Blair stands. "How do you know about all that?"

"You know how she knows, Blair," Nyta says.

"Yes, but I want to hear her say it."

My eyes burn with fury. Is she purposely trying to provoke me? I smile. I'm not going to play these games. "Yes, Blair you do know. Nyta told me I projected from my body. It's why I couldn't heal myself." I can feel the friction, and it makes me want to hurl fiery flames. I fork more food in my mouth right away because I know if I don't, I might.

My eyes dart to Rory.

The silent pause is deafening.

"We can't see ghosts," Blair says, glaring. "And Cole apparently can. That day in the circle there were wraiths all around us. We didn't know until after we ported that they had cursed our entire group. Redmae saw them too, and she's the one that saved us."

"Are you saying the wraiths are what has made you all ill?" I ask.

"We think so," Nyta says.

"Any idea how to cure it?" I ask.

"No. I have, however, been able to stop the progression."

"I can't help but think it has something to do with the Super Blue Blood Moon," Arryn says. "It's happened before."

"What? When?" Rory asks.

"Ah, yes, I do seem to remember reading about the great Tora'Nari plague," Dom says. "It was a horrid time in history. Nearly wiped out the entire race, am I correct?" He looks at Arryn.

She nods. "Yes, you're correct. My sister and I barely escaped with our lives. All of the symptoms we are experiencing are identical to what I remember."

"So, what do we do?" I ask. "How did your people survive?"

Arryn looks saddened. "They didn't. The only survivors were the ones who made it to the portal gates of Ladorielle right before it was permanently destroyed."

"Well, we have to do something. I can't help but think the events of Cole's actions propelled some kind of curse or spell."

A sound from the circular room of portal doors grabs everyone's attention and all eyes watch as one of them lights up around its frame.

"Isn't that a broken door?" Thom asks in alarm, dropping his fork to the floor with a loud clank.

"Yes, it is," Garrick answers. He draws his sword. "Everyone, prepare to arm yourselves. We don't know who is coming through."

Most of the servants and others who were hiding from the war exits through the doors to Ladorielle, afraid.

"Who would have access to this door?" I ask.

"No one," Garrick answers, "it's been dormant for centuries." He eyes the dwarves motioning them to gather at the opposite side of him.

Nyta casts a protective shield over the entire room. "This will only hold for so long," she says.

Garrick nods.

The doorframe completes its activation, revealing a bright light and a water-like substance filling the interior within. Like all the other portals, this shows a picture of the other side with two people coming through.

I notice the name above the doorframe: Crimson Moors.

29

THE LAST PRINCESS

Two people step through the portal door, wearing clothes I'm unfamiliar with, dressed in all black leather attire. The woman wears a long dark blue cloak with golden stitching around the edges along with a bag that sits on the side of her hip. Accompanying that, is a dagger housed in a golden sheath. The hilt has a rounded tip with the letter S embedded in labradorite. She's young, like me. Not much older than twenty. Her hair is black and her eyes blue, like mine. She looks a lot like me, except she is taller. Her companion wears the same attire in addition to a black leather jacket underneath his cloak. He has blond hair jutted back, a square jawline, and a dimpled chin. He carries a sword on his back. It isn't hard to see they have come from the dark side of the world. *Assassins.*

"We mean no harm," the man says holding up his hands. "My name is Bryce, and this is Petra. We've come to warn you. There has been a time shift of the recent past that may send us all into a tailspin once more."

Nyta lowers her shield and comes for a closer look. "It can't be. Are you Storms?"

Petra raises her chin and looks at Bryce.

He nods. "We are."

Nyta points to the portal gate that they just came through. "That door has been broken for hundreds of years." She looks around the room. "Gentlemen, lower your weapons."

She gestures to our guests. "Come, we were all about to eat. I'm sure you are hungry. You can tell us about your warning."

"They both look a lot like Sir Bryce and Lady Petra," I say.

"I agree." Redmae comes to lie by my side. *"Something tells me they are one in the same."*

"I'm curious, who are you two exactly." Blair scowls. "Petra and Bryce Storm have been dea—"

"Blair, don't be rude," Uncle Chad scolds. "Let them speak."

"I'm a time traveler," Petra says. "I was torn from my world a few years ago and told to search for twelve books, and only when I found them could I return."

"A few years ago?" Rory whispers. "Clearly that isn't possible."

Petra lifts her chin. "Time is spun differently when you're a time jumper."

Nyta eyes Arryn and she nods. Arryn and her cat leave through the Ladorielle door.

"Sounds fascinating," I say. "You must know Aoes then?"

"Wait, Aoes is here?" Petra asks.

"You know Aoes?" Nyta asks.

"Of course. He owns a shop in Wisteria Keep. Or use to. It was destroyed."

"I see." Nyta raises a brow.

"What do you mean? Wisteria—"

Nyta raises her hand and cuts me off. "If you know Aoes, then you must know Thermyah. They're close friends."

"Yes, of course," she says.

Bryce clears his throat. "She was my mother."

"Was?" Nyta seems concerned.

"Oh... Well..." Petra appears confused. "The last we saw of her, she was sucked through the portal that also captured us. We just assumed she was—"

"Dead?" Nyta smiles. "We haven't heard from her in years." She takes a sip of water. "This may become very complicated if we're not too careful."

"I'm sorry. I'm a bit confused," Petra says.

"As are we," Garrick answers. "If I'm correct, you're from the past and of Storm Blood—" He's cut off by the sound of the bell.

"Please rise for Queen Sara," Arryn says.

"Enough of the formalities, Huntress. We don't have time." The queen enters wearing black leather bottoms and a black tunic. A breastplate in our coat of arms décor cover her middle and a long black cape is clipped to one shoulder. "You're absolutely right, Garrick, these two are from the past. And there is only one reason why that would happen.

"You may be seated." Queen Sara smiles. "This is Petra. You might know her as the runaway Princess of the House of Zhir. It's good to see you again."

Gasps and question flint around the room.

Dom stands in protest. "What in Ladorielle is going on here?"

"Quiet, please," she says. "I can understand your concern.

"Treasonous, is what this is." A man I don't recognize yells and is immediately apprehended by two guards.

"Silence!" The queen pounds her fists on the table. "I will not have this room in discord. You all know as well as I, if she were a true Princess of the House of Zhir she would be burning to ash as we speak. This hall is protected. You of all people should remember that, Kollin."

Kollin's face still shows anger. He bows his head in respect. "Forgive me, Your Majesty."

Queen Sara looks about the room, finally landing on my face, and smiles.

"Why are you looking at me?" I ask.

"You're the key to all of it." My grandmother doesn't elaborate, instead, she acknowledges the strangers. "Bryce, Petra, I see you have found the artifacts and have repaired The Book of Secrets to the Crimson Moors.

They bow.

"Permission to speak, My Lady," Petra says.

The queen nods. "As you wish."

"We were met with great resistance from the Zhir army. Many casualties. We request Wisteria Keep, be protected."

"Aye. You have my support. You know that."

Petra looks my way. "My Lady, if Wynter is to pull off finding your great nephew Cory, they will need reinforcements."

"Pardon me, My Lady," Dom asks. "But how do you know these—"

She puts up her hand. "I can understand your confusion, Dom. Petra and Bryce have visited me once before, and we had a splendid conversation. I agreed to help her in finding the Book of Secrets that would unlock the Crimson Moors." The queen appears stoic and spreads out her arms. "But look around. How can we find Cory, my son, and daughter-in-law and help our allies if we cannot find the cause of this current curse plaguing us? But we have a plan."

Queen Sara looks back at Petra and says, "She is the last of her bloodline. She is also the beginning, and she is the mother of all Storms, and also the last Ice Dragon shifter." My grandmother nods. "Show them, my dear."

Petra closes her eyes and stands. She clasps her hands together with her elbows out, chanting in another language. A language I know. *Valjw.* Which means transmute.

"You do not need to say the words out loud," a voice says.

It's the voice I heard earlier when coming through Nyta's village. *"It's you. You, were the one calling my name."*

"I had a feeling I'd finally be able to connect with you once the portal gate was enacted. I've been trying to reach you for some time, now."

In seconds the wind kicks up and ice forms around the walls. Petra transforms into a white dragon.

People step away in awe, stopping short of chaos.

"Wait!" the queen calls. "She means none of us any harm. She is one of us."

I look in awe at the magnificent creature. Her wings glide effortlessly, making a swishing sound with every wave. Her scales glisten like ice crystals and her eyes are bright blue. *This must be why the Storms have blue eyes. It's not because they are Nytemires.*

The ice dragon answers my thoughts, telepathically. *"You must find a way to show them, Wynter."*

"I don't understand." She shows me a vision of her past. Of how she escaped the House of Zhir. How she discovered, like me, her life was based off deception. She shows me the before and after of Wisteria Keep and how it endured such a wicked war.

"In time you will come to understand your true calling, but for now your path leads you in another direction. Trust your instincts and you can call upon me anytime with one simple word. 'Teljw'"

"It means guidance in our language, doesn't it?"

"Yes. Tell no one of our telepathic connection. When the time is right, I will come to you."

Then, just as quickly as she transformed into a dragon, she reverts back into her humanoid self. "Now that you know who I am perhaps we can resolve the many issues at hand?"

Queen Sara nods.

Petra sits. Bryce holds her hand tight and smiles.

"What about you, Bryce?" the queen asks. "Our history books tell us that you were a member of the King's court. Am I correct?"

"I was. I still am." He looks at everyone seated before going on. "I come from a long line of knights. My family were the protectors of the Storms' court..." He pauses as though the memories are painful. He lowers his eyes and wrinkles his brows. His eyes glisten. He clears his throat and continues, as though to brush off his demons from the past. "...before King Zhir of the House of Zhir destroyed all Storms' territories. I am the last of the Knights of the Rose, King's Guard of the Northern Veil. Oath-bound for life to protect and defend the Storm crown. I will always be by Petra's side. It is my sworn duty."

"Thank you for the introduction, Bryce. It sounds like we have work to do." Queen Sara instructs Arryn to guard the door to the portal of Ladorielle, and Garrick to guard the one to Dragonscale Island. "Who volunteers to protect the Crimson Moors portal?" Queen Sara, asks.

Kollin stands. "I will volunteer, Your Majesty."

"Very well." She nods, tilting her head in the direction of the new activated portal. "Now, back to the issues at hand, let me first ask, Petra, how much time do we have?"

She looks down at her hand. "An hour at most."

"What do you mean an hour?" I ask, fear once again creeping down my spine. All this time travel manipulation is playing with my head.

Queen Sara holds up a hand. "We don't really have time for explanations, so I'll keep this brief. Because Petra is a time traveler, it is her gift to wander the pathways of time. Wynter, your gift is to see what cannot be seen by the naked eye—namely entities such as ghosts, wraiths, and the like. It also provides you with the means to interact with these entities through projection, the power to visualize the undead, and the ability to heal others." She looks over at Petra. "She is a—"

"Travelling Mage?" Dom says out of turn. Queen Sara gives him an eye. "Forgive me, Your Majesty." He gets down on one knee.

"Oh, get up, Dom. I told you we can all speak freely in this room, as long as we maintain some sense of decorum. I understand that we are all feeling a bit of excitement over what we've just discovered."

Petra continues, "I've been nicknamed the White Dragon, because unlike most dragon shifters, ice dragons can change into whatever creature they desire And I travel best in bird form. But enough about me." She looks down at her hand. "We're wasting time."

"Rory, how are your porting abilities?" the queen asks.

"Not up to what they should be." She looks down as if she is ashamed. "My jumping spell seems to be the only thing that works." I can tell that Rory doesn't want to look me in the eye, and I feel her heart rate speed up. It's not in her nature to look away. She'll hold her stare with confidence against anyone, even me.

"I see. Well perhaps we should find another Druid. I can't risk you not bringing my great granddaughter back safely," Queen Sara says.

"What is she talking about?" I ask Redmae. Petra looks over at me as though to hear my thoughts as well.

"Not sure."

"Pardon me, Your Majesty, but where should we be going now?" I ask.

Queen Sara points to the Crimson Moors door. "Through there. That is where you must go now. That is where you will find Cory. Without him, we will fail."

My heart weighs heavy, fearing the worst. "Do you know if he's alive?"

"Yes, he's alive," the queen answers. "The only thing saving him now is the Blade of Hope." She lifts her chin and stiffens as though she's about to give more bad news. "And the only one to release the blade is the one who stabbed him."

I look at Cole, his eyes staring into nothingness. "But that's impossible. Look at him. He's in no condition to travel." A vision of the watch Cory wears comes to mind. "Still, Cole presented himself in my nightmare, warning me that he knew where Cory is in Scarlet Hollow. That's where we are going isn't it?"

"Yes," Queen Sara replies, "but first you must be prepared for what you will encounter."

The Ladorielle bell rings.

"Lord Jeoffrey and the Lady Geneviève," Arryn announces.

They stride in with slight joy on their face. I can see a sense of relief from my dad.

"Did you get it? Were you successful?" Queen Sara asks.

"We did." My dad pulls from his pocket a watch identical to the one Cory wears.

30
BOOK OF SECRETS

"**D**AD," I SAY, AND I run to him.

"Wynter you're awake." He hugs me tight. "I'm so relieved you're alive and well. You gave us such a scare."

I giggle. "I have to keep Sarmira guessing, don't I?"

He pulls back and clutches both sides of my cheeks, grins, and kisses my forehead. "Don't ever scare me like that again."

"Dad, I'm fine. I see you have the watch to free Cole as well."

He holds up the time piece for all to see, bringing it back to our full attention. "Yes, it seems we may have run into a bit of a problem along the way, too." He looks over at my great grandmother. "A conundrum, really." He straightens his stance and looks back at Geneviève for a moment and says, "Permission to speak, Your Majesty."

She nods. "Of course."

"Although Moyer has been defeated—"

"Defeated?" I turn to look at everyone else. "Does that mean that Moyer is truly dead—now that Sarmira is no longer a host in her body?"

"Moyer's death was the reason Cory was stabbed," Blair says. "Something in Cole, snapped and that is why the boys dueled it out."

I shake my head. "No. If there is one thing I know, it's this...Moyer isn't dead. I'd see her soul pass. I'd see Sarmira in the physical world—rather I'd see her in my mind roaming. It's the gift of seeing ghosts." I gasp at the realization of my true power. I exhale, pausing as if the world stood still. "How did I not figure this out until now?"

"Wynter?" Rory questions, "What are you saying?"

I'm a bit stunned at my own epiphany. "I thought seeing ghosts was the weakest gift a person could get, but it didn't occur to me until now just how unique it truly is." I guzzle a glass of water before continuing. "Moyer isn't dead, and Sarmira isn't free. Yes, the report of her wreaking havoc on Earth and building a secret army might be true, but she hasn't released Moyer, because I would have seen my evil grandmother pass if she was."

The air in the room grows still.

Staring down at my hands, I say, "I'm not sure why I'm allowed to see some things and other times I don't...perhaps it's because I still need training, but what I do know, Moyer isn't dead." I look at all the eyes in the room staring at me. "And don't ask me how I know, because I don't even know, how I know."

I stiffen as the memories slide back into my head. "I think she—meaning Sarmira—wanted you all to believe that Moyer's vessel had perished. It bought her time."

"Then who was the person Cory stabbed?" Chad asks.

I shake my head. "I wasn't there. You tell me."

"A clone is my guess," Petra says. "My uncle Artan escaped the House of Zhir long ago. Was this Moyer, wearing a cape, with unusual markings in the stitching?"

"Cory and I have such cloaks," Rory says. "They were given to us by Arryn."

Attention is brought to her, where she guards the gate to Ladorielle. "I was instructed by Her Majesty to give them to you," Arryn answers.

"It's true," The queen admits, "but Petra, are you saying Moyer had such a cloak?"

"I can't be for certain, but it is the only logical explanation. Moyer grew up on Elleirodal as a girl and during that time she would have had access to—"

"Yes, I see your point, Petra. Very interesting indeed." She raises a brow. "In that case, we shall assume Moyer is still alive."

"What about the Super Blue Blood Moon?" Blair asks. "We all saw the Underworld army pouring into Earth the day we escaped with our lives."

"I do believe that is the reason the balance of power has been tipped. Somehow that event has played into our moon's forces, and unintentionally been placed into our leverage. Sarmira won't see it coming if we play our hand correctly," Queen Sara says.

Gasps and grunts flit around the room.

The queen smiles. "Now that we are all here, I can officially say we are at war with the Underworld. And we have a plan to stop it." She sits at the opposite end of the table. "I've received information from our allies from every region of Ladorielle as well as the rebel bases on Elleirodal. And so far, the enemy is winning." She pauses. "It has come to my attention that one way we can save the magic is by fighting back the evil Sarmira has unleashed and beat her at her own game."

Chad curves a devilish smile. "You're implying we split into groups?"

Dom speaks out of turn, looking quite nervous at Chad's remark. "Your Majesty, forgive me but—"

She puts up her hand. "Please be patient and let me finish."

Thom takes Dom's hat and smacks his brother with it over the head.

"We have fought many battles, and with each loss, we are weakened and yet strengthened at the same time." She leans in, eyeing all of us. "I'm talking about magic. We fight back with magic."

The news I'm about to hear can't be good. The people around the table are just as eager to know, their faces worried.

"Nyta came up with a brilliant plan, and the council and I agree that it's the best option for the people of Ladorielle."

"What's this option?" This time, Thom gets a whack from Dom.

I whisper to Nyta, "That's the errand you said you had to run earlier today, isn't it?"

"Shh, let the queen finish," she says.

"When a soul dies, the Underworld gains strength. It's what powers Sarmira's undead army. When a magic soul dies, the power it provides them with is even greater."

"What do you propose we do?" Dom interrupts again.

Queen Sara stares at him with an unpleasant expression.

"Sorry." He takes his hat off and bows his head where he sits.

"Countless lives will be lost if Sarmira finds Wynter and ends up taking her soul."

"I keep hearing you all say that, but the necklace will protect me."

"What are they up to?" I ask Redmae.

"I don't know. They haven't revealed their thoughts to me yet."

"The necklace can only do so much," Sara counters. "Soon the magic will be siphoned, never to return, and our planet will die." Sara stands. "I don't think you quite understand, my child. Sarmira isn't after you for your body, she's after your soul, and if she has her chance, you will be the ruler of the Underworld."

"What?" My body goes ice cold.

"It's true," Petra says. "I saw the prophecy back in my grandfather's study. It was the reason I stole the Book of Secrets in the first place."

"Wait, you stole the Book of Secrets?"

"I stole it from my grandfather Vothule, the King of the Underworld and ruler of the House of Zhir." There are gasps of amazement and fear from the crowd at this announcement. "I returned to Wisteria Keep, not knowing the power of that book would set off a series of events. Thermyah, my mentor had no idea I had the book. I still don't know who originally stole the book from the Hall of Secrets."

I turn around, looking at that book now where it lies on the pedestal. "But no one is capable of lifting it off of there now, so how was someone able to do it before?"

"That is the big question, isn't it?" Petra answers. "No one seems to know."

"Our guess," The queen answers, "it has something to do with the destruction of Nevis' Lazoria."

"The planet of dragons? But that's just a myth. A fairy tale. It doesn't exist," Thom says.

"It was explained to me by Thermyah," Petra says. "It wasn't until I landed in another world that I began to put the pieces together through hidden texts, and tomes."

I clear my throat. "So, your visit with us today means—"

"That I have found the fourth book of the twelve portal books lost," Petra interrupts. "I've eight more to go. With each book I find, the stronger Nevis' Lazoria will become."

I turn to Queen Sara. "And you think Cory disrupted the timetable?"

"Not Cory." She looks over at Cole. "His brother."

We shift our attention to him sitting quietly. Still staring at the same wall, not moving an inch since I got here.

"You see, when he stabbed Cory, he didn't just stab him with any old dagger. It was the Blade of Hope. A blade that never should have been used on its intended charge."

Whispers begin and my great grandmother continues to reveal more hidden secrets. "Silence, please." She takes a moment to collect peoples' attention before continuing.

"There are three daggers, each possessing a fraction of the Power of Three."

Rory and I gasp together. *"Red, are you hearing this."*

"Yes. I find this all rather interesting. It's all beginning to make sense."

"The Blade of Truth and Blade of Peace are still missing." My great grandmother narrows her gaze at me. "Find those and you find the Sword of Valor."

"Where do we start?" Rory asks.

"By finding Cory. If he has the Blade of Hope it will lead you to the others. The three blades will be drawn to each other," she says.

I gulp. A cold chill rises up my spine. "I don't understand." My head throbs thinking of all the different tasks ahead of us. "Are you saying because the Blade of Hope has been revealed that soon the other will be, too, and we need to find Cory first, otherwise the underworld will find the missing blades before we do?"

"That's a horrifying thought, Wynter," Dom says.

"Her thoughts are correct, though," the queen confirms. "Chad, you will lead a team back to Storm River Manor and find a way to seal the portal that has opened. Once Moyer is free, Sarmira will be trapped. If we can hold her off long enough, I'm hopeful it will buy us more time to turn the tide with the current war that continues beyond the door of Ladorielle. Isalora is still there, else

Wynter would have known otherwise." The queen looks at me. "Am I right?"

I nod. "I haven't seen her cross over, if that's what you mean."

"Good. That means she and Fran are still holding the gates secure to Scarlett Hollow. Your best outcome is to defeat Sarmira. By doing that, we will send Sarmira there. At least then we might have a chance."

Is that where my aunt has been this whole time?

The hall shakes vigorously, startling many of us in our seats. "We need to get this done before it's too late," Queen Sara says. She braces herself, looking up at the rafters, as some debris falls, while many others—including myself—take cover under the table until the quake stops.

After the walls calm and the rumbling ceases, I ask, "What was that?"

"What humans call an earthquake," Blair says. "It means Sarmira is getting more powerful."

"No, Blair. It means our work here is done," Petra says. "I do wish I could stay and chat, but as a travelling mage, I have no control over what the rune says." She holds up her hand revealing the greyish black stone in the shape of an eye, imprinted into her palm. "It's beginning to glow which means it is only mere seconds before Bryce and I will be whisked away on another adventure. Quakes seem to follow us. It's our indicator that the task we have sought to complete is finished." She smiles at me. "Wynter, we will meet again soon, at another unexpected time. Stay the course, be brave, and never forget who you are."

A breeze flows through the sealed chamber of the Hall of Secrets, followed by a portal bubble opening behind Bryce and Petra. It swallows them both and then closes as quickly as it opened.

We're all left speechless.

"What do you suppose Petra meant by, 'We'll meet again soon?'"

"She's the travelling mage my dear," Queen Sara says. "And she's on quests of her own, just as you are. We stick to the plan."

I stare at her. "What plan?" I whisper.

"To find Cory."

Dad holds up the watch. "And to free Cole."

31
POWER OF THREE

COLE ROCKS BACK AND forth, humming and looking down at his empty plate. He starts mumbling words that don't make any sense.

I attempt to reach him telepathically.

"Cole, please, if you're in there and can hear my thoughts, hold off this demon as much as possible. We're coming back for you, I promise."

"I don't think he can hear you," Redmae says.

I look at the people in this room. They're all probably just as overwhelmed by the information given to us today. *"People are on edge."*

"We all are."

The servants clear away the dishes as my mind fogs, thinking of what is about to happen.

"Do you think it will be painful for him? Placing the watch on him, I mean?"

"I wouldn't think so."

Cole's moaning is an ominous reminder of what happens when a soul becomes possessed, and it sends chills down my spine. I look down at my necklace, and it glows the shade of blue that warns of danger approaching. *"Something tells me Cole is fighting the demon within him."*

My mind immediately wants it to be Cory, but I know it isn't him. Cole sways, mumbling jumbled words until his words finally form. "Wraiths, they're coming for us," he shouts. His black aura spreads around his body.

He startles everyone. Many voices whisper in the hall, and I feel their anxiety as tensions rise. Again.

"Cole's about to go through one of his episodes. Jeff you better make this quick before it's too late." Blair works to calm him. I can feel her heart quicken.

"I'm worried. Do you think she can hear us?"

"You mean Sarmira? You think she's inside his head?"

It takes but a second for me to clue in. "Wait," I say. "I think Cole can hear us, and although he's frozen, he's listening." I turn to look at my great-grandmother. "I can see his black aura. At first, I didn't put it together, but I think I get it now."

"How is that possible?" Blair asks. "No one evil can enter this hub."

"The balance of power has been weakened, Blair," Sara says.

"I think they are both in there. Cole and the demon possessing him," I say. "The demon part of him is listening."

"Are you saying that everything we have said in this room, Sarmira knows about already?" Dom asks.

I nod. "I think so. It isn't too clear, but I just remembered something."

"Something in your dream?" Nyta asks.

"It sounds impossible, but I remember Cole mentioning that a demon possessed his body, and he was trapped like his brother." This propels me to remember what Cory said back when we were still at Storm River Manor. "Sarmira knew the shadow walkers every move, they were an extension of her," I say. "I realize dreams are not always accurate, but this is the only thing that makes sense. How else would Sarmira always seem to be one step ahead of us?" I stand, making eye contact with both Chad and Blair. "If we have jewelry to protect us, then the only missing link" —I look back to Cole— "is him."

"And here I thought it was the cameras," Blair says, smirking.

"Then Sarmira knows we're about to visit Storm River Manor," the queen says.

"Unfortunately, I believe so. Yes," I say. My throat goes dry.

I overhear Queen Sara whisper to herself. "How did I not see this coming?" She penetrates my thoughts. *"Are you sure about this?"*

"I know she can hear us, Great-Grandmother. I didn't grasp it at first. But Cole is in there and so is the demon, and I think he's relaying everything we say to Sarmira."

"Then it means this demon possessing Cole, also knows where Cory is, and knows what we're about to do, too."

"Precisely," I add.

"Might I suggest we blindfold him, your Majesty," Thom offers, "so we do not add to the information Sarmira is so sneakily trying to obtain?"

"And ear plugs?" Dom adds.

Cole screams, "No." He gets up onto his feet and runs right for me. His eyes glow bright blue and beams shoot forth. The light from him is so bright that it has me afraid they're laser sharp—sharp enough to sear through the stone walls surrounding us.

Dad thwarts Cole's attack and slams him to the floor, but Cole is quick and before Dad has a chance to put the watch on him, it's knocked out of his hand and tossed across the floor. Cole then goes for Dad's throat.

"Dad, watch out!" My thoughts rush through a multitude of past life-threatening experiences. This is another test, isn't it? My first test was to learn to shift, and my second was truth—I know who I am. My third is trust my inner peace and allow my instincts to guide me. Trust my instincts, else I will char every man, woman, and child who walks in my path that may upset me. It's something Dragonscale said to me after I charred the floor while practicing. I take another swig of the medicine that is nestled inside the pocket of my jacket, before shouting, "Cole!"

His neck snaps in my direction and his laser eyes strike me. But they don't seem to affect me. Interesting. I tuck this revelation away for later. I return with a blast of my own magic, encasing him in ice, and it knocks him unconscious. "Do it now, Dad!"

He places the watch on Cole.

Nyta huffs, as though she's pleased. "Perhaps that spell worked better than I thought."

"Huh? What spell?" I look at her, confused.

"The spell that was cast before you woke. Your trial is complete."

"Hang on a second… I can transform now, or do you mean I can leave the Island?" I feel the rage inside my veins, but I have better control than before. I can feel it bonding to my soul.

"You have the temperament to control the rage," Nyta says. "I have to admit, I was expecting something different."

"How so?"

"It may not make any sense to you right now, but Wynter, you're fully charged, and free to roam the world as you please. Cole's soul is back in his body which has given the Power of Three, some energy that was lost."

"Are you saying that is why magic was tipped?"

"No, I'm saying you passed a test, and Cole passed a test within Scarlet Hollow which allowed the both of you to gain more magic that will ultimately help us all."

The room grows quiet again. All the attention is focused on me, as though I'm going to burst into flames at any moment.

Shock permeates my body as a sudden realization comes to me. "I know what to do," I say, lifting my chin. My stomach sloshes, and I put my head between my knees. "I know what we need to do."

"So, do we," Nyta says, looking at Dad. "The watch you placed on Cole will protect him."

"So, the demon in him is gone?" Blair asks.

"Only one way to find out," I say. Cole is still knocked out from my ice blast. "Shall we wake him?"

I look at Redmae.

She grunts, lying down by the fire.

One of the doors lights up in the hall. It's the one from Storm River Manor

"Who can that be?" Blair asks.

I feel my body tense. "Relax," Dad says. "It's probably Derek."

"Wait, he's alive?" Chad asks. "I saw Cole kill him in the fight at Storm River Manor."

Derek and another woman comes through. She is unfamiliar to me.

"Mom? Is that really you?" Blair asks.

The woman takes in a deep breath, setting her eyes on Blair. *"Her birth mother?"* I ask.

"Yes, it's Drena. We all thought she was dead. I watched her die myself. So. I'm just as surprised as you."

"Drena, it's good to see you again. We have a lot of catching up to do," the queen says. "Now that we have you two here, we can proceed as planned."

A cry rings out and it draws our attention.

"What?" Blair asks, confused.

"Your skin, it's—" one servant says.

"What about my skin?" Blair panics and runs over to the mirror above the buffet. "It's back to normal," she adds, turning around and smiling. "Your complexion is clearing, too," she says to Dad.

Everyone gasps in awe.

"The magic is reversing. It may have something to do with the watch Jeoffrey put on Cole's wrist," Nyta explains. "It means Cole's spirit must be free."

"But what has that to do with this reverse aging that's happening to me?" Blair asks.

"Honestly, Blair, I don't know," Nyta answers. "Cole is your son. There must be a connection between you and him." She looks around at the rest of us. "Not everyone is affected by this. Jeff and others are still aging. I'll need to study this more. Until we find the cause of our problem, the magic will continue to drain. All it means is that Cole and Wynter share the power of balance." She looks at Blair. "You're somehow connected in this webbed mystery. My guess is magic will still be drained as long as Sarmira has power on Earth."

"How long before you think Cole will wake?" Dad asks.

"I don't know, but we can't wait for that—we also need to find Dragonscale. He's most likely the reason magic is dying," Nyta says.

"We haven't heard from Dragonscale since the day you and the others fought off Lira and Miles in the War Room," Queen Sara says.

"Where do you suggest we start this whole grand adventure?" I ask.

"Your locket should tell you the way," Nyta answers.

I open the amulet to see that Nyta is correct. The compass needle turns in an uncontrolled spin. "What's it doing?"

"It appears to be undecided. Hmm, interesting," Nyta says.

Cole seems to be coming to and he begins to hum again.

"Nyta, I thought you said the watch would work?" Dad asks.

"Yes. It's supposed to. I don't understand." She looks at me.

Cole opens his eyelids, and a beam of blue light shoots from his eyes, still encased in my icy blast.

"Stay out of his gaze," I say. "It's her, Sarmira. She's taken over his body. The demon that once possessed Cole is no longer there."

"How do you know?" Chad asks.

"Because I hear her laughing in my head. Rather in his."

"That explains why the watch isn't working; she's much too powerful," Nyta says. "Her magic might destroy Cole's soul."

"I'm onto you, Sarmira. I will free Cole from your miserable grasp, and then I'm coming for you."

"You think you can beat me, child?" Her malevolent laugh rings through the cavities of my brain. *"Cole and Cory are with me now—there is no saving them. And soon, I'll have you, too. You're playing right into my hands."*

"Get everyone out of here, now." I move toward Cole.

"Wynter, what's going on?" Rory asks.

"Rory, you need to get everybody out. She's here, she's in Cole's head. In this very room with us."

"I will find you, Sarmira, and when I do, I will kill you."

"Good luck with that." A shock of electricity ripples through the hub. Shrieks of panicked voices follow.

"Everyone out, now!" Neither water nor fire will absorb the shock; I have but a split-second to decide.

I grab onto Cole and absorb the hit, while many in the portal hub flee, screaming.

"No, Wynter," Dad shouts. "She'll take your soul, too."

He runs toward me and attempts to knock me from Cole's grasp. I feel someone tug at my hand. Before I have time to react, I'm suddenly ported out of the Hall of Secrets.

32
OUT OF ASHES

WE LAND IN A strange area, and I'm wondering where I am. Are we dead? Not possible, this doesn't feel like a spiritual experience. Besides, my body throbs in pain, like I did a two-hour workout at the gym.

I struggle to stand, assessing the environment I've jumped into. I appear to be at the edge of a forest. The trees are a variety of fir and maple with colors of oranges, yellows, and reds blending together. The eerie part is I don't hear the sounds of any birds, only the rustling of fallen leaves.

The absorbed shock I took through Cole's mind still reverberates through my brain. I can still feel the evil of Sarmira's presence trying to penetrate my psyche, although it's fading quickly.

Looking at the maroon sky with its dark cherry clouds, I have an eerie feeling I'm no longer on Dragonscale Island. Lightning ignites behind the cumulus clusters, giving me reason to suspect

I'm no longer on Ladorielle. This looks all too familiar. I've been here before but cannot place when. Did I dream all this again? Am I back at Scarlet Hollow? Was the meeting with Nyta, Red, and everyone in the Hall of Secrets all another illusion?

"No, you're not dreaming," Redmae says.

I hear her grunt and whine in pain but can't locate her. *"Red, are you okay?"*

"Um, I think so?"

"Where are you?"

"I don't know."

I spot Rory lying in some bushes, rising unsteady to her feet. "Hey, are you okay?" I dash to help her up.

"Yeah." She grunts. "Oh, my head." She places her hand on her skull. "Where's my sister?"

"I haven't found her yet. But I hear her in my mind. She's good. Let's hope everyone else made it out safe, as well."

I turn a full circle assessing our surroundings once more. "Rory, how did we get here? What happened, back at the portal hub?"

Still a little disoriented she says, "I panicked. I didn't want a repeat of the past blasts Sarmira has managed to create, so I pulled you out before Cole—Sarmira could destroy you." She places her hand on her skull again. "Oh, my head. This feels like a migraine."

"Here, let me help." I place my hands around Rory's temples, hoping my curing abilities will work. Plus, it will confirm I'm not dreaming this time. "Feeling better? I'm still new at this healing stuff."

"Yes, thank you. That ability of yours may come in handy in the future."

Movement a short distance away alerts me to a pair of scarlet eyes glaring through the dark forest. It's Redmae. At least I hope it's her. *"Have you seen anyone else?"*

"No, not yet." She comes forth through the bushes. Her coat is covered in leaves, dirt, and brush.

"You okay?"

"No broken bones that I know of."

A wicked laugh calls out, and we all turn to see nothing. "Please tell me you guys heard that?" I ask.

"Yes," Rory says.

"I heard it, too," Redmae confirms.

"We're not alone. Someone else is here in the woods with us," I say.

I feel my feet lift from the ground and lose control of my movements. "What's going on?" I flail in the air, attempting to gain control, and notice Redmae and Rory are levitating as well. "Wait, I know we can't be dead. I healed you, Rory. I can't do magic like that when dreaming." I look down to see our bodies huddled on the ground. Both Rory, Red and I are slumped over. "Apparently it's another twist, in the many we have encountered lately." The memories of my nightmare return.

"What? No, I'm not dead!" Rory's screams echo.

"Red, can you hear me?" I ask telepathically.

"Yes. And my sister is being dramatic as usual."

"I heard that," Rory says.

"Hang on a second, you can hear us, too?" I ask.

"Loud and clear," Rory confirms.

"That begs the question, why are all three of us in the air, and how can my sister hear us?" Redmae questions.

"Not possible." I look down again at our bodies lying on the ground, appearing lifeless. "I agree, Red. How are we all experiencing the same thing?" I say aloud.

"Wynter," a voice whispers.

"Cory? Is that you? Who's there?" I ask and look behind us. There is nothing there. Rumbling clouds thunder, and deep red shadows move rapidly across the sky.

"Wynter, who are you talking to?" Rory asks. She appears a little stunned that all three of us are floating, then looks below her. "Please tell me we're not dead." I feel Rory's worry. Her heartbeat is panicked. "This is all my fault." Her eyes widen. "Wait, what did you just say to me?" she asks.

"I didn't say anything," I reply, raising my brow. This is a little creepy. "Are you hearing voices too?"

Rory seems unsure. "I–I don't know. I heard your voice, but you're right in front of me. But your voice sounded malevolent." She squints. "Wynter, what's going on?"

"Either we all projected, or we're dead. Whichever it is I am in no mood for round two at being a ghost." I look down at our physical forms lying unconscious on the ground. "I think we're in the Crimson Moors and on our way to Scarlet Hollow."

Rory protests, "Impossible. That would mean we're—"

"Dead?" I finish. "Precisely." I look at Redmae and gasp. "You're not a wolf anymore."

She doesn't notice until I point it out to her. "Guess I know now when I die, I won't be in wolf form," she jokes.

"Not funny, Red. We're going to fight and get back to our bodies." I look down, and they follow my gaze.

We see smoke scale upward toward the sky, not too far from us.

"What's that burning over there?" Rory points.

The plumes are dark. "I don't know, but if it's a fire, then we need to wake up before the flames reach us," I say. I work hard to keep calm.

Rushing sounds of water distract me, and I hear multiple voices call, *"Wynter!"* All of them whispering in different directions. Fearing that this is becoming another nightmare, I ignore them and instead focus on how I'm going to get my body back. *Please, don't let this become another dream stamp. I'm sick of this.*

I swim through the air, weightless, but I don't gain any distance. I know it's not my time to go. I refuse to allow the darkness to consume me. The voices become more prevalent and forceful the more I ignore them. It's like my will isn't my own.

"Let's link hands. Don't listen to the voices calling. Ignore them. We need to will ourselves back to our bodies," Rory says.

My mother Isalora appears. *"Come with me."*

"Wynter, it's a trick. It isn't her. Close your eyes," Rory says.

Isalora gets angry and pushes Rory, breaking our hands apart. Rory sails back to the ground, and I watch her slam back into her body and take a deep breath.

She scrambles, getting up, saying, "No." Rory looks up to where we both hang above her. "I can't see you, but I know you're up there. Fight back!" She looks down at my body and checks my pulse and looks up at me again, as though she can see me. "You're not dead. You're projecting again. Wynter, fight!"

"Wynter, can you hear me?" a different voice says in my head.

"What is with all these voices? Who are all of you?" I look up to the sky.

"I hear them, too," Redmae confirms, *"but Rory is right: we have to fight this."*

The silhouette posing as my mother extends a hand. *"I'll show you."*

"Don't go to her. It's a trap. She's just an illusion," Redmae says.

Again, like with Rory, the Isalora-spectre slams Redmae, severing the connection between us, and sends Redmae back to her body. She howls, confirming she's back in wolf form. I hear arguing and yelling coming from Rory.

I look at this entity that resembles Isalora. *"You're not real."* Dragonscale taught me discernment, and my senses tell me this is false evidence appearing real. Fear.

Isalora's rage increases, and she sends more whispers, trying to get inside my head. She attempts a different tactic, changing her image to look like Cory, and holding out a hand for me to come forward. *"Reach deep into your soul. Concentrate. Visualize where I might be and come."*

My necklace glows blue, warning me of the danger. "You're not Cory. You're not my mother. And you're not going to get what you want. Now leave!"

I hear the faint sounds of birds singing. The rush of the water becomes softer. A mist appears, and I lose sight of everything in front of me, including the image of faux Isalora.

A powerful force pushes me, and like with Rory and Redmae, I'm slammed back into my body. I gasp for air, sitting up.

Rory strangles me with a hug. "You're back! You had us worried."

I struggle to breathe. "R-Rory."

Redmae brushes up against her sister, encouraging her to ease up.

"Oh, sorry." She smiles. "Forgive me, but I've never been more relieved than I am now. We at least had Nyta last time. This time, there was no way to heal you. What was that all about, anyway?" Rory asks.

"I don't know, but something tells me it's not over."

We all hear a moaning call out behind some brush, a few feet away.

Red growls.

"Who's there!" I call.

"Cole," the voice answers in my head.

"Impossible. Show yourself."

"Wynter, what is it?" Rory asks.

"They claim to be Cole."

"Impossible."

"That's what I said."

Redmae paces ahead. *"Wait here."*

"Are you kidding me right now? I'm coming with you." Ignoring her, I follow.

Redmae grunts.

Cautiously we pass through thick brush to find Cole lying face down on the ground. His body is badly burned. Fabric clings to his skin and his face is almost unrecognizable. Smoke escapes what little clothes are left on his body.

"Is he still alive?" Rory asks.

I check for a pulse and nod. "Barely. But how did he come through?" My stomach clinches at the thought of those we left in the Hall of Secrets. Seeing Cole this way ignites a fear far too great, and I lose my footing and fall backward. Realizing who was left behind in the horror of the electrical storm, I say, "Let me try and heal him."

"Are you serious?" Rory exclaims. Her anger rises. "After what he just pulled?"

He opens his eyes and we all gasp.

Seeing me, he smiles. "I'm finally free from her grasp." He swallows hard and coughs.

"He's dying. Can you see into his thoughts, Red?"

"You mean can I see the demon? No, it's gone." Redmae circles around to the other side of Cole. *"But Wynter, he's a vampire, and the only way they can die is—"*

"By fire." Aloud I say, "Rory, relax. It's truly Cole. Putting the watch on him worked." Cole's heartbeat is so faint I can barely feel it. *"We can't let him die. He's the only one who knows where Cory is."*

I reach deep into my mind and use my healing magic and attempt to heal him. "Sara was right. The magic isn't as strong as it used to be. Even mine is fading." My hands glow to heal Cole. *"Nothing is working. Red, I can't heal him."*

Cole's breathing speeds up as he attempts to grab my hand. "House of Bloodbane."

Before I have time to react, Cole's body bursts into flames, singeing him to ash.

"No!" I scream.

Rory grabs my arm to pull me from the burning flames. "Are you nuts? You will burn like him."

"Yeah, I guess I am, Rory. Cory's brother just died. My family is dying. Every time we think we've made progress; something pulls us backward. Forgive me if I'm a little distraught, okay?"

I back away, knowing we will never find Cory now. "Sarmira was right. She will never allow us the upper hand. She knew we would find a way to reach Cole, so she eliminated him before we could get to Cory."

"Listen to me, Wynter, we will find another way." Redmae brushes up against my side to try and comfort me.

"People don't spontaneously combust like that." I'm taken aback by what's happened.

"I don't think he spontaneously combusted. He was caught in the electrical surge like all of us, except Sarmira finished him off.

It was probably her plan all along. Wynter, we will find Cory. Redmae and I both know how to track." She puts a hand on my shoulder. "Trust me. We will find him."

"I know, Rory. It just feels like it's two steps forward and one step back in everything we do."

"I don't understand any of this, either," Rory says. "If Cole was free from the demon, how did he burst into flames like that? None of this makes any sense."

"The Underworld is what happened," I say, throwing a fireball at the bush next to Cole's remains. "Now, what are we going to do? I have no idea where we are."

"I do. We're on Elleirodal, the identical planet to Ladorielle," Redmae says. And those hills will lead to the Crescent Mountains. But what's between them is the Crimson Moors.

"How do you know that?"

"Because of that." She points her nose in the direction of a ledge where a lighthouse overlooks the ocean below. *"My mother told us stories of when she was a young girl, and how she escaped a tracker—a dark witch that marked her for life. She has no memory of it. The journals she left behind gave her clues that she allowed a seer to wipe her memories. It was the only way to keep her hidden from the House of Shadow Raven."*

The setting is eerily similar to the one in my dream stamp. A breeze wisps through my hair. *"It's déjà vu, again."*

"Wynter, why do I get the feeling you've been here before?" Rory asks.

"Because I have." I turn to look at Rory. "Both Redmae and I were here in my dream. And I find it a little creepy that the dream I had is unfolding before my very eyes." Chills run down my spine thinking about it.

"I wonder if there is a cave, too?" I ask.

"Guess we should find out."

"Hang on a second. Are we just going to leave Cole's ashes here?" Rory asks.

"You have a better idea?" The smell and taste of ash lifts in the winds. "And why do you suddenly care about Cole? Rory, he's dead. What more do you want me to do? It's not like we have an urn lying around. Besides, possessed or not, Cole was a vampire. I'm guessing he's permanently in Scarlet Hollow now."

"Have you forgotten the prophecy?" Rory presses. "And what are we going to tell Blair?"

"What prophecy? I haven't a clue how to find Cory, defeat Sarmira, or find Dragonscale, let alone complete some prophecy spoken of my future. The three to be one isn't Cory, Cole, or myself. Isn't that obvious? Because he's dead." I stare back at Cole's ashes. "As for Blair, I have no idea how I'm going to tell her about this. Now, come on, we need to focus on how to get out of here."

The lighthouse ahead looks farther than we anticipated, and we're quickly halted by a large gorge between us and it.

"Now what?" Rory asks. She, too, looks unsure. "I don't think I can jump us across that." She turns, looking at me with curiosity. "What's so appealing about that place, anyway? I mean, I know you think you've seen it before. But we're in a strange new place. I don't have a good feeling about this."

"Neither do I." I tilt my head, looking down at the crevasse. "But something tells me that place is our ticket out of here."

"If what you say is true, and we're on Elleirodal, then—"

"Doesn't matter. Cory and Dragonscale are still missing. And we have to find them." I turn around once more, peering in the direction where we left Cole's burning ashes. "I know you don't understand, and neither do I for that matter, but there's someone in the lighthouse we must see."

"How can you be so sure? And what makes you think you failed?"

"I don't know. Maybe because Cole is dead. This wasn't in the plans."

Rory nods, taking a deep breath. "So, what's so interesting about this lighthouse you're so eager to see?"

Flashes of memories flit across my mind. "The lady in my dream predicted I would see this place in the real world."

"And how do you know it wasn't Sarmira disguising herself yet again?" Rory asks.

Rustling sounds in the brush behind us grab our attention. "We're not alone," I say.

Rory flinches, grabbing her quiver. "What was that?"

I hear her heart race, as does mine, and her sister growls. *"Red?"*

"I don't know." She prowls. *"Stay behind me."*

Vicious growls and multiple red eyes poke through the shadows from the dark forest edge before us.

"I know those glares, Red."

"So do I," she says, growling back defiantly at the trees.

Behind us, I hear the ocean waves crash against the cliffs below. "There's nowhere to go but down, guys."

A rumbling laugh echoes and a familiar female voice coos. "You will never escape my wrath." We can't see her, but that voice of hers is deafening. Sarmira.

"How are we not in Scarlet Hollow, Red?"

"I'm just as lost as you. It's as though we're in the undead world, yet we're not ghosts."

"Sarmira! You won't get away with this," I say.

"Hmm, now, where have I heard this before? Ah yes, I remember your mother said those words to me right before I stole the heart from her body." She gives a wicked laugh.

The wind kicks up and a funnel cloud descends the lands between us and the forest. Sarmira appears.

Her black hair and green eyes accentuate her emerald gown. She appears just as she did in my dream. But her beauty is clouded by evil intentions. She smiles, her glare malicious. "It's simple, your soul for his."

"Never. Tell me where he is," I demand.

Rory brings her bow out and prepares for a fight. Redmae growls louder.

Sarmira notices Redmae's demeanor. "It's a shame you left. We could have had so much more fun together, Redmae."

Redmae paces in front of both Rory and I while Sarmira steps slowly back into the dark woods, passing through a host of ghouls that assemble in front of her.

The ruby eyes, filling the forest behind her, glow brighter as they begin spreading out to either side, revealing their true forms. Sabretail Prowlers.

Moments later, a gigantic, winged beast emerges from the trees, roaring behind Sarmira and the sabretail prowlers. The ghouls fade like ghosts evaporating with the wind and disappear while the prowlers scatter through the woods. They look as startled as us.

Smoke rises from between the black scales of its plated skin. The creature is massive. and circles about, as though taunting us, yet it hasn't tried to kill anyone.

"A dragon," I whisper under my breath.

Rory prepares to shoot.

I throw my arms up. "Wait."

"Wait? Wynter, have you lost your mind?"

"Perhaps, but if it wanted to harm us, it would have done that already."

Redmae continues to pace back and forth, looking up and growling at the creature.

Sarmira and the a few remaining prowlers glare at the beast. Clearly, they were not expecting this monster to appear. Sarmira disappears, leaving the sabretails to defend themselves on their own.

"What do you see, Red?" I ask.

"That's just it. I can't see anything. I failed to mention I cannot read the mind of a dragon."

"Right. Somehow I knew that," I say, thinking back to when Namari once told me that dragons have their own inner language.

"Shoot now and ask questions later." Rory releases her arrow between my outstretched arms, and I can't stop her this time. It hits the flying lizard in the chest. The shaft breaks in half upon impact, angering the beast.

It roars, opens its mouth, and breathes out a massive fiery blast, igniting the trees around us and causing the prowlers at the edge of the woods to all go up in flames with it.

"Rory, I told you not to shoot!"

"I know, but it was too close for comfort."

"Well, you managed to make it angrier."

"So, what now?"

"Run!"

The dragon circles around and makes a beeline toward us.

We all race for cover but before we have a chance, the dragon swoops in, grabs us all in its massive talons and takes us high into the sky leaving behind fire and ash. "Got any other bright ideas, Rory?"

33

THE LETTER

"Excuse me, might I have a word?"

He turns, looking shocked. She smiles. Good, it's him. Her long black cloak hides her features.

"Who are you? How did you get in here? Are you a spirit, too?

"I have my ways." She's amused by his wonder and comes closer. "You're Cory, right?"

"Yes, how do you know my name?" He stands.

She can't help but notice his physical body lying on the dais. The Blade of Hope sticking from his chest. Her plan must work. She must play her cards very carefully. "Again, I have my ways." Her eyes glow blue. It's almost hypnotizing.

"What do you want?"

"I have a message for you." She pulls something from her pocket.

"Is Wynter coming?"

The stranger is confused for a moment by his words. "Ah, Wynter, yes. I have seen that path take place, and if she continues that route, you will see her soon. But that isn't why I'm here."

"Then why are you here?"

"I've come to warn you." She moves closer, holding out her hand.

"What is it? Is my family alright?"

She ponders a bit. "Family. I believe all is well, but there is something you should know. It's about your father. Here, take this."

Cory laughs. "Now that's funny. I don't have a father."

"Oh, but you do. And he wants to meet you. Would you like that?"

"Hang on. My mother believes he's dead."

"He's very much alive." She inches closer, and hands him the note. "It was nice meeting you, Cory."

"Wait, who are you?"

The woman grins. "I'm The Eye of the Raven. She transforms into a beautiful bird with sparkling blue eyes and flies off, disappearing into the Scarlet Hollow mist.

He opens the note:

Cory,

I know you probably have many questions. If you want the answers, seek out the Keeper of the Lighthouse. They will tell you how to find me.

Sam

The letter ignites in flames, and Cory drops the note as it crumbles to ashes.

GLOSSARY

The Storms

Ailbert Storm: The middle sibling of the three Storm brothers, Gavin and Bram. His Wife: Sara Deagon. Their Son is Ian. Great grandfather to Wynter Storm.

Arik Storm: Son of Gavin Storm and Isobel Deagon - Storm Wife: Maura Moyer.

Blair Storm: Mother is Drena (Vampire). Father is unknown, but she knows she's a Storm. Adoptive Mother: Madame Moyer. Her sons: Casey, Cole and Cory. Born a vampire.

Bram Storm: The youngest son of Bryce and Petra Storm. His wife is Clarice. Their sons are Derek and Daniel.

Bryce Storm: The knight that killed Sarmira's original body, causing her to exile her remaining years as a wraith. Bryce is married to Petra. They have three sons: Gavin, Ailbert and Bram.

Casey Storm: Son of Blair. Born deformed. Redmae's best friend. Father unknown at this time. Cory and Cole's older brother.

Chad Storm: He is the son of Madame Maura Moyer-Storm and Arik Storm. Jeoffrey's younger brother. Wynter Storm's uncle.

Clarice Storm: Married to Bram Storm. Died in childbirth.

Cole Storm: Son of Blair and twin brother to Cory. Born a vampire. Father unknown at this time.

Cory Storm: Son of Blair and twin brother to Cole. Born a vampire. Father unknown at this time.

Daniel Storm: The son of Bram and Clarice Storm and Derek's older brother.

Derek Storm: He is the Son of Bram and Clarice Storm. Daniel's younger brother.

Eleena Storm: Married to Ian. Mother to Isalora and Francesca Storm. Grandmother to Wynter Storm.

Francesca Deagon-Storm (Fran): Older sister to Isalora and Daughter to Eleena and Ian. Sara Deagon Storm is her grandmother. Wynter Storm's aunt. Her formal name is Drelanda.

Gavin Storm: Oldest brother to Ailbert and Bram. Parents are Bryce and Petra Storm. Son is Arik.

Ian Storm: Son of Ailbert and Sara Storm. Husband to Eleena. Their daughters are Francesca and Isalora. Wynter Storm's grandfather.

Isalora Deagon-Storm: Mother to Wynter Storm and wife to Jeoffrey Storm. Her parents are Ian and Eleena Storm. Her grandmother is Sara Deagon-Storm. Younger sister to Fran.

Isobel Deagon-Storm: Sara's younger sister. Wife of Gavin Storm and mother to Arik Storm. She's the grandmother to Jeoffrey and Chad Storm. Both sisters married Storms in secret. Causing a great scandal among the Houses.

Jeoffrey Storm: Son of Madame Maura Moyer-Storm and Arik Storm. Husband of Isalora Deagon-Storm. Chad's brother. Wynter Storms father.

Madame Maura Moyer: Married to Arik. Mother to Jeoffrey and Chad. Adopted mother to Blair. Grandmother to Wynter Storm. Possessed by Sarmira.

Petra Storm: Wife to Bryce. Mother to Gavin Ailbert and Bram.

Sara Deagon-Storm: Married to Ailbert Storm. Mother to Ian Storm. Grandmother to Isalora and Fran, and Great grandmother to Wynter Storm. Oldest sister to Isobel. Her father is the slain King of Ashengale. Her father was killed during the great battle.

Wynter Storm: Daughter of Jeoffrey Storm and Isalora Deagon-Storm.

First cousins: Arik, Ian, Derek, and Daniel.

Ladorielle Community

Drena: Elvin daughter to Gage was turned to a vampire. Blair's mother.

Gage: Elvin: Drena's father.

Garrick: Head commander guard of Ashengale City.

Geneviève Fernshadow: The Royal Storm's porter. Her father is Gage and mother is Laveena (Dryads).

Gretta: A Dryad.

Huntress Arryn & Akira: Queen Sara's Royal Guards.

Kyla: Gretta's sister, also a Dryad.

Laveena: Geneviève's mother.

Nora: Iknes Shaw. Wynter's Lady's Maid, and a Shadow Walker.

Nyta: (Nigh-ta) One of the last of Sara's court. The medical doctor for the Storm Castle and its surrounding people. High Priestess to the castle. A Diviner of magic.

Nytemire: (Night-my-er) A cross hybrid of a Necromancer and vampire.

Redmae: A wolf. Rory's sister.

Rory: Wynter Storm's best friend.

Stella: Wynter's friend from Storm River Manor.

Thom & Dom: Dwarf twins and warriors.

Zak: Nora's brother. Also an Iknes Shaw

Underworld

Iknes Shaw: Snake-like creatures that are of a humanoid form. They have the head and arms of a human, and a body of a snake. They have the ability to look like a human.

Sabretail Prowlers: Invisible demon dogs that work for Vothule the Underworld King. They have the body of a dog and a tail like a sabre.

Sarmira: A powerful Necromancer sorceress: Ultimate power of evil. Has the ability to raise the dead, create chemistry poisons, read minds of anyone. Often places memory stamps on her victims. Necromancers see the undead and can possess the bodies of others. As long as they breathe the essence of life they can live forever. Weakness is Labradorite.

Trek: Ogre-like creatures that can have skin shades from green to a pale white. They have the innate ability to shift into anything.

Vothule: King of the Underworld. Sarmira's superior.

Ladorielle

Ashengale: City of dragons

Elleirodal: (Elle- ir o dal) Elleirodal and home of Zhir and the twin planet to Ladorielle.

Giant Country: A heavy mountainous terrain where giants and Iknes Shaw live among each other.

Geneviève's Ranch: An Elvin city

Grengore Mines: Area where minerals are located and the tunnel to the Lake of No Return.

Ladorielle Territory: An area that is at war with the Underworld that's trying to overtake the land.

Ladorielle: (La- door - ē – elle) Twin planet to Elleirodal. Ladorielle is divided into three continents. Ladorielle Territories, Storm Castle Realm, and Dragonscale Island. The Storms once ruled all of Ladorielle, with Dragonscale Island coexisting on the same planet. Elleirodal realm and the house of Zhir plan to take over both realms.

Pine Willow Valley: The place where Geneviève's ranch is located.

Scale Rock: The crevasse cavern where the Iknes Shaw live.

Shadow Vine Forest: The home of the Dryads, and haven for fairies.

Songbird Meadow: The meadow where the killer birds sing their prey to sleep.

Storm Castle: Where the Storm family resides.

Dragonscale: Ruler of the universe, and the balance of power with good vs. evil.

The Council: the circle of balance: the ruler of each realm seats at the table of balance. They are the high courts of the universe. Each house have their own set of rules, and leaders. If a decision cannot be made, it is brought up to the council for a vote.

The Houses

- House of Storm ~ Nytemires (hybrid Vampire/Necromancer)

- House of Deagon ~ Dragons

- House of Fernshadow ~ Elves

- House of Fae 'Oria ~ Dryads

- House of Grengore ~ Trek (aka ogres and goblins)

- House of Zhir ~ Vothule's Underworld and Sarmira's home. (Necromancer)

- House of Silverback ~ The wolves

- House of Bloodbane ~ Vampires

- House of Ashburn ~ Witches

- House of Shaw ~ Iknes Shaw snake people.

- House of Dhor ~ Giants

- House of Odewyn ~ Wizards

- House of Ironstone ~ Dwarves

STORM BLOODLINE SAGA

The written order

Book 1: Eyes of Wynter

Book 2: Different Shade
of Wynter

Book 3: Wynter Reign

Book 4: Wynter's Fury

Prequel: Eye of the Raven

House Trilogies

Vol 1: House of Shadow Raven

Part of the Storm Bloodline Saga

Mirror of Fate

Other Books

Middle Grade Book

The Fairy Mermaid and the Crystal Key

ACKNOWLEDGEMENTS

Thanks again to God for giving me the thoughts to write this story.

There are so many people to thank: to my husband and kids, you are the world to me. A huge shout out to my beta team who have helped me through the painstaking rough drafts.

Denise

Olivia

Sharon

Mel

Thank you, Rebecca Jaycox, and Gail Delaney my editors.

Also, I would like to thank these readers for reading and helping me catching the last-minute errors.

Bobbi

Veronica

Shan

Laura

Elizabeth

I hope you enjoy the story.

About the Author

Emmy R. Bennett lives in the Pacific Northwest and grew up in Washington State in a Lutheran household. Although she's strong in her faith, she believes everyone has the right of free will, in their beliefs.

When she isn't at her desk writing, she's spending time with her family, gardening, crafting, or reading.

She loves to study genealogy and her family line has been traced back to the Vikings. It's one of the many inspirations from which she's drawn to write.

©2018 Photography by Mel Sabarez